Caught in the Snare of the Hunter

Caught in the Snare
of the Hunter

A Christopher Worthy/Father Fortis Mystery

———◆———

DAVID CARLSON

coffeetownpress

Kenmore, WA

coffeetownpress

A Coffeetown Press book published by Epicenter Press

Epicenter Press
6524 NE 181st St.
Suite 2
Kenmore, WA 98028

For more information go to:
www.Camelpress.com
www.Coffeetownpress.com
www.Epicenterpress.com
www.davidccarlson.net

Cover watercolor by Kathy Carlson
Interior design by Melissa Vail Coffman

Caught in the Snare of the Hunter

ISBN: 978-1-68492-071-6 (trade paper)
ISBN: 978-1-68492-072-3 (ebook)

Printed in the United States of America

Caught in the Snare of the Hunter *is dedicated to the students, faculty, staff, donors, and all those who love Franklin College, a small liberal arts college in south-central Indiana that I am proud to call my academic home. Franklin College is more than a college; Franklin College is a community that has transformed lives, including mine, since its humble beginnings in 1834.*

For he (God) will deliver you

from the snare of the fowler.

Psalm 91:3 (American Standard Version)

✝

ACKNOWLEDGMENTS

ONLY THE AUTHOR'S NAME APPEARS ON the cover of a book, but supporting and assisting every author are many people. I am indebted to my wife, Kathy, who is my first editor and my main supporter. I am also grateful for the encouragement of our two sons, Leif and Marten; our daughter-in-law, Mandy; and our grandchildren, Felix and Freya. I have felt your support for this series from its beginning.

Jennifer McCord is not just my contact at Coffeetown Press but also a trusted advisor on all things related to writing and publishing. Sara Camilli is the type of supportive literary agent that all authors hope to find. Fortunately, I did.

Finally, I want to thank faithful readers of the Christopher Worthy and Father Fortis series. Knowing that readers are as curious as I am to discover how Worthy and Father Nick will solve the next mystery is what sustains me when I write late into the night—and sometimes in the middle of the night.

NOTE TO READERS

———◆———

*C*AUGHT IN THE *S*NARE OF THE *H*UNTER is set in the near future when the Covid pandemic is over. All restrictions have been lifted, all borders open. May that day come soon.

CHAPTER ONE

———————◆———————

FATHER NICHOLAS FORTIS GAZED AT THE happy couple across the restaurant table and thought, *Do I really want to ruin their evening?*

He knew he should wait until Lena Fabriano's three-week visit with Christopher Worthy ended. He knew his friend Worthy had taken vacation leave from homicide cases, had cleared his schedule so that he could spend every precious hour with Lena. And Nick knew the only feeling he should have on this night was gratitude.

Worthy and Lena had driven down from Detroit to his monastery in northwest Ohio to take him to dinner. He wasn't surprised that Lena looked as beautiful as he remembered, her dark eyes sparkling, but Worthy, despite the gray appearing at his temples, looked younger.

Unfortunately, overshadowing the joyous occasion was the dread Nick was feeling. Two days before, he'd sat with Brother Paulus, another monk of St. Simeon's, and listened as the monk shared that his younger brother, a parish priest in Saginaw, Michigan, hadn't been heard from for nearly a month. Brother Paulus had done more than share his worry; at the end of his confiding in Nick, he'd grabbed his hand and pled, "My family fears the worst, Father Nicholas. I beg you to help."

Nick also knew that he'd never been good at hiding his feelings from his closest friend, Worthy. The two had worked too many cases together, had hunted killers and even faced death together. But this was a night to celebrate, not to burden Worthy and Lena with what was troubling him.

"Do you realize it's been almost a year since we saw each other, Nick?" Lena asked. "I've always felt bad that I didn't say a proper goodbye in Jerusalem."

"It was a crazy time, my dear. We were heading off in different directions—you to Ireland, Christopher back to Detroit, and me eventually back to my monastery in Ohio. And, of course, I knew you both wanted to spend every moment together."

Worthy looked over at Lena. "I was afraid we'd never see each other again, but, as I remember, you didn't seem worried about that at all."

Lena clutched Worthy's hand. "Then I must have hid my feelings. I was terrified, but I also believed we'd do whatever we could to hold on to each other."

"And looking at you two now, I'd say you were right, Lena," Nick said. "I know it can't be easy, not seeing each other unless one of you flies across the Atlantic." He raised his wine glass for a toast. "To you both."

The three glasses clinked against each other. "And here's to strong friendships," Lena said, smiling at Nick.

"And here's to the three of us solving that mystery together," Worthy added.

"Um. . . we'd better stop," Lena said, setting down her glass. "Too many toasts and you'll have to carry me to the car, Chris."

"Speaking of the car, we should be heading back to Detroit soon," Worthy said. "I thought we'd go sailing in the morning."

As much as Nick hated to admit it, he was relieved that, in a few minutes, he could stop pretending. "It means a lot that you came down to see me," he said. "I know you know this, but I love you both."

They sat for a moment in silence before Worthy said, "There's just one problem, Nick. In the whole time we've known each other, I've never seen you not finish a meal or fail to order dessert. What's going on?"

✠

THAT NIGHT, WORTHY AND LENA DIDN'T return to Detroit, and, the next morning, they didn't go sailing. Instead, they sat for the rest of the evening in the restaurant listening as Nick related Brother Paulus' story.

"I'm sure Paulus won't mind me sharing what he told me, but the details are vague. And honestly, Christopher and Lena, I don't want to burden you with his problem—and maybe my problem—especially as the two of you have so little time together."

"Trust me, Nick, we're not going to leave until we hear the story," Worthy said. "We can go sailing another day."

"Chris and I both noticed you aren't your normal self, Nick. I worried you might be ill, so I'm relieved it isn't that," Lena added.

Forcing a smile, Nick said, "No, no, my doctor says I'm sound as a horse—a horse who needs to lose about seventy-five pounds, though. I think he's been talking to my abbot." He paused before adding, "But are you sure, Lena? My problem can wait until you leave."

Lena smiled at Worthy. "That would mean three weeks of Chris trying to guess what this is all about. Don't keep us in suspense."

Worthy nodded. "Nick, all I'm promising is that we'll listen. If you need something from me, and I know it can wait three weeks, I'll put it out of my mind."

"I'm not sure I believe that, Christopher, but I'll try. And maybe I will have dessert then."

After they ordered, Nick explained that what Brother Paulus had told him was serious enough for the police to get involved. "But for all I know, it could be more a matter for a woman's magazine than a crime."

"Now, that's got our attention, Nick. We're all ears," Worthy said.

"I warn you, this could be the proverbial molehill being made into a mountain. But here's what Paulus told me. He has a brother, Joseph, who's been a priest in Saginaw, Michigan, for the past year. Before that, he studied for a year in Greece."

"Is he married or single?" Lena asked.

"Ah, you remember that Orthodox priests have a choice. Father Joseph is single, and that's important. After Paulus and I talked, I wanted to get another perspective on Joseph. I called the office of the Metropolitan-Bishop in Detroit. I got hold of the Chancellor, the Metropolitan's right-hand man, who was noticeably evasive with me. But what I was able to piece together is that the church's hierarchy has . . . no, I guess it's fairer to say they *had* big plans for Father Joseph. That's why he was sent to Thessaloniki. He was in a doctoral program in liturgics."

"I don't know of any doctoral program, at least, any reputable one, that can be completed in a year," Lena said.

"No, you're right. You see, Father Joseph already has one doctorate, from Boston University in Greek History. The one in Greece was to be a second. But he was sent home early."

"Ah, so that's where the woman's magazine angle comes in," Worthy said.

Nick nodded. "All the Chancellor would tell me was that things didn't work out in Greece. So, I spoke to Paulus again and told him that I couldn't help unless he told me everything he knows about what happened in Thessaloniki. That's when he told me that Father Joseph became friends with a Ukrainian woman, a fellow doctoral student. I don't know the woman's name, but she was . . . well, she was married to a Russian. Father Joseph told his family that what happened in Greece was a colossal misunderstanding."

"But we should take that with a grain of salt, right?" Lena asked.

"That's what I don't know. What is clear is that this woman began to come to Joseph for support. She claimed her husband abused her."

"True or false, Nick?" Worthy asked.

Nick shrugged. "Again, I don't know, but Father Joseph believed her. Joseph also said someone sent him a threatening note about his relationship with the woman. When Joseph said he'd be happy to go with the woman to the police, she panicked. Her husband, she said, is ex-military and has been involved in some shady dealings —arms smuggling that might have involved a murder back in Russia—but he was never charged. She said her husband had connections in the police."

"This is beginning to sound like a movie," Lena said.

"Yes, but is it fiction or a documentary?" Worthy asked. "What else do you know?"

"Not much, Christopher. Father Joseph was sent home in disgrace because of a decision he made that was either heroic or foolish. In his last week in Thessaloniki, this woman knocked on his door around two o'clock in the morning. Joseph said that when he opened the door, he found her hysterical. 'He's going to kill me; he's going to kill me,' she kept saying. So, Joseph let her stay the night."

"I think we can guess what happened next," Lena said. "Her husband turned Joseph in to the authorities."

"Not to the police, but to the Church hierarchy in the city. In less than a week, Joseph was on a flight home. He told his family and the Metropolitan-Bishop in Detroit that he'd only let the woman stay the night to protect her, that protecting her was his only motive. It looked bad, and once he was home, there was a chance that Joseph would be defrocked. But the church hierarchy wanted to give him another chance, and there was an opening for a priest in Saginaw, not all that far from Detroit. Brother Paulus told me he thought the Metropolitan-Bishop did that so that he could keep an eye on his brother."

"Any idea what happened to the woman?" Lena asked.

"Joseph told his brother that he doesn't know, and when I called the Chancellor back, he told me the woman's whereabouts are irrelevant."

They sat in silence for a moment before Worthy asked, "How was this Joseph settling in up in Saginaw?"

"Paulus said he spoke to his brother several times. Apparently, Joseph also came down to St. Simeon's once on a retreat. I wish I could say that I met him, but I didn't. Paulus said his brother knew his future in the church would always be under a cloud, but he wanted to put the sorry mess behind him. Other than telling the story of what got him sent home, Joseph never mentioned the woman again."

"And now he's missing."

"Yes, Christopher, for almost a month. The police finally treated the situation as a missing person's case, but they've found no trace of his whereabouts or his fate. What we know is that he didn't take his car or passport."

"And the church?" Lena said.

"According to Paulus, initially, the church in Saginaw was worried. I could tell that the Chancellor and probably the Metropolitan-Bishop in Detroit believe his disappearance is another chapter in the life of a messed-up young priest. I think it likely, if Joseph ever returns, that his life in the Church is over."

"What does the brother think happened?" Worthy asked.

"Paulus and their mother fear the worst, that Joseph was kidnapped for some reason . . . or . . ."

"Or that he's killed himself," Lena said in a soft voice. Turning to Worthy, she said, "How far is Saginaw from Detroit?"

Before Worthy could answer, Nick said, "No, no, I'm not expecting you to go up there."

"Nick, please. Let us do this," Lena replied. "You'll be doing us a favor."

"A favor? I don't understand."

"It's something Lena and I talked about on our drive down from Detroit," Worthy said. "When we're together, whether it's here or in Rome, every minute that passes is like a grain of sand falling inside an hourglass. We both need something to think about besides how quickly our time together is fleeing. Anyway, didn't you say after last year in Jerusalem that your abbot said enough was enough, that he wouldn't give you permission to investigate another crime?"

"My abbot says a lot of things, but yes, you're right. And if he consulted the Metropolitan-Bishop in Detroit, I don't think he'd consider the disappearance of Father Joseph to even be a crime."

"Okay, then, it's settled," Worthy said. "We'll drive up to Saginaw and make some inquiries. Nick, you can help by talking again with Brother Paulus about his brother. We have to get a better sense of him. Is he a hopeless romantic, a playboy, the victim of a kidnapping, a suicide, or something else?"

Nick sat back, relieved. *Worthy said "we." The three of us are in this together, but I wonder where this will lead.*

CHAPTER TWO

⸻◆⸻

OCTOBER 6

O N THE DRIVE DROVE NORTH FROM DETROIT TO SAGINAW, Worthy asked, "You're sure you're okay with this?"

Lena reached over and squeezed his arm. "Actually, I was relieved that we both feel the same way. If we happen to be on a bit of an adventure while I'm here, well, why not? Anyway, you took me sailing yesterday, just like you wanted."

"I hope you don't feel you had to like the sailing, just because I do."

"No, of course not. But I liked what you said when we were out on the lake, that bit about how when you're sailing you feel alert and relaxed at the same time."

"That doesn't sound too flaky?" Worthy asked.

Lena shook her head. "No, it's close to what I'm feeling right now."

"Really?"

"Yes, I think so. When we met last year in Rome and fell in love, we were both caught up in a complicated case. Now, having this missing priest to think about seems a lot better than sitting in your apartment or driving around Michigan just to be driving around. The important thing is that we're together, so right now driving to Saginaw seems to be a bonus."

Worthy laughed. "I've never heard Saginaw described as a bonus. The city has seen better days economically, and it's had more than its share of crime."

"Then maybe I should expect the scenery to take my breath away."

"Sorry once again. If Saginaw sat on the shore of one of the Great Lakes, you'd be right. Here, let me show you," he said, holding up Lena's hand. "What we call lower Michigan is shaped a lot like your hand. And Saginaw is right here, not far from Lake Huron, but far enough," Worthy said, pointing to the soft skin connecting Lena's thumb to the rest of her hand. "Saginaw is right where people get painful cracks on their hands, especially in winter."

As if she could feel the wintry cold, she withdrew her hand. "I wonder if this priest found Saginaw to be a painful place."

NICK OFTEN THOUGHT THAT FEW MONKS MATCHED THE STEREOTYPE held by many outsiders. He considered himself a good example. Yes, his long beard and equally long hair bound in a ponytail were nearly identical to that of other Orthodox monks from Mt. Athos in Greece or monks in Australia, but his weight, broad smile, and talkative nature didn't match the image of the thin and somber ascetic.

Brother Paulus, however, with his permanent frown and soft voice, fitted society's impression of a monk to a T. Whereas Nick, in his senior class of high school, was voted "most likely to become a professional wrestler," he imagined that Paulus was earmarked for monastic life from the cradle. Even now, as the two of them sat alone in the monastery's library, the sun's rays slanted down on Paulus' head like a halo.

All this made Nick curious about the missing brother, Father Joseph. Was the family one of the rare ones in the modern age that willingly offered its sons to the Church? Nick knew that his own mother wept angry tears before the icon of Christ when she lamented that her one surviving son would never give her a grandchild.

"Joseph and I aren't very much alike," Paulus said. "His given name was Aristotle, so we always called him Aris. Joseph is his middle name and the name he took when he was ordained."

"I think I remember you saying your brother is younger than you," Nick said.

"Six years. There's another brother in between, Soter, and the two of them were both crazy about sports. Sports and I didn't mix," Paulus said with a shrug, "but Soter was good enough at rowing to get a scholarship to a small college in New York. Aris, though, was exceptional. He won a full scholarship to University of Maryland. He made All-American and holds some record at the school. That made his decision to become a priest all the more puzzling, at least to our Papa."

Nick could tell that Paulus was in awe of his brother, and he also knew that Joseph, by not marrying before ordination, had accepted a permanent life of celibacy.

"What can you tell me about Aris' relationship with women?" Nick asked.

Paulus blushed, and Nick understood that here too Aris had outshined his older brother. "The girls in high school called him 'Adonis.' And he was in a fraternity at Maryland, so, in the pictures I saw, Aris always seemed to be with beautiful women."

Nick tried to imagine the family of three sons, two athletic and maybe extroverted, and one, Paulus, studious and introverted. It wasn't difficult imagining Paulus as a celibate monk, but Joseph as a celibate priest? Celibacy didn't mean a priest disliked the company of women, but the vow would make the priesthood a tricky dance for someone, maybe someone like Joseph, who was used to the attention of the opposite sex.

"Brother Paulus, what did you think when you first heard your brother was being sent home because of a woman?"

Brother Paulus reacted to the question by looking down and folding his hands in front of him tightly. *Whatever the answer is, I know it's painful,* Nick thought.

"Aris is the type who looks out for other people. When he told us this woman's life was in danger, I wasn't surprised that he protected her. I always thought, if Aris had lived in the Middle Ages, he'd have been a knight."

A knight with a damsel in distress? Nick thought. He knew every seminarian was warned about how rumors related to sexuality, even baseless ones, could scuttle a vocation. But maybe at two in the morning, a young man who answered the knock on the door in pajamas, not a clerical collar, wasn't Father Joseph as much as he was Sir Aris.

"From the way you describe your brother, I picture him as the kind of person who would run toward a burning building, to see if anyone is inside, instead of running away."

Paulus looked up. "That's Aris exactly. And that's why I wasn't surprised when he announced that he believed he had a vocation. But I knew he'd want to be a parish priest, not a monk."

"The thing is, I'm wondering if your brother, in wanting to save others, could be the type of priest who would ignore the dictates of his superiors. In other words, for someone like Joseph, the vow of obedience to a Metropolitan-Bishop might be more difficult to observe than the vow of celibacy."

For a few seconds, Paulus shook his head vigorously, but then stopped and sat in silence for a moment. "I was going to say that Aris isn't a rebel, but what you said . . . I can see what you mean. So many people, those who don't know Aris, assume he was sent home because he slept with this woman. As a priest, he's now a person of danger to himself and to the Church, someone who has to be monitored. But Aris isn't the type to forget his vows and just hop into bed with a woman—even if the woman wished that."

Nick tried a different tack. "Might your brother ignore the guidance of his superiors, such as the Metropolitan-Bishop, if he thought that was what God was asking of him?"

Brother Paulus' lips trembled as he looked toward the window and the setting sun. "Yes, that's Aris."

LENA AND WORTHY'S FIRST STOP IN SAGINAW WAS AT ST. GEORGE, the only Greek Orthodox church in the city. The domed church was small, the parking lot accommodating no more than fifty cars. On this Thursday afternoon, there was only one car in the lot. Worthy rang the buzzer by the door marked "Office" and waited until a middle-aged woman opened the door a crack to ask, "Can I help you?"

Worthy introduced himself as a policeman from Detroit and Lena as his associate before asking if the woman would be willing to answer some questions about Father Joseph.

"Oh, my, I don't know. Father Gregory is doing hospital visits," the woman replied, even as she let them into the building.

"Was Father Gregory here when Father Joseph was at St. George?" Worthy asked.

The woman walked them to a small office where, on the desk, Worthy read, *Florence Reston, Administrative Assistant.*

"No, Father Gregory came as his replacement. Where did you say you were from?"

"Detroit. I work in the homicide division there."

Florence Reston's hand flew to her throat. "Good heavens, is there bad news about Father Joe?"

"No, nothing like that. Father Joseph's brother asked us to help," Worthy explained, stretching the truth a bit. "So, as I said, we have some questions. They'll only take a few minutes."

Mrs. Reston's brow furrowed. "Well, seeing as you're from the police, I suppose it's okay." She pointed to two chairs before moving around the desk to sit in another.

Worthy thanked her before asking, "How long did you work with Father Joseph?"

"Oh, I've been at St. George for ten years. So, we worked together the whole time Father Joe was here."

"How would you describe him?" Worthy asked.

Mrs. Reston shook her head. "I'm not a member of this church, but I share their feelings that maybe we never really knew the real Father Joe. You see, nobody here knew about what happened in Greece until after he disappeared. That was something a local reporter dug up. And now, because of the worry and then all the hurt feelings, it's hard to remember how we felt about Father

Joe when he first came to Saginaw."

Reaching into a drawer of her desk, Mrs. Reston pulled out a brochure and handed it across the desk to Lena. "This is the program of Father Joe's installment."

Worthy and Lena looked at the brochure together. On the cover was an icon of St. George and then below that the face of a priest identified as Father Joseph Kouris. Worthy wondered if his first reaction was triggered by the photo or by what he knew of the priest, because the smile on Father Joseph's face looked forced.

"Father Joseph was . . . is very intelligent," Mrs. Reston said. "I remember parishioners saying his sermons were an improvement over those of Father Leonites. He was the previous priest, you see. More than one person at the time told me they were surprised that a priest with such gifts—we were told Father Joe has a Ph.D.—was assigned to such a small parish. But I'm a member of the Baptist church, so I never heard him preach."

"What about around the office? What was he like?" Lena asked.

Mrs. Reston pursed her lips in thought. "The whole time I worked with his, he was organized. Every morning, he would show me his schedule for the day, so that I would know where he would be in case an emergency came up when he was away from the office. At one of the hospitals or nursing homes, I mean."

"Would you describe him as friendly? Did he get along with people in the parish?" Lena asked.

Mrs. Reston nodded without hesitating. "He was always friendly. Not just with those here at St. George, but also in town. Everyone liked Father Joe, even though . . ."

"Yes?" Worthy asked.

Mrs. Reston shrugged. "Sometimes, he seemed . . . I don't know. He could be silent."

"Withdrawn, as if he had something on his mind?" Worthy asked, thinking how much that also described him.

"Yes, that fits. He could go quiet, like he caught himself, if that makes any sense. But maybe that's what made him a good listener. Of course, since the newspaper articles . . . well, some people in the parish feel betrayed, and not just by Father Joe. The Metropolitan-Bishop in Detroit should have told the community about his past."

"Do people in the church think he left on his own volition?" Worthy asked.

"Oh, yes, I think most do—now."

"How did he leave the office? Did he clear out his personal articles before he disappeared?" Lena asked.

Worthy was pleased that Lena seemed as keen to understand Father Joe as he was.

"It did look like he took some of his things. I remember when the police were looking through his office, I saw the photo of his family was gone."

"How about his calendar?" Worthy asked.

"Now, he left that, and the police have it, I imagine."

"Did the police show you the calendar?" Worthy asked. When Mrs. Reston looked confused by the question, he added, "Did you see if he'd noted down meetings or visitations for the days or weeks after he disappeared?"

"No, I don't rightly know that. Now, just a minute. I do remember there was a wedding scheduled for the following Saturday, because he met with the couple the week before."

Worthy glanced over at Lena, who nodded. *Yes, that could be important,* he thought.

"Is there anything else?" Mrs. Reston asked, obviously finding the questions upsetting.

Worthy thought for a moment before answering. "My father was a minister; in fact, he was a Baptist minister, Mrs. Reston. I remember he always gave his secretary the contents of the Sunday bulletin by Wednesday. You said Father Joe was organized, so can I assume there was a set day when you received those sorts of details?"

"It was Thursday, always Thursday. But Father Joe left . . . he disappeared on a Tuesday, so no, I didn't have it for that week."

"Do you still have the bulletin for the Sunday before he disappeared?" Worthy asked.

"I'm sure I do," Mrs. Reston said, as she rose and walked to a filing cabinet. After a few moments, she returned with two bulletins.

Worthy looked at the date: September eighth, two days before the priest disappeared.

"Did the police ask to see this?" he asked.

"No, but then I don't know how that bulletin could help you."

Worthy turned toward the back page and pointed. "Here is what he put in the bulletin about upcoming events at the church. There was to be a Bible study and then a parish council meeting for Wednesday, and on Thursday, a morning liturgy."

"Does that mean that Father Joseph expected to be here?" Lena asked, looking at Worthy. "Or, he planned to run off, leaving the impression that everything was normal."

Worthy shrugged. "I don't know. "Mrs. Reston, do you know if Father Joseph left things in his desk?"

Mrs. Reston shook her head. "For a week after he left, the police told me to stay at home. When I returned, his desk was cleaned out. Whether the parish council or the police did that, I don't know."

Worthy removed a small pad of paper and a pen from his shirt pocket. "Can you give us the contact information of whoever heads up the parish council?"

"That would be Demetri Fragouli, the president," Mrs. Reston replied after a moment's thought "Maybe he should have answered your questions instead of me."

"No, Mrs. Reston. A church secretary knows a priest or minister in a different way from others in the parish. Which leads me to my final question. You said Father Joseph is well-liked outside the parish. Are there anyone in the community with whom he is particularly close?"

Again, Mrs. Reston pursed her lips in thought. "There's a cycling club in Saginaw, and I know he liked to ride his bike on outings with them. I don't know if they became close friends, though."

Worthy nodded and smiled. "I expect the local bike shops would know the name of that club." Both Lena and he thanked the secretary who escorted them to the door leading to the parking lot.

As they drove away, Lena said, "The saddest part of that interview for me was that Mrs. Reston didn't ask to hear back from us if we discovered anything new. I imagine a lot of those in the church have already made up their minds about Father Joseph."

AS THEY PULLED OUT OF THE PARKING LOT, Worthy said, "Lena, before we go into the station, let's check the stats on missing persons for Saginaw for the past three months."

After five minutes of checking on her phone, Lena said, "None were reported for the month of September. What does that mean?"

"That Brother Paulus was right about what he told Nick. The police haven't treated Father Joseph's disappearance as suspicious, which is why we're going to talk with them next."

A ten-minute drive brought them to the police station. As they entered the front door, Worthy noticed Lena dig in her purse for a tissue, which she then raised to her nose. *I guess police stations, at least those this part of Michigan, smell the same,* he thought, recognizing the mix of odors emanating from the wait area—alcohol, sweat, anti-bacterial cleaner, and despair.

He showed his ID and asked the sergeant at the desk where he could find the officers in charge of missing persons. The sergeant, a mouth breather who looked close to retirement, squinted as he studied Worthy's ID.

"Happy to meet you, Lieutenant," he said before glancing at Lena. "You also a cop?"

"No, but I'm with him."

"Still have to see some ID, ma'am."

Lena handed her passport to the sergeant.

"Magdalena Fab-ri-an-o," he said aloud. "I hope you don't mind. I'm the curious type. It says here you're a dottore. What's that?"

"It means I'm a university professor with a doctorate."

"Huh, don't think I've seen that before. From Italy, I see."

"Yes, Rome, actually."

"Well, I'll be. You're from Rome, Italy. My, your English sure is good. I'd have never taken you for an Eye-talian."

"I earned my doctorate in the States."

"Well, once again, I'll be. What in?"

"Abnormal psychology," Lena said.

Worthy understood why Lena did didn't go into detail, trying to make the sergeant understand that her specialty was actually mysticism and those who claimed to be mystics.

The sergeant laughed and then leaned over the counter to offer a loud whisper, "We get a lot of abnormal psychology around here. Yes, we sure do."

Worthy was about to break into the conversation when the sergeant said, "Missing persons is on the second floor, two doors to the left once you get to the top of the stairs. Ask for Sergeant Maaki."

Worthy was already heading in that direction when he stopped. "Do you mean Freya Maaki?"

"One and the same, Lieutenant. You know her?"

"Uh-huh, we worked a case together a couple of years ago."

"As I always tell the missus, 'small world,'" the sergeant said. "I'm sure the sergeant will be happy to see you."

The desk sergeant was right. Freya Maaki was as pleased to see Worthy as he was to see her. When Worthy saw Freya, any suspicion that the Saginaw police failed to take Father Joseph's disappearance seriously evaporated. He knew Freya when she was a new officer in the Houghton Police Department in Michigan's UP. Two years before, she worked closely with Nick and him on mysterious deaths at a remote monastery on the shore of Lake Superior. He knew her well enough to know that whatever caused the Saginaw police to dismiss Father Joe's disappearance, it wasn't because Freya prejudged the case.

"So you're in missing persons now," Worthy said, as Freya came around her desk to give him a hug. After he introduced Lena, he added, "And you're no longer fighting those two up in Houghton. Funny, I've forgotten their names."

"Please, have a seat, sir, and you too, Dr. Fabriano. I wish I could forget their names, but they're Fanchon and Freeman. Oops, I'm forgetting my manners. How about some coffee?"

As Freya walked to a small table with a coffeemaker on it, Worthy tried to decide how she'd changed since he last saw her. Freya had let her hair grow longer, but it still had the blonde translucence of those with Finnish ancestry. Worthy thought she looked happier, especially around the eyes.

"No need with the 'sir' and 'doctor' business, Freya. It's Chris and Lena."

Freya returned with two cups. "Just because you give me permission doesn't mean it's going to be easy to do that," she said. "But I'll try."

"Chris doesn't bite," Lena said with a smile.

"Oh, I know that. Lieutenant Worthy—Chris—never scared me," she said, smiling at Lena. "But he was the world's greatest mentor."

"Enough of that. We did good work together, and we got lucky. What surprises me is that your captain let you go. His name was Milton, as I remember," Worthy said.

Freya shrugged. "In a way, Captain Milton didn't let me go. He retired not long after our case closed. That's when the powers-that-be decided to promote Fanchon. It didn't take her long to approve my transfer request."

"Jealousy?" Lena asked.

"My guess it was also shame," Worthy said. "Fanchon and Freeman did their best to force the evidence on that case to fit their pet theory. Freya wouldn't go along. And, in the end, Freya was right. I don't think Fanchon would want a reminder of her mistake hanging around."

"Doctor . . . Lena, the reason I didn't bow to Fanchon and Freeman was because of Chris and Father Nick," she said. "I can almost guarantee you that if they'd hadn't been there, an innocent monk would be in prison right now. Fortunately for me, I haven't been handed such a complex case since then."

"Which brings us to why we're here, Freya. The priest Father Joseph Kouris, who disappeared a month ago, is the brother of a monk in Nick's monastery. The brother asked Nick to help, and after Nick told us what he knew, Lena and I agreed we'd look into it."

Freya's eyebrows raised as she slowly nodded. "I wouldn't be surprised if the family thinks we waited too long to investigate. But we didn't wait. The problem was that, at first, we had a lot of contradictory testimony, and we didn't know what to make of his disappearance."

"Once I realized that you were working missing persons, I knew the case hasn't been mishandled," Worthy said.

"Thanks for that," Freya said. "We waited our standard forty-eight hours in case the priest had a good reason for being away from Saginaw, and by that time the church authorities in Detroit steered us in another direction."

"You mean the story of what happened in Greece," Lena said.

"Right. I'm not being defensive when I say we stayed open to all possibilities, but as soon as the media got ahold of the story from Greece, the public decided he'd run away, if not *with* the woman at least *for* her." She passed a series of photos of Father Joseph across her desk. "Have you seen these?"

Worthy and Lena looked at one photo after another of the priest.

"Freya, I bet you'll agree that he's a good-looking priest . . . no, a good-looking man," Lena said. "He could be a model."

Worthy could also see the man's attraction. His dark eyes and strong jaw reminded him of an actor whose name he couldn't remember. "What do you think happened to him?"

"Well, we have his passport, so we never thought he left for Greece," Freya said. "I know that's not an answer to your question. What do I think? I think the media and the public decided very quickly that our case was a soap opera. That version of the story went national, and, I expect, had some traction in Europe as well. All that means is that we've been inundated with sightings of the two. Kissing at Niagara Falls, walking the beach in Brazil, camping in Alaska, and being seen on more than fifteen different flights to Athens."

"I'm familiar with how theories, especially for people out of the ordinary, become the accepted narrative," Lena said.

"So, you help out with law enforcement?" Freya asked, before taking a sip of coffee.

"No, I investigate stories, past and present, of supposed mystics. That means that a great deal of my research or interviews has to do with peeling back the layers of the legend surrounding the saint or mystic. I'm thinking that maybe what you're up against in the case of Father Joseph is something like that—tales, different stories that people want to believe."

Freya nodded. "That sounds about right. And we are, as you say, 'up against' it. As sad as it will be for the family, I've thought this case might end when some hunter finds his body out in the woods."

"Suicide?" Worthy asked.

Freya took a moment to answer. "We've considered that, but no one in the church described him as depressed. A bit quiet at times, but that's not all that unusual. We know he liked to cycle, so maybe he was out on one of our trails and had an accident. He could have fallen over a precipice, or maybe he accidentally got between a momma bear and her cub."

"Is his bike missing?" Worthy asked.

Freya smiled. "I should have expected you to ask that. No one remembers clearly if he had one or two bikes. I've been given both answers. All I know is that we found one of them in the rectory's garage with his car. It's possible another one is missing, but we're not sure."

"If that's what happened, that he fell off his bike in the woods, people are going to be very disappointed," Worthy said.

"An accident isn't sexy like a romance is," Lena agreed.

They sat in silence for a moment before Worthy said, "I was wondering if you collected what was in his desk."

"We did, but after we looked through it, we gave it back to the church. I think the parish president has that."

"Did you find anything significant?" Worthy asked.

Freya removed a file from a desk drawer. Opening it, she said, "The usual odds and ends—staples, paper, pens, and rubber bands." Turning a few pages, she added, "I forgot that we made copies of everything in the desk that was typed or hand-written. The secretary told us that the handwriting was Father Joe's, so we thought they might tell us something. But we didn't find anything helpful."

Worthy knew his next question would be taken by some police officers as rude, but he thought his history with Freya might offer him some grace. "Would it be possible for us to take a look at those? You see, my father was a minister," he said, as if that explained his request.

Without hesitating, Freya passed the pages over to Worthy who accepted and placed them so Lena could also see.

"I hope you do find something, Lieutenant . . . I mean, Chris. We've hit a brick wall."

Worthy looked at each of the sheets slowly. "I'm not expecting to find anything dramatic." After a few minutes, he stopped. "This might be something."

Lena bent down closer and read aloud the one line on the sheet of paper. "*The Saints of the Church. Different personalities, all used by God. We are all*—he doesn't finish the sentence."

"Just that one line? What do you think it means?" Freya asked.

"I can think of a number of possibilities," Worthy said. "This page could mean he was planning an upcoming service and these words, few as they are, were his initial thoughts for a homily—for the sermon. If that was the case, your suggestion could be right, Freya. He wrote this before heading out on his bike where he had an accident. You'd think his body would have been found by now, though."

"There's a second possibility, though I think it's unlikely," Freya said. "He might have left this page in his desk as cover, to suggest he intended on being in Saginaw for the service."

"Why do you think that unlikely?" Lena asked.

"If I wanted to give that impression, I'd have written more than just a few words."

The three sat in silence as Worthy glanced through the remaining pages. After he closed the file, Lena said, "I think there's another possibility. It's possible Father Joseph started to write his homily, but before he could finish it, something happened—maybe he received a message—that changed his plans. He left on his own accord."

Worthy frowned. "If you're right, Lena, whatever triggered his decision was so important that he was willing to throw away his career, his vocation."

OCTOBER 7

ONCE AGAIN, NICK SAT ACROSS FROM BROTHER PAULUS in the monastery's library.

"I suppose what you're saying is positive," Paulus said, even as he looked neither happy nor relieved by the news.

"We can never make promises in cases like this," Nick said, "but no one is better than Lieutenant Worthy at getting to the bottom of mysteries."

"I was hoping that you'd be the one to look for my brother," Paulus said sheepishly.

Nick didn't reply immediately, tempted as he was to ask if the monk had ever spoken up in support of the previous times when Nick had been away from St. Simeon to assist Worthy. But now, he realized, wasn't the time to pour salt into Paulus' open wound. "I think we both know that the abbot isn't likely to let me do that," he said. "Of course, if you made a personal appeal to him, sharing your family's concern, there's a chance he might change his mind."

Paulus looked down at his hands, calloused by his years working in the monastery's woodworking shop.

No, he's not going to make that appeal, Nick realized. The abbot never opposed Paulus' long and solitary hours in the shop where he made wall crosses. After all, those crosses brought in consistent revenue to St. Simeon's. From the abbot's point of view, the only thing Nick's detective work with Christopher Worthy brought to the monastery was media attention, and the abbot had made it clear many times that a monastery has no business seeking worldly fame.

"Even though I can't leave St. Simeon's, I can help on the case," Nick said. "And so can you."

Paulus looked up. "How?"

"The more you tell us about Joseph . . . Aris, the better our chances to discover why he disappeared."

Paulus shrugged. "I already told you everything that might be important."

Something in the way Paulus said that suggested to Nick that the statement wasn't totally true.

"It's often something that doesn't seem important that will be the most help."

The monk sighed and didn't say anything.

"It's natural for family members to shield one of their own, but you have to know, Paulus, now isn't the time for any of that. The greatest help you can give to your brother is to be candid with us."

Saying nothing, Paulus returned his gaze to his hands, folded on the table.

Nick sat forward. "You might as well share what you're holding back. We'll likely find out anyway."

Paulus' sigh ended in a groan. "It was a long time ago," he said, his voice no more than a whisper.

"What was?"

The monk sat back in the chair, his face red. "Once I tell you, you'll see that it has no bearing on my brother's disappearance."

"Let me make that decision, Paulus. I can't tell you the number of times people complicated an investigation by assuming that what they knew had no bearing on a case. Sometimes they're right, and sometimes they're wrong. But what I know for sure is that keeping family secrets is never more important than solving a case."

The room was silent for a few moments, Nick's long experience in hearing confessions telling him that Paulus was weighing the choice he'd set before him.

"Aris was sixteen, a junior in high school," he began, the words coming out slowly. "My family didn't realize how serious his relationship was with a girl he'd known since middle school until she . . . until she became pregnant."

Paulus paused as if those few words had sapped all his energy, but after an-other moment, he added, "Abortion was out of the question, so the two families agreed to give the baby up for adoption. The baby, a boy, was born and imme-diately taken away." Paulus paused, and Nick waited in silence. "We found out a year later that the baby had died of meningitis. I remember that the adopted parents were suspected of neglect. It was horrible for everyone."

"That's understandable, Paulus. I would imagine that it was especially hard on Aris."

"After he heard, Aris nosedived. He was so depressed that we wondered at times if he should withdraw from high school for a semester. I know it sounds odd, maybe cruel, but the only two things that pulled him through were weightlifting and rowing. Whatever he was feeling inside he released in the weight room and on the water. He became a kind of terror, both in single and double sculls. He was a good rower before the pregnancy, but in his senior year, he was considered one of Pennsylvania's best. That led to the scholarship to Maryland."

"Did he keep contact with the baby's mother afterwards?"

"No, her family moved out west somewhere. Arizona, I think."

"But Aris changed, is that right?"

Paulus grimaced. "Not completely, and not always. He was still popular. But he could also withdraw into himself. Even if the baby hadn't died, Aris might have been that way. Who knows?"

"Tell me how your family reacted."

"Ah, Papa," Paulus said, leaving it at that for a few moments. "I think some men are hardwired to focus on the future. My Papa's mantra was 'the past is the past. It's over. Nothing you can do about it.' That was how my Papa tried to help Aris, and maybe he did help."

"Let me guess. Your father never missed one of your brother's rowing competitions."

Paulus nodded. "When I told Papa I felt a call to be a monk, he gave me a look. I knew what he was thinking. 'This is the son I've never understood. Sure, go be a monk.' But when Aris decided to go to the seminary? All Papa could say—no, scream—was that Aris had just been invited to tryouts for the Olympics. Momma cried, but she accepted it. But Papa? Never. From what my mother told me, Papa kept going at Aris when Aris moved home after college graduation. As you know, Nicholas, Greek families get pretty loud when there's a disagreement. Papa wanted Aris to be the star Greek-American Olympian. But more than that, my father saw Aris' Olympic success as just the beginning. He talked of Aris, with Olympic credentials, succeeding in business or sports-casting. But instead of becoming a famous Greek Olympian, Aris kept repeating that he wanted to become a Greek Orthodox priest. Eventually, he moved out and lived with a friend before seminary started in the fall. I honestly believe that if Aris hadn't been in such good shape, Papa would have tried to beat what he called Aris' 'goddamn, crazy decision' out of him."

"Hmm," Nick said, not saying anything else for a moment. "I understand this wasn't easy for you to tell me, but it might be helpful. You said your brother could withdraw."

Paulus shook his head fiercely. "If you're thinking suicide, you're wrong. Don't even consider that. Aris would never take that path, never."

Nick knew there was no point in arguing, but given all that Father Joseph had been through, suicide was a possibility—a sad end to a sad story.

CHAPTER THREE

That same morning, as Worthy drove from their motel in Saginaw, he listened as Lena read off the contact information for Demetri Fragouli, the president of St. George's parish council and a partner in the Saginaw law firm of Naylor, Naylor, and Fragouli.

"It's nine o'clock. Let's see if he's in his office," he said.

The law office was in the center of town, one door down from an upscale restaurant. Stepping through the front doors, Worthy and Lena approached an unoccupied reception desk.

From an office toward the rear of the room, a female voice called out, "I'll be with you in a minute, if this printer will cooperate." After a few minutes, a tall, middle-aged woman in a well-tailored business suit emerged, wiping ink from her hands, as she asked, "Do you have an appointment?"

Worthy took out his ID and showed it to the woman. "We need to talk with Mr. Fragouli."

"May I ask what this is about?" the woman asked as she looked from Worthy to Lena and gave no indication that Worthy's ID impressed her.

Worthy looked down and read the nameplate on the desk—Darla Helgeson. "Well, Ms. Helgeson, it's about a case that we're helping with," Worthy said. "One that's related to Mr. Fragouli's role in his church."

"Mr. Fragouli is a very busy man. I can see if he has any openings, but that wouldn't be until next week."

Before Worthy could respond, Lena began to tap with her bright red nails on the counter. "Ms. Helgeson, perhaps you recognize Lieutenant Worthy's name from the media," she said. "I can assure you that the lieutenant, as a prominent and decorated homicide detective in Detroit, has fewer openings in his schedule than Mr. Fragouli. So, if Mr. Fragouli is in his office, I suggest you tell him that Lieutenant Christopher Worthy is here and wishes to speak with him about the disappearance of Father Joseph Kouris."

Worthy forced himself to keep a straight face as Ms. Helgeson stared at Lena's tapping nails for a moment before picking up a phone on the desk. In a few minutes, Lena and Worthy stepped out of the elevator on the building's third floor to be greeted by Mr. Fragouli.

"Lieutenant Worthy and . . .?"

"I'm Dr. Fabriano, a psychologist and a friend of Lieutenant Worthy."

Mr. Fragouli looked from Worthy to Lena and back again. "Please come into my office. Would you like coffee or tea?" he asked, pointing to a long table and chairs.

Lena accepted tea and Worthy declined the offer as they entered a spacious office with glass-fronted bookshelves and original art on the wall. As Mr. Fragouli walked to a small kitchenette set against one wall, Worthy noted that the lawyer could be a relative of Nick, sharing his Greek friend's substantial girth and similar powerful voice. And in that moment, Worthy realized, despite Lena's effective bluff, that Nick would probably gain more from this conversation than the two of them.

"I didn't realize the Detroit police had taken an interest in our problem," Mr. Fragouli said as he set the teacup and saucer on a small table. "And the fact that you work homicide has me worried, Lieutenant. Has there been a development in the case?"

"No, we don't come with any news, and our involvement is on behalf of Father Joseph's brother."

"Which one—the financial advisor in Lansing or the monk in Ohio?"

"The monk. You know Brother Paulus?" Worthy asked in return.

"I know of him, but we've never met. I hope the family isn't still fantasizing that Father Joseph was abducted."

"I think it's fairer to say that the family wants some fresh eyes on the case."

"I have no problem with that. All of us at St. George would also like to know why he left." The lawyer paused for a moment before adding, "Whatever Father Joe did or whatever happened to him has divided the parish. And St. George is a small parish that can ill afford divisions. His . . . his whatever we call it—his fleeing or his tragic accident—has remained a cloud over the community. For some of us, it's hard to think about anything else. Even in the worst-case scenario, which I don't have to spell out, we'd at least have an answer. We could grieve, lament, or shake our fists at the heavens, but we could move on."

Worthy could empathize with the man and the weight he carried as the parish council president. And maybe that weight was even heavier for a lawyer trained to get to the bottom of things.

"We talked with Mrs. Reston, the church secretary. She said something interesting."

"I expect she would. She knows the parish like no one else," Mr. Fragouli said. "Please share, if you don't mind."

"When I asked her what Father Joseph was like in the days and weeks before he disappeared, she said she could hardly remember those days."

Mr. Fragouli nodded and looked at Lena. "As a psychologist, you're probably not surprised by her comment. That's only human nature, don't you agree?"

Lena nodded. "Confusion isn't a mental state that any of us enjoy. We would prefer an answer, even a wrong one, to no answer at all. My guess is that once the media uncovered Father Joseph's problem in Greece, that became the controlling narrative."

Mr. Fragouli nodded appreciatively. "I couldn't have put it better myself."

"And you, Mr. Fragouli? What do you believe?" Worthy asked.

The lawyer waited for a moment before speaking. "I will give you the answer I give everyone at St. George who can't seem to get past it. I say we might never know why Father Joe left, but we have to accept that he did."

Worthy wondered if the parish president took his own advice. "How would you describe Father Joseph before he disappeared?" he asked.

The lawyer paused and picked up his phone. "Darla, call my ten o'clock and tell them I'll be a few minutes late."

After putting the phone down, Mr. Fragouli walked to the kitchenette and poured himself a cup of coffee. "Can I get you more tea, Doctor?"

"Yes, thank you."

"And you, Lieutenant. Are you sure you won't have something? Sparkling water, perhaps?"

"Water would be fine. Thanks."

After Mr. Fragouli returned to his chair, he leaned back and looked at the ceiling. "I'll be brief. We were happy at St. George to have a young priest, one who related well to the youth and young families. He was good at sports, which impressed the kids. They'd see him cycling around town, you see. In terms of the services, Father Joe was more than competent in leading the liturgy, and his homilies were first-rate. Fifteen to twenty minutes max, they were thoughtful and practical."

"How about in his relationship one-on-one with parishioners?" Worthy asked.

"Those in the hospital or a nursing home liked his manner. He seemed empathetic, very caring."

A very rosy picture, Worthy thought, wishing again that Nick, with his own background as a priest, were here to probe further.

"What about his moods?" Lena asked. "Mrs. Reston said he was withdrawn at times."

"Withdrawn? Well, maybe that's exaggerating things a bit. He was a single man who lived alone, remember. I wouldn't say he was ever aloof with us, yet . . ."

Worthy waited a moment before asking, "Yes?"

"Again, what I say might just be tainted by the media, but I'm not sure any of us would say—at least now—that we truly knew Father Joe. Was that just a matter of his only being with us for a year before his disappearance, something that would have changed if he'd stayed longer? I don't know if any of us can answer that question, Lieutenant."

Worthy thought back to his own days growing up in a parsonage. His father, a Baptist minister, had more than once said, "A pastor and his family must be friendly with everyone, but close friends with nobody."

The memory of his father led Worthy to ask, "What about with other clergy in the community? Sometimes clergy find support there."

Mr. Fragouli nodded. "An interesting question, one that has both a 'no' and 'yes' response to it. The 'yes' part is that Father Joe, as I said, was a committed cyclist. He rode his bike whenever he could, and I know he sometimes went cycling with a club here in Saginaw. But I don't think any of them were clergy from other churches. Yet I could be wrong about that."

Lena cleared her throat. "This might be a delicate question, but we need to understand how he related to women."

"No problem, as far as I could see. I think some of the middle school and high school girls had a crush on him, but he knew how to deflect that."

"Was there any woman in the parish who seemed especially close to him?"

Mr. Fragouli didn't respond for a moment. "I think that's a question better left to Mrs. Reston. She knows better than anyone about the people who came to talk with Father in his office, but I never heard of anything like what you're suggesting. As I said, Father Joe didn't give off any warning signs that any of us detected. And with that, I'm afraid I'm going to have to beg off. I have one appointment after another this morning."

At the door, Worthy paused and turned back to the lawyer. "As parish council president, were you surprised by how often the Metropolitan-Bishop in Detroit asked for an update on how Father Joseph was settling in?"

For the first time, Mr. Fragouli seemed to hesitate. "No, no, not at all. He was young, and St. George was Father Joe's first assignment as a solo priest. I just took the Metropolitan's interest as part of his pastoral duty."

As Lena and Worthy drove away, Lena turned to Worthy. "My questions didn't bother you? I don't want to be in the way, Chris."

"Are you kidding? What you said in there, the psychological angle, that was important."

"It's hard for me to gauge. Promise me you'll tell me to shut up if I come on too strong."

He reached over and caught her hand. "I don't think that's going to happen, but okay, I promise."

They rode in silence for a few moments before Lena asked, "How did you know that the Metropolitan-Bishop was checking up on Father Joseph?"

"I didn't, but I thought it was likely, given what happened in Greece. And I imagine a lawyer like Mr. Fragouli would have sensed something, would have asked for an explanation. But I think it's pretty certain that Mr. Fragouli isn't going to tell us what the Metropolitan-Bishop told him."

"Do you think we'll do better with the other names on the list?" Lena asked.

"No, because Mr. Fragouli will be calling all of them by now, warning them about us. As a lawyer, he's undoubtedly coached them to repeat what he already told us."

"Of course, that's exactly what he'd do. Where does that leave us?"

"Call Nick, Lena. Ask him to get contact information from this third brother in Lansing. We can drive there and talk to him tomorrow. After that, I think we should head back to Ohio to talk with Nick."

"Are we sure that the abbot won't let him leave St. Simeon's?" Lena asked.

"I think it's time I found out, once and for all. I'm going to look the abbot squarely in the eye and tell him his attitude toward Nick is pure bullshit."

OCTOBER 8

NICK WOKE THE NEXT MORNING WITH THE NAME "ELIAS" dancing in his head. *Of course,* he thought as he sat up in bed, *why didn't I think of Elias before?*

Father Elias had been a fellow seminarian of Nick's twenty years before. Even as Nick had felt called to monastic life, Elias had taken the path of marriage and then parish ministry. In fact, Nick had been a groomsman in Elias and Sophia's wedding.

More significant, given what was weighing on Nick's mind, was the fact that Elias had been the Metropolitan-Bishop's right-hand man, the Chancellor, fourteen years ago. If anyone could uncover the details of Father Joseph's debacle in Greece, details the present Chancellor was keeping from Nick, it would be Elias.

After early morning prayers and breakfast, Nick found the directory of Greek Orthodox clergy serving in North America in the monastery library. He discovered that Father Elias was the proto-presbyter, or chief priest, at St. Mary's parish in Santa Monica, California, having accepted that assignment three years before after serving more than a decade in Bismarck, North Dakota.

Southern California, that's a sweet assignment, Elias, Nick thought as he pictured his friend walking the beach instead of shoveling snow in North Dakota.

Communicating with his old friend was something Nick could contribute to the case from St. Simeon's, but the limitation chafed. He'd much prefer to be on the road with Worthy and Lena, able to travel without needing his abbot's permission to join them in Saginaw and Lansing.

Once again, as he sat in the monastery library, he was aware of the chasm that separated him from his superior. On one side of the gulf was Abbot Lucas, who reminded Nick repeatedly of the vow of stability, the promise to remain in one's own monastery unless moved by the abbot. On the other side was his own sense that he was called to be a monk who helped solve homicides. He thought of the saying that was placed prominently on one of St. Simeon's walls: "The only purpose of human life is to help heal the world."

What frustrated Nick was his inability to convince Abbot Lucas of two things. One, instead of leaving St. Simeon's behind when investigating cases with Worthy, he felt he was bringing a bit of the healing solace of the monastery to victims and their families.

And two, he understood that if anyone with a religious calling could help the police solve cases, that person would be a monk or nun, not a parish priest. The numerous duties of a parish meant that a priest was tied more to a specific location than monks or nuns to their monasteries.

As he closed the directory and left the library, Nick wondered if Father Joseph had felt chained to the parish in Saginaw. What if Father Joseph were someone who felt, as Nick could feel, compelled to deal with a serious problem, but, unlike him, was prevented from even requesting a leave? What if Father Joseph hadn't abandoned his calling but left Saginaw to somehow fulfill it?

FROM HIS CAR, WORTHY CALLED SOTER KOURIS' NUMBER and heard a receptionist say, "Kouris Wealth Management, how can I help you?"

Wealth management, Worthy thought. One brother a priest, another a monk, and the middle son living in the world of high finance. *Was Soter the one son the Kouris family was proud of?* he wondered.

After Worthy requested a meeting with the financial advisor, the receptionist put him on hold for a moment before coming back on the line. "He has a half-hour opening at 4:30 this afternoon. Will that work?"

Lena and Worthy drove hurriedly to East Lansing and found Kouris Wealth Management nestled between a pizza parlor and a college bar in a strip mall near the university. The location gave Worthy the impression that Kouris Wealth Management wasn't managing much wealth.

Soter Kouris might have been an athlete in college, but the years since college hadn't been kind to him. Psoriasis on his hands and neck was coupled with a belly that protruded over a tightly cinched belt.

"Before you arrived, I reached my brother Paul down in Ohio. He told me that you," Soter said looking at Worthy, "are helping with Aris' disappearance." Turning toward Lena, he said, "But I don't know who you are."

"I'm Dr. Fabriano, a psychologist," Lena said. "Lieutenant Worthy and I have worked on cases together before."

Worthy nodded in agreement, thinking that was close enough to the truth.

Soter Kouris wet his lips before speaking. "Thank you for not saying anything to my receptionist about . . . well, about my wayward brother, Aris. An embarrassment is never good for business."

The brother's use of the words "wayward," "embarrassment," and his calling his brother Aris instead of Father Joseph made it clear to Worthy how Soter Kouris interpreted his brother's disappearance. He decided to wait to hear what else the financial advisor would say. After an awkward moment, Soter added, "Aris has been a mystery to the family for some time—at least to Papa and me."

"When did you last see your brother?" Worthy asked.

Soter looked up to the corner of the ceiling spotted with moisture stains as if the answer were written there. "I didn't make it up to his installation at the church in Saginaw—neither did my father, come to think of it. Snowed under with business, you see." After he paused, he added, "So, the last time I saw Aris must have been when the family was together the Christmas before last. Yes, that's about right. Papa and Aris got into it again, about Aris becoming a priest. This past holiday, my family and I were with the folks in Pennsylvania, but Aris, of course, had services at the church in Saginaw. But maybe he didn't want to get into another fight with Papa."

So, this brother lives no more than two hours away from his younger brother in Saginaw but has never visited, Worthy thought.

"Mr. Kouris, you used the word 'embarrassment,'" Lena said. "Do you blame your brother for his disappearance?"

Soter's face turned red. "Did I say that? Well, this isn't the first time Aris has embarrassed the family. His time in Greece—well, what was that, but a royal fu—, a royal mess."

"What do you think happened in Thessaloniki?" Worthy asked.

Soter sighed heavily. "Aris should never have become a priest, much less a celibate one. No, that never made sense to me."

When Worthy and Lena nodded that they did know that, Soter continued. "For my other brother, Paul, yes, celibacy is no surprise. Paul was never comfortable around girls. But Aris? Aris always liked women, and women have always liked him. I'm not saying Aris should have married, but he's all male, if you know what I mean." He paused before glancing toward Worthy, "What was it you asked me?"

"I asked what you think happened to Aris in Greece, but maybe you answered that. You think your brother and this Ukrainian woman were involved with one another, is that right?"

"What else am I to think? You do know that Aris was engaged twice in college."

Worthy remembered what Nick told him over the phone the afternoon before, that Brother Paulus described Aris as popular with women. But there had been no mention of Aris being twice engaged.

"No, we didn't know that," Worthy said. "What happened?"

"The first one, to Candace, was at the end of his second year of college. He brought her home over Christmas to meet the family, and I have to tell you, she was gorgeous. She was just the type I'd expect Aris to go for, but I could tell pretty quickly that that relationship wasn't going to last. She was Irish-Catholic. No way Momma was going to give her blessing for that."

"You mean, because she wasn't Greek?" Lena asked.

"She wasn't even Orthodox," Soter said, raising his hands in emphasis. "I can't remember who ended the engagement, but is made sense."

"You said your brother was engaged a second time," Lena said.

"Right, right. That was in his senior year; in fact, that engagement ended just before he graduated. Phyllida was Greek, from an Orthodox family from out East, so when they split, the folks were devastated. Papa and momma really liked Phyllida, and wedding invitations had already been sent out."

"Who broke off the engagement?" Lena said.

"Aris did, and, as I said, that was a shocker. All I know is that a month later, Aris announced he was going to become a priest. Papa flipped out—ended up in the E.R. with panic attacks."

They were silent for a moment before Worthy said, "Let's go back to what you believe happened in Greece."

Soter Kouris frowned as he looked out the window. "My brother Paul and I never agreed on Aris' so-called vocation. I agree with Papa—that decision was the beginning of Aris going off the rails—his instability, I mean. Did you know he was offered a tryout for the Olympics? But being a celibate priest? No, Aris isn't made for that life. Did I say that he always liked the ladies, and the ladies always liked him?"

Worthy could sense a note of satisfaction in Soter's comments about his younger brother, a brother who was more gifted athletically and who'd turned down an Olympic tryout. "Are you saying you think your brother left Saginaw for a woman?"

"I'm not saying he did, but I'm not saying he didn't. I won't go into details, but it doesn't take a genius to see a pattern with my brother."

Before Worthy could reply, Lena spoke. "If you're right, Mr. Kouris, why hasn't your brother come forward? Being with a woman is a violation of his vows as a priest, but it's not against the law."

"Look, my brother Paul has been a monk for what—ten years? And I've been developing my business for the last six. Life's about being stable, choosing something and sticking with it. But Aris? As Papa says, Aris makes decisions without thinking them through. So, I'm not saying Aris is living with some woman, but I believe when you find Aris, there's going to be woman in the mix."

CHAPTER FOUR

———— ◆ ————

THAT AFTERNOON, LENA AND WORTHY DROVE FROM LANSING to Detroit to have dinner with Amy, Worthy's younger daughter. Unlike her older sister, Allyson, Amy seemed less damaged by her parents' divorce. She hadn't cut her father out of her life as Allyson had initially done, and she said, at least, that she was glad her father had met someone. Their evening together wasn't the first time Amy and Lena had met, and Worthy sensed whatever her true feelings were, Amy had decided to play the role of the mature adult. And maybe, Worthy wondered, that explained why Amy wore make-up for the dinner and tailored slacks rather than jeans.

After the waiter brought tea and coffee, Lena said, "So, tell me how your second year of college is going. Do they still call it the sophomore year?"

"It's funny. When you're starting college, everyone calls you a freshman. And if you're getting ready to graduate, they call you seniors. But the years in between just seem to be the years in between. Maybe it's because so many take four and a half or five years to graduate. But about my year? Let's see. Over the summer, I lost my two favorite professors, which bummed me out pretty bad. One decided to be a full-time artist, and the other retired for health reasons. Their replacements are okay, I guess. Other than that, I was elected recruitment chair in my sorority for next year. That's a lot of rah, rah, if you know what I mean. I guess I can play the part at least for another month, when recruitment is over."

"We don't have fraternities and sororities in Italy," Lena said. "But when I was in grad school at Notre Dame, I taught several undergrad psychology classes. That was my introduction to the fraternity-sorority system. I was warned that those groups kept old tests and notes on file, but I heard the same about athletes."

Amy smiled. "My lips are sealed on that. But anyone can find the same kind of help on the internet. I think it's up to the person if they want to cut corners or not."

"And that's true whether you're a student in Italy or the States. But you like your college?"

"Franklin College? Yes, it's small, but the college is great at helping students set up internships. And that's actually something I wanted to talk with you about, Lena."

"Oh?"

"My first choice for an internship is to work in Italy, maybe even Rome, in a firm that restores paintings. If I can find something like that for next summer, I can combine that with my senior year experience. That's a research paper on feminist perspectives on the Renaissance painter Gentileschi."

Lena nodded. "Oh, I like that topic. There's a lot of interest in Gentileschi now." After a pause, Lena added, "If you choose Rome, you're welcome to stay at my place."

Amy shook her head. "Thanks, but if I get the internship I'm applying for, I'll have student housing near the university. No, what I'm thinking is that it would be nice to know someone in Rome. Unlike Allyson, I've never been to Europe. Actually, I've never been out of the U.S., and I don't know Italian. I did take three years of Latin, but I don't think that's going to be of much good."

"A bit, mainly to read the words on the monuments, which is more than I can say for most Italians. Does it affect your plans if your Dad comes over to Rome for a few weeks next summer? You see, this is my time to be here, but next summer is your Dad's turn to visit me."

Amy looked at Worthy. "What do you think, Dad?"

Worthy had enjoyed sitting quietly, listening to his daughter and Lena. Amy seemed years, not months older, than she did on her last Christmas break. She was now as tall as her sister, Allyson, and, like Allyson, played college-level volleyball. Her hair was also shorter, cut in a style that was longer on one side than the other. But Amy's question of him brought back painful memories of the time he and Allyson overlapped on a case in Venice. Although they eventually worked through the tension between them, he remembered how much Allyson had resented his presence.

"I promise to stay out of your way," he said. "No college student wants a Dad hanging around. So, it's up to you."

"Look, Dad, I'm not Allyson. I'd be happy to have you hanging around," Amy said.

"I'm sure your mother will miss you," Lena said.

Amy nodded. "Yes, but with me being in college, I think she's used to the empty nest. But just to be on the safe side, I probably won't tell her anything until I find out if I get the internship. Anyway, enough about me." Smiling, she added, "Tell me, Lena, what exciting things does my Dad have planned for you while you're here? I can only imagine how thrilling it is to be in Detroit after Rome. Ha!"

While they ate, Worthy and Lena described, without offering names, the case of the missing priest.

"This is an Orthodox priest, like Father Nick?" Amy asked.

"Yes, even Greek Orthodox," Worthy explained.

"Then, why isn't Father Nick here with you?"

"That's something I'm working on. We could have used him when we were in Saginaw. He would have seen through the smokescreen we faced. But Nick is helping out, even if he's stuck in the monastery."

"But this missing priest could show up tomorrow, right? Like Allyson did when she ran away back in high school, I mean."

"If he does, Amy, he's not going to get away with just giving the silent treatment," Worthy said. "This guy has a lot of explaining to do."

Amy looked at Lena and shook her head. "This is Dad's idea of giving you a good time?"

Lena shook her head. "No, it's fine. Really. Your Dad is letting me do more than tag along."

"Because you're a psychologist, you mean," Amy said.

"Lena is a specialist on unusual religious behavior, so I think a priest who disappears fits that category perfectly," Worthy explained.

Amy's hand with a buttered roll in it froze between her plate and her mouth. "But you work homicides, Dad, and missing persons sometimes end up . . . that way. Murder victims, I mean."

Worthy looked down at his wine and slowly nodded. "Yes, Amy, they do."

OCTOBER 9

THE NIGHT BEFORE, NICK HAD ARRANGED THROUGH FATHER ORDO, Prior of St. Simeon, for Nick and Lena to be allowed into the monastery's archive room the next morning. Monks were allowed to have visitors, but if too many visited, that was considered a problem. Father Ordo approved his request, but Nick knew that the prior would fill the abbot in on the disappearance of Brother Paulus' brother. Nick could imagine the awkward conversation with his abbot that loomed ahead.

At least I'm helping out from inside St. Simeon's, he thought. But Nick knew the abbot would expect for him to ask, once again, for permission to leave.

Nick let Lena and Worthy begin the meeting by sharing what they'd learned from the parish council president, Mr. Fragouli, as well as from Soter Kouris.

"There's obviously a considerable amount of sibling rivalry between Soter Kouris and Father Joseph," Lena said. "He didn't try to hide how much he was enjoying his brother's downfall."

"That's how I read him as well," Worthy added.

Nick considered the point. "I'm curious, Lena. You said this brother kept saying that he and the father saw the situation the same way. Do you think that's the truth?"

"He might have overemphasized how close his view of Aris—Father Joseph—used to be with his Dad's. Maybe he's thinking about what he might gain from his brother's predicament. I'm guessing it could be closeness with his father."

"Soter and Aris were both athletes, but Aris came out on top. Soter mentioned a tryout for the Olympics," Worthy said. "A lot of fathers would favor that kind of son."

"Yes, the golden boy until he decided to become a priest. That's when he became a puzzle to his family," Lena said. "Did you learn anything more from Brother Paulus, Nick?"

Nick shared what Paulus told him about the pregnancy when Aris was in high school, the death of the baby, and Aris' reaction of throwing himself into athletics, especially rowing. At the end, he described Aris' two failed romances and his sudden decision to attend the seminary.

When he finished, Lena looked up from the notes she was taking. "We also heard about his romantic failures. Those broken engagements might fit Father Joseph's pattern." The brother in Lansing said both he and his father saw Joseph as unstable."

"What do you mean by his pattern?" Nick said.

"Soter told us his version of his brother's life. Aris was the popular and athletic son, the golden child, all the way through college. The fact that Soter didn't even mention the pregnancy in high school suggests it wasn't a big deal to Soter and probably the father. The focus was still on the rowing, the scholarship, and the offer of an Olympic tryout—everything a papa would be proud of. That is, until . . . Nick, how did Paulus describe the father's reaction to the decision to go to seminary?"

"The father called it 'his goddamn crazy decision.'"

"And it would be exactly that to their dad," Lena said. "In one moment of instability, the golden child became the destroyer of his own myth."

They were silent until Worthy said, "Lena, you said that was Soter's version of his brother. Is there another?"

"The idea of Father Joseph being impulsive and unstable serves Soter's purposes. But it's not the story Paulus tells, is it, Nick?"

"No, but if you're right, Paulus' version could be just as biased."

"That can't be helped, Nick," Lena said. "Every story is a filtered story. When people tell stories, they're always revealing something about themselves."

Nick sighed. "Paulus' version is certainly different. In his eyes, his brother Aris was his opposite—an extrovert, popular, the star athlete. But for Paulus, the pregnancy and the death of the baby were more than minor blips in his brother's life. They affected Joseph deeply. But is that the truth, or was that how those tragedies would have affected a sensitive introvert like Paulus?"

Lena shook her head. "Two brothers, two versions not just of Father Joseph but of a family."

"Which leaves us with the big question. What version is the right one?" Worthy asked.

Lena shrugged. "What we're missing, Chris, is Father Joseph's version of the story, his narrative. Even so, his version is probably as biased as the others, but until we know that, we won't know why he left."

"It's like a multi-dimensional maze," Nick said.

"Welcome to the daily life of a therapist," Lena said.

"Then I don't know how you do it," Nick said.

"The answer to that is simple, Nick. I don't do it. Yes, I'm a psychologist, but I'm not a therapist. I research people we call mystics, and I have the advantage of studying most of them after they've died."

"Except when you're studying a living mystic, like last year in Rome," Worthy said.

"Right, that was an exception. As strange as it is for me to say, I would have understood her far better if she'd been already dead."

Nobody spoke for a few moments before Lena shuddered. "Sorry, I think I just suggested that we'd understand Father Joseph better if he were dead."

LATER THAT AFTERNOON, WHILE NICK WALKED LENA AND WORTHY to St. Simeon's parking lot, he said, "I feel so useless sitting here."

"We could have used you up in Saginaw," Worthy said. "I'm sure you'd have gotten more out of the parish council president than we did. And we haven't begun to interview people in town who knew Aris."

"Christopher, don't make me feel worse than I do. The abbot is adamant."

Worthy stopped walking and looked back at the monastery. "I think it's time I had a chat with your abbot," Worthy said.

CHAPTER FIVE

———— ◆ ————

A FTER WORTHY HEADED FOR THE ABBOT'S OFFICE, Nick and Lena walked down the hallway to the monastery's chapel.

"If you don't mind waiting in the library, Lena, I need to pray."

"Of course, Nick."

Kneeling before the icon of St. Simeon, Nick prayed for God's will to be done, even though he had little hope that Worthy would change the abbot's mind. Instead, he worried that Worthy's well-meaning attempt would backfire and lead to a permanent ban on him helping Worthy in the future.

He could understand that his times away from St. Simeon's could look to other monks as if he were getting away with something, like a schoolboy playing hooky. To those who chose to view him in this way, Nick was feeding his ego by pretending to be a detective. The media's interest in him, a monk who worked on homicide cases, hadn't helped.

All monks are charged with praying daily for the world and the souls in it. As Nick saw it, the only difference between his fellow monks at St. Simeon's and him was the place where he offered his prayers. If anything was true, he prayed more when he was working with Worthy on a case than when he was in the monastery.

But, if the will of God as channeled through his abbot was for him to no longer help Worthy, Nick knew he would accept that verdict. What pained him most about such a verdict was knowing that his relationship with Worthy would slowly wither. Nick had no doubt that Worthy was even then regaling the abbot with how much he, Nick, contributed to his investigations.

But what Worthy couldn't share with the abbot would be how much he, Worthy, meant to Nick. Worthy had become a brother, in many ways as much a brother, if not more, as the monks of St. Simeon's.

Over the years of their friendship, Nick knew many people assumed that Worthy was a spiritual project for him, a soul needing to return to God. Yes, it was a fact that Worthy, having lost his faith nearly a decade before, pursued his cases without the benefits of prayer or belief. From their first case together, however, Nick understood that much of Worthy's upbringing as a minister's son remained in his bones. Because of this, Worthy had an uncanny ability to solve cases where murder occurred in churches or monasteries. Over time, Nick found it easy to accept what Worthy couldn't—that the God Worthy had lost track of had not lost track of Worthy.

"Purity of heart." It was a phrase from the gospels that became the goal of all monks, for Jesus had said, "Blessed are the pure in heart." What bonded him to Worthy was the knowledge that Worthy, in his own way, sought purity of heart, devotion to truth, as strongly as any monk did. There was disappointment, guilt, and pain in Worthy's life—less now that Lena Fabriano had brought love back into his life—but not once had Nick observed duplicity in his friend.

He shook his head. How could he ever explain to his abbot that Worthy, operating without faith, had taught him so much about the spiritual life?

☦

THE LATE MORNING SUN SHONE DOWN FROM A CLOUDLESS SKY when Worthy found the abbot in his office, scowling as he studied his computer screen. The abbot's face didn't improve when Worthy asked that Nick be allowed to join him in searching for the missing priest. The abbot glanced up, looking as if he'd bitten into something sour.

"What you don't understand, Lieutenant, is that I'm responsible for the spiritual development of Father Nicholas."

Worthy anticipated that the abbot would initially oppose his request, but not in this way. "I don't understand," he said.

Abbot Lucas closed his laptop and folded his hands on the desk. "By definition, a monk is one who has withdrawn from the world for the sake of his soul and, indeed, for the sake of the world. In a sense, a monk seeks to disappear from the world's gaze in order to more fully love and pray for the world. Now, in Father Nicholas' case, the opposite has regrettably happened. Father Nicholas has become a kind of celebrity. I didn't put my foot down when his picture with you was on the front page of *USA Today* last year—but I should have."

Worthy wasn't sure how to respond, given that what the abbot said was the truth. But it wasn't the whole truth.

Before Worthy could reply, Abbot Lucas continued. "Because you're not Orthodox, Lieutenant, you may not understand that we take our cue from the holy icons. When we stand before an icon, what we don't see is as important as what they do see. We are in the presence of the saint, not the iconographer, the artist behind the icon. In most cases, the iconographer's signature won't be found. In a similar way, any focus on a particular monk's specialness is damaging to a monk's soul and also to his monastery. You see, the values of society have no place here. Your notoriety, Lieutenant, after solving the case in Rome last year is to be expected. The fact that Father Nicholas experienced the same notoriety, however, is a serious problem."

"Are you saying Nick returns to St. Simeon's expecting to be treated as special? If so, I don't believe it."

Now it was the abbot who paused before continuing. "No, I agree. Father Nicholas doesn't do that. But can't you see that his coming and going disrupts the peace of our community?"

It was only then that Worthy realized he was arguing for Nick's help not only on this case, but on all future cases.

"Reverend Father, because of Nick, we've been able to close some very difficult cases." Worthy sought for language that the abbot might better understand. "Nick is especially gifted at finding missing young people. It's uncanny how deeply he grasps the thinking of young people in particular. He told me more than once that hearing confessions at St. Simeon's has helped on our investigations. He calls it 'prayerful listening.' It's incredible what he brings to these cases."

"And I'm sure you're genuinely thankful, Lieutenant. But you must understand that at some point, Father Nicholas is going to have to decide if he's a monk or a detective."

Worthy felt he was losing ground in the argument. It was no wonder that Nick often felt stymied by the abbot. "I, I know it's unusual, but Nick is both of those—a monk and a detective. He's saved lives, and I mean both body and soul. Are you sure the problem isn't lack of imagination or maybe . . . maybe jealousy here at St. Simeon's?"

The abbot bowed his head, closing his eyes before rising to his feet. "Mr. Worthy, I think our conversation has come to an end."

Not until I've tried everything, Worthy thought.

"Reverend Father, you must think I have a lot of nerve. It's not nerve, but something else—desperation. With all due respect, if you think Nick stops being a monk when he's outside these walls, you're mistaken. I've won a number of commendations and a certain reputation for solving difficult cases. But that hides the truth, a truth that Nick would likely deny, and that is that I'm most effective when he is on cases with me. My guess is that Nick has never told anyone in St. Simeon's what he contributes to our work."

The silence of the room made Worthy wonder if he'd gone too far. But instead of insisting Worthy leave his office, the abbot sat down again.

"All right, Lieutenant, now is your chance. Tell me what Father Nicholas offers that is so important."

Worthy took a deep breath. "Reverend Father, it's hard for those unfamiliar with homicide investigations to grasp how stressful and discouraging the work can be. First of all, there is the family of the victim. Their world has just come to an end, and it's hard to describe the look they give us. They're begging for answers, and many times I can't give them answers for weeks or months. Meanwhile, I'm so focused on the case, tracking down clues and interviewing witnesses, that it's easy for me to feel that these same families are draining me. And yes, I know that police departments have chaplains that can meet with grieving families, but I wonder if you can imagine what it's like for families to be consoled by Nick, a compassionate priest who is also investigating the case. More times than I can count, families whom I thought had told me all they knew, share something with Nick that they'd forgotten."

Worthy paused and tried to read the expression on the abbot's face, but the abbot gave nothing away.

"But there's so much more. I can be a loner, and I withdraw more and more as I work a case. Every partner I've had except Nick has complained that I shut them out. Some see me as a glory hound, a cop who doesn't want to share the limelight. I don't mean to be defensive, but that's not true. What I'm trying to say is that Nick is the only one I've worked with who doesn't abandon me when I go . . . when I have to go into myself. Somehow, he understands that I have to withdraw if I'm going to get into the mind of the killer. Nick stays with me when I take that . . . that descent."

The longer the abbot didn't say anything, the more Worthy wondered if he was getting through at all.

"You have to know something before you decide, Reverend Father. Two years ago, my older daughter was abducted on a case that Nick and I were working. Because of problems that my daughter and I had after my wife divorced me, I was paralyzed with guilt. I was of absolutely no use."

Worthy felt a lump in his throat and he waited until he was sure he was in control. "What I know is that my daughter Allyson wouldn't be alive today if Nick hadn't been with me on that case."

Worthy tried to steady his voice before continuing. "What Nick does is save people. I'm sure he's given comfort and encouragement to many who come to St. Simeon's. But when he's working with me, he saves people too. Sometimes, it's getting a daughter back. Other times, it's giving a family comfort and something even more than comfort—hope. And more than once, Nick has faced killers and given them a chance to confess, even at the risk of his own life. Nick doesn't stop being a priest when he's working with me. Can you honestly deny that he's living out his calling when he's working with me?"

Worthy stopped, feeling gutted. The abbot said nothing for a long moment, then surprised Worthy by bowing his head again and muttering what seemed to be a prayer. When he finished, he looked at Worthy with tears in his eyes.

"It's no secret that I've resisted Father Nicholas on this matter. Even when the Ecumenical Patriarch requested his presence with you last year in Rome, I thought His Eminence was wrong. I thought I knew Father Nicholas better than the patriarch . . . and better than you. But now I wonder. Have I a mote in my own eye when it comes to Father Nicholas?"

Worthy watched as the abbot seemed to struggle to explain himself.

"You're wrong on one point, Lieutenant. The issue is simpler and maybe sadder than jealousy. Most monks are introverts; we are the type who prefers solitude. I'm not telling you anything you don't know, but Father Nicholas doesn't fit that mold. It's been too easy for me to hear the complaints of some of my monks who say Nicholas talks too much. My predecessor as abbot left specific instructions on how I was to treat Father Nicholas. I was told in clear terms to rein him in and force him to choose between helping the police and being a monk. Until this moment, I've never questioned that advice. But now? Yes, I think now I do question it."

The room was silent for a moment before Worthy said, "It's funny. Nick is criticized for talking too much, and I'm criticized for keeping too much to myself. My daughter Allyson, the one I was talking about a minute ago, once said that I should have been the monk and Nick should have been the detective. But I've worked with Nick enough to know that when Nick is talking, he's always listening. He hears things in other people's silences, and they sense it. I know this because, as I said, he understands my silences, which I'm told are too many."

For the first time, Abbot Lucas smiled, though weakly. "You're asking a lot of an abbot to expect him to agree that a person can have too much silence in his life."

Worthy returned the smile but said nothing.

Finally, the abbot rose and sighed deeply. "I think you just heard my confession, Lieutenant. Someone said the wise person is one who is willing to change his mind, especially when he's been so sure that he was right. I ask for your forgiveness, Mr. Worthy, and I promise that I'll ask Father Nicholas for his. I cannot promise that Nicholas will escape criticism by some of his brother monks or by my successor, but it's time, I now see, that St. Simeon treats Father Nicholas with more grace—and, when he is away, that we offer more of our prayers for his work with you."

CHAPTER SIX

————◆————

OVER LUNCH IN ST. SIMEON'S REFECTORY, Nick sat stunned as he looked from Worthy to Lena. He opened his mouth, but nothing came out.

"Oh, ye of little faith," Worthy said with a smile.

"Little faith, indeed, Christopher. But how did you ever manage to change the abbot's mind?"

"I thought I'd failed, but then I realized neither the abbot nor maybe the other monks have any idea what you contribute to our cases—as a priest, I mean."

"That's kind, my friend, but until now, Abbot Lucas has resolutely stuck to his belief that a monk belongs in his monastery."

"Oh, he made that clear, but when I described what you do for the victims' families, for me, and maybe especially for the perpetrators, he started to see things differently." Worthy looked down at his plate of food before adding, "It's when I told him how you saved Allyson's life two years ago. . ."

Nick put his fork down on the plate, shook his head and gazed up at the ceiling. "I don't know what to say but 'Thank you, God, for small miracles.' Although, given the grilling I've usually gotten when I return from a case, I'd say the miracle is anything but small." He paused before shaking his head again. "Are you sure you didn't misunderstand the abbot?"

Lena laughed. "You can ask him yourself. The abbot told Chris that he's going to ask for your forgiveness, Nick."

"If that happens, then I'll know I'm not dreaming."

Worthy reached across the table and jabbed Nick's arm gently. "There, see? This is no dream."

"Okay, okay. I believe you both, but I feel a bit like a convict walking out of prison. I don't know how to celebrate."

"Oh, we have an idea. Let us take you out to dinner tonight."

"That would be lovely, Lena, but I don't want to abuse my new freedom with the abbot, so let's make sure I'm back by 8:30 for prayers." He shook his head again in disbelief. "I can hardly believe this, Christopher. Before we go for dinner, I want to spend a few minutes in our chapel, and I want to make a phone call to my friend from seminary. If anyone can uncover what the Metropolitan-Bishop believes happened last year in Greece last year between Father Joseph and the Ukrainian woman, it will be Elias."

Twenty minutes later, Nick heard Father Elias answer his phone. "Father Elias speaking."

"This is an old friend calling. Do you have time for a game of racquetball and a few beers?"

"Who is this? Wait a minute. Good Lord, is this Nick?"

"It is, but I was just kidding about the racquetball."

"Were you kidding about the beers? Tell me you're out here in Southern California," Father Elias said.

"Unfortunately, no. I'm still at St. Simeon's. How are things in Santa Monica?"

"Well, it's just so boring to see the clear skies and sunsets over the Pacific."

"Yes, it's clear you're suffering for the faith," Nick said with a laugh. "Not everyone is blessed to spend the winter here in northeastern Ohio."

"Spare me, O Lord. You do know I was in Bismarck, North Dakota, before being assigned here, so winters I know."

"I did see that in the directory. From Bismarck to Santa Monica. How did your family take the move?"

"Thanks, Nick, for not assuming that everyone would love to leave one of the coldest spots in the US for Southern California. My son and daughter made great friends in Bismarck, and Gail, my daughter, struggled here at the beginning. The Southern California high school scene isn't the easiest to get used to, but the youth group at church has helped."

"Actually, Elias, I'm calling about someone having a difficult time adjusting to a new environment, or, at least, I think I am."

"Okay, you have me intrigued. Someone from our seminary days?"

"No, but you're in the ballpark. Have you heard about Father Joseph Kouris?"

"Of course, Nick. He's the missing priest from Michigan, right? Oh, wait a minute. Are you working with the police on that?"

"As of about an hour ago, I'm officially on the case."

Elias' voice dropped. "Do you think he's still alive?"

"He's been missing for a month, but obviously, that's what we're hoping. But so far, no one seems to know where to look."

"Now I'm even more intrigued about why you called," Elias said.

"Before I tell you that, I need to give you some background information. Father Joseph was on the fast track for big things in the Church. I'm talking about being Metropolitan-Bishop someday, or maybe even higher. If you've seen photos of him, you know he's a good-looking man. He's also quite charismatic. I've been told that young people especially like him. Eighteen months ago, even though he already had a doctorate in Greek History, he was sent to Thessaloniki for a second PhD, this one in liturgics."

"Charismatic, good-looking, and highly educated. Yes, I can see him doing well. So, what happened?"

"That's what I'm hoping you can help us find out. What we know so far is that Father Joseph became friends with a Ukrainian woman, a fellow grad student at the university."

"And Joseph was celibate?"

"That's half the problem, and the other half is that the woman is married."

"Ouch. Was there impropriety or just rumor?" Elias asked.

"Father Joseph said the woman was being abused by her husband. Then the woman came to his apartment in the middle of the night in hysterics. Father Joseph let her stay in his apartment for safety and claims nothing else happened. The husband complained to everyone who would listen—the university officials, church leaders, just about anyone. Father Joseph was on a flight home within days."

"With his brilliant career down the drain."

"Nearly. He was assigned to a small parish in Saginaw, Michigan. But a month ago, he disappeared without an explanation."

Elias sighed. "There are a lot of what-ifs here, aren't there?"

"That's what I'm hoping you can help with. You worked under the Chancellor in Detroit after seminary. Then you were elevated to the post of Chancellor."

"I think I get the picture, Nick. The Metropolitan-Bishop's office in Detroit is saying little. They're focused on damage control, right?"

"Let's just say I don't think we've been told everything they know."

"I'm happy to help if I can, but what specifically would you like me to find out?"

"For starters, anything you can find out about the Ukrainian woman. But the second thing is more important. The Metropolitan-Bishop must have required counseling for Father Joseph, wouldn't you agree?"

"Without a doubt. But I'll have to be careful how I ask them back in Detroit."

"What I'm hoping is that you know someone still in the office who's good at picking up gossip."

Elias was silent for a moment. "I think I know just the person, Nick."

✝

BROTHER PAULUS WAS RELIEVED TO LEARN THAT NICK could work more openly on his brother's case, but he also felt a pang of guilt. In past years, he'd been one of the monks at St. Simeon's who looked askance at Nick's frequent departures to work with a homicide detective in Detroit. And once, he remembered with shame, he'd relayed to the abbot a question asked him by a group on retreat at St. Simeon's: "Can you point out the monk who solves murders?"

Paulus knew that every monastery in the country has to deal with what is known as the "Merton syndrome." Named for Thomas Merton, the Trappist monk from Kentucky, this "malady" occurs when a member of a monastic community achieves worldly fame and notoriety. Visitors flock to such a monastery not to experience God in solitude, but to catch a glimpse or maybe exchange a word with the monastery's "celebrity."

Without a doubt, Nick was that monk at St. Simeon's. True, other monks at St. Simeon's had achieved some distinction—the community had two writers, a potter, and a poet—but only one had been on the front page of *USA Today* and been awarded—Nick had declined the honor—commendations from not one, but three police departments.

Now, however, with Nick permitted to fully investigate his brother's disappearance, Paulus could only be thankful that God's mercy, like the rain, fell on the undeserving and the deserving alike.

Mixed in with his thankfulness were his dark thoughts about his brother's fate. He knew, should Joseph's body be found, that this would devastate the family, but was death, he wondered, the worst possible outcome? From the questioning that he'd been subjected to by the Chancellor in the weeks after his brother's disappearance, he understood that the Church's greatest fear was a sexual scandal—no, a second sexual scandal, given what the church hierarchy believed happened earlier in Greece.

His prayers for his brother hadn't changed over the weeks since his disappearance, that Joseph would be found alive and with a plausible explanation for his disappearance. The longer the search went on, however, the more he thought he was asking God for the impossible. Did he honestly believe his brother was a John Doe, suffering amnesia in some hospital? That seemed unlikely, yet it was no more bizarre than his mother's belief that her son had been kidnapped and was being held for ransom somewhere.

The truth was that there was *no* plausible explanation for his brother's disappearance. And as the days and weeks went by, Paulus had come to accept, regardless of what he voiced in his prayers, that his brother was a complete mystery to him.

CANDACE JAKES RESENTED THE PAST BREAKING INTO HER PRESENT LIFE, and that was what the phone call from Lieutenant Worthy, a Detroit detective, had done. She chastened herself for not telling the detective that she couldn't help him. Instead, she'd allowed herself to be talked into a Skype interview the next day.

Now three years into a marriage that had produced a son and a daughter, a marriage she thought, if not great, was better than most, Candace still found the memory of her engagement eight years before to Aris Kouris to be painful. She thought back on the eleven months of that engagement, the last month the most difficult because she knew at some level that something was wrong.

She'd learned of Aris being missing only when another detective, a woman from Saginaw, called her two weeks after his disappearance. Candace hadn't, in fact, known Aris had become a priest until the call, and she remembered laughing when the Detroit detective asked if she'd kept contact with Aris since college. Not likely.

Sometimes she'd awake in the morning, seeing his face in her mind and shuddering as she thought, "What if I'd married him?" If she had, it wouldn't have worked, but that was something she could see only in hindsight. Aris' joy in being engaged had never seemed genuine, which, of course, was something she assumed was her fault. *He's holding something back, something I have yet to earn,* she thought at the time.

It was only when the Detroit detective shared that Aris had been engaged a second time, again unsuccessfully, that she could accept that the problem lay with Aris.

Having come from an Irish family that showed love by verbally fighting, as she assumed Greek families did as well, she realized soon after the glow of love faded a bit that Aris would never fight with her. When they disagreed, he would look down as if he deserved her anger. When she shared her frustration about this with her sorority sisters, they told her she was crazy to complain. Aris was not only good looking, which she couldn't deny, but would obviously be a considerate husband. Why did she need him to get angry, to yell at her, or, worse, to threaten her with violence as some of her sorority sisters' boyfriends did? She remembered one sorority sister who said, "Candy, if anyone ever had a storybook romance, it's you and Aris."

Over the eleven months of their engagement, Candace did feel that the two of them were living out a story, each playing an expected role. More and more, she listened to Aris and thought, "Well, isn't that what I expected him to say?" Two nights before she returned the ring, she had a dream of Aris sitting alone in his dorm room, studying a script. In the dream, she tore the script from his hands to find his name before a line that read "I love you" and then her name in front of the next line that read "And I love you too."

Phyllida Tismanakis also wished that she hadn't answered the phone call from Lieutenant Worthy, a Detroit detective, and heard the name Aris Kouris again. Not that there'd been a day since he broke off the engagement one week before their college graduation that she hadn't thought about him. In her closet, safely stored in a protective dress bag, hung the wedding dress and above it, on a shelf and also in plastic, were the two crowns worn in a traditional Greek Orthodox wedding. Her mother had insisted that she keep them "at the ready," but in the more than four years since her engagement to Aris, neither the dress nor the crowns had been out of the plastic. She knew that there they would remain until her mama died.

Aris had told her about his previous engagement to an Irish-American, explaining that the main reasons that had fallen through were their religious differences, she being Catholic, and her fierce temper. At the time, Phyllida felt relieved, knowing she was her predecessor's polar opposite. She, like Aris, was Greek Orthodox, and she was also a person with a quiet voice and an aversion to conflict.

But in the end, those factors hadn't saved the relationship. After a period in which she felt him increasingly withdraw, he told her of his plans to become a priest. It was after dinner one spring night, when they'd been walking hand in hand by a small lake on the university campus. While his decision had come as a shock, given that he'd been offered a tryout for the Olympics in rowing, she said that she'd support his decision and be willing to be a presbytera, a priest's wife.

How could she ever forget his next words: "No, Phylli, you don't understand. I'm going to be a celibate priest." She remembered laughing, sure that he was joking. But when he dropped her hand and looked down, avoiding her gaze, she realized he was serious.

"But you can't," she remembered saying. "Aris, you can't. My dress and the crowns. The arrangements . . . Think of all the arrangements."

Somehow, she'd gotten through those last days of university, passing—barely—her final exams. Sleep deserted her as she realized she was facing a future without a plan. For the following summer and fall, she'd lived at home, managing to do nothing but sit in front of the TV and eat sweets. And, although she soon began a library job and moved to an apartment across town from her parents, she hadn't taken the weight off. When she opened her closet, she looked at the dress that she could no longer fit into and felt condemned.

CHAPTER SEVEN

---◆---

WHILE WORTHY AND LENA WERE CONNECTING WITH ARIS' two fiancés, Nick waited for his friend Elias to return his call. After that, he planned to borrow one of the monastery's cars and drive to Saginaw. There he would begin to interview or re-interview people who knew Father Joseph.

As Abbot Lucas had promised Worthy, he called Nick into his office to explain his change of attitude regarding his absences. He sensed that the abbot feared he would respond triumphantly, but all Nick felt was gratitude.

"Reverend Father, I promise not to abuse this trust," he said at the end of their time together.

"Father Nicholas, I was wrong to accuse you of that in the past. I know better now. And I won't embarrass you by asking why you didn't make the case yourself. I'm sure I know the reason for that."

Nick had accepted the embrace of his abbot before retreating to the chapel to offer his gratitude to the Theotokos, the Mother of God. After that, he returned to his room and began to pack for his trip to Saginaw.

As he did so, he realized he was spending more time wondering what kind of man Father Joseph was than wondering where he might be. He suspected that some of those he would talk to in Saginaw, both in the parish and in the town, no longer considered the man to be a priest. What Nick believed, until proven otherwise, was that Father Joseph might have left Saginaw, but that didn't mean he'd left the priesthood.

OCTOBER 10

WAS THAT A DREAM OR A MEMORY? WAS IT BOTH? Worthy asked himself as he lay, staring at the ceiling. Next to him, Lena slept peacefully. As more of him woke up, he realized it had been both a dream and a memory all tangled up. In the dream, he was about ten years old, sitting on his side of the breakfast table as his father, a Baptist minister, led the family prayers.

He sat up in bed, the memory his unconscious had dredged up slowly clearing. That morning, when he was ten, his father had prayed for Rev. Billy Whitely, who'd been Worthy's summer camp pastor. His father's tone of voice suggested something was wrong. When his father finished the prayer, he asked his father what had happened to Pastor Billy. He remembered his father looking out the window as he replied that Rev. Whitely had left the church he was pastoring.

When he asked if Pastor Billy had taken another church, his father said that he'd just gone, leaving his wife, kids, and the church a little over a week before.

Worthy remember the chills that ran down his spine at the time. Only bad dads, he'd thought at the time, would do that kind of thing, dads who were drunkards or who were criminals. Dads who were ministers would never do that, would they?

After a moment, he remembered the end of that story. Pastor Billy, after being missing less than two weeks, had returned to his family and his congregation, saying he'd needed time away to think and pray. Pastor Billy wasn't at church camp the next summer.

Worthy lay back down again and thought about Father Joseph, who he still thought of as Aris Kouris. This clergyman hadn't returned in two weeks; it was now a month since he'd last been seen.

Lena's arm fell across his chest. "You're up early," she said in a groggy voice.

"Not by choice. Ever had a dream that wasn't really a dream?"

"Hmm. I can't believe you're giving me a quiz this early in the morning."

"It's not a quiz. I'm just wondering how common it is for priests or ministers to run off."

"I don't answer any questions before I get a kiss," she said, drawing herself closer to Worthy.

Worthy kissed her and then kissed her again. "There. Now tell me what you think."

"I think I'd rather go back to sleep."

"Okay but don't blame me if you dream about runaway priests."

"As long as they're young and handsome, I won't mind," she said as she rolled over and pulled a pillow over her head. Little more than a minute later, Lena threw the pillow off the bed and onto the floor. "I can hear the wheels churning in your head, and they're keeping me awake." She turned back to Worthy and said, "Ask me the question again."

"How often do priests and ministers run away?"

Lena yawned. "Do you mean because of an affair or because they're pedophiles?"

"Do you think those are the only reasons?"

Lena didn't answer for a moment. "What if we ask why any adult runs off? Are priests and ministers all that different?"

"Okay, that makes sense. So, in my experience, embezzlers tend to run off with money, and so do blackmailers or those being blackmailed. But the church finances in Saginaw are apparently all in order, and Aris' bank account in Saginaw hasn't shown any activity since he disappeared."

"And no one we talked to in Saginaw has suggested he did anything to one of the children or, for that matter, one of the adults," Lena added.

"Freya would have looked into that right from the beginning. No, there's nothing."

They lay in bed without saying anything for a few moments. "If this were Latin America, priests go missing all the time," Worthy said. "But I don't think we can assume a terror squad kidnapped this priest."

"And if this were Italy, someone would have brought up the Mafia by now," Lena said.

Worthy exhaled slowly. "People do just run away, not from any crime they've committed, but from their lives. It can be an act of pure selfishness, or maybe the person feels stuck or trapped. That's another reason we have to get to know Aris better. Until we do that, we won't know if he ran away *from* something, ran *toward* something, or *both*."

IT WAS EARLY AFTERNOON WHEN NICK RECEIVED THE CALL from Father Elias.

"Hey, Nick. I did get hold of one of my friends in the chancellery. There's no trouble if she remains anonymous, is there?"

"No, not at all. We're just trying to establish some direction on the case. What did she say?"

"Some of it was what you'd expect, that the silence about Father Joseph in the office speaks loud and clear."

Nick sighed. "The hierarchy's way of trying to move on. How long has that been the case?"

"The way my friend tells it, Father Joseph seemed to be the only topic of conversation in the week after he disappeared. They had to contend with the police and then the media. But when the police stopped coming around and the news cycle moved on, the office was told to direct all calls about Father Joseph to the New York office."

"Ah, to the Archbishop himself," Nick said. "As you said, that's what we'd expected. And it explains why the current Chancellor stonewalled me when I asked about what happened in Greece."

"I don't know if this is helpful, but my friend remembers seeing Father Joseph in the Metropolitan-Bishop's office several times. That must have been during the first days after he returned from Greece. Of course, no one outside a few people in the Detroit office knew about the Greece part of the story, but my friend knows a friend who knows the secretary who typed up the minutes of those meetings. According to this person, there was just the Metropolitan-Bishop, the Chancellor, and Father Joseph at some of the meetings, but in at least one more there was another fairly young priest who's also a clinical psychologist."

"Ah ha. Yes, that's helpful. Any chance of getting his name?" Nick asked.

"I'm working on it. My friend has to be careful about not seeming too curious."

"Thanks, Elias. Did the secretary describe what Father Joseph looked like when he first got back?"

"Nick, that's something I was saving as my big reveal, but, as long as you asked, she said he was quiet, but he didn't act guilty or ashamed. If she hadn't learned later what had happened in Greece, she'd have thought he was just another young priest having a meet-and-greet with the Metropolitan-Bishop. Oh, and she also said he was drop-dead handsome."

"Interesting. Not the handsome part, but the part about not acting ashamed. By the way, how was the incident in Greece described?"

"The one who took the notes remembered recording that Father Joseph had been 'indiscreet.' But we all know that's code for a priest being involved with a woman—a woman not his wife, I mean."

Nick was silent for a moment before saying, "Elias, if you're willing, I'd appreciate it if you find out two names for me. First, the name of the psychologist who met with Father Joseph and then the name of the Ukrainian woman from Thessaloniki."

Now Father Elias was silent. Finally, he said, "You think the Detroit office has the name of the woman?" Elias asked.

"I'm sure that someone in the hierarchy has it."

"If the Metropolitan-Bishop's office does know that name, that would be under lock and key in the files. Sorry, Nick."

"No, no, don't be sorry. I was thinking there might be another way of getting that name. Is it possible that the secretary who took notes in the meetings still recalls that woman's name?"

"Hmm. If I thought you were just being nosy, Nick, I'd tell you to take a hike. But we've all read about your talents. It turns out my racquetball partner from seminary has a gift for solving crimes. So, yes, Nick, I'll try, but I make no promises."

CHAPTER EIGHT

———◆———

"CHRIS, I WANT TO WARN YOU. Talking with the two fiancés isn't going to be easy," Lena said over dinner that evening. "You and I both know what it's like to go through a divorce. Granted, yours was worse than mine, but most people assume a broken engagement is less traumatic than a divorce. But I saw what my sister went through when her fiancé broke off their engagement. It made my divorce look like a picnic."

"But that doesn't make sense," Worthy said.

"Why? Because you think a broken engagement is easier to endure than a broken marriage?"

"Well, yes."

"Ah, men," Lena said with a sigh.

"Why? What am I missing?"

"How should I put this? Chris, you're confusing standing before the gate of paradise with the garden itself."

"What is that—an Italian proverb?"

"Not that I know of, but it should be. Engaged couples look ahead to marriage as if they are on the verge of entering paradise. A broken engagement feels like you've been turned away at the gate. So close, but then denied. Anyone who has experienced a broken engagement can't help but live in an eternal state of 'what if.'"

"And marriage? That's paradise?"

"Married people walk through the gate of what they think is paradise, but they soon realize that what they've entered is a garden. A lot of marriages are pleasant, don't get me wrong, but gardens can be filled with weeds—choking weeds, in my case. What I'm saying is that married people know what those with broken engagements never know—that marriage is at best a well-tended garden. But it's not paradise."

Worthy was silent for a moment, and Lena wondered if what she'd said caused him pain. She was consequently glad when his next comment was about the two fiancés, not himself. "According to the one brother, Soter, the finance guy, Aris' first fiancé broke off the engagement and then got married. You think she still feels robbed in some way?"

"Of course. 'What might have been' is always in the background. But you're right, if you're thinking it was much worse for Aris' second fiancé. She's still single. God only knows how much she's living her life 'East of Eden.' I forget who coined that phrase."

"I know Steinbeck used it, but if my memories of Sunday School are correct, the phrase is from the Bible. But you're saying the second fiancé lives outside the garden."

"Worse than that," Lena said. "She believes she's been barred from paradise."

October 11

Nick had always loved driving, but the vow of a monk to remain in the monastery made this chance to drive to Saginaw an even bigger treat.

Two years before, Worthy and he had worked a case in Michigan's Upper Peninsula, and he hadn't forgotten the dense forests and the shore of Lake Superior. He'd also not forgotten Freya, then a new police officer in the Houghton Police Department and now in Saginaw. She had risked her career to help Worthy and him solve several gruesome murders, and he knew she would be just as helpful now.

Of the various interviews that Worthy and Lena had already conducted in Saginaw, Nick considered it worth his time to re-interview Mrs. Reston, the parish secretary. He would not, however, re-interview Mr. Fragouli, president of the parish council, even as he wouldn't bother calling the current Chancellor in Detroit again. Those with official positions would repeat official and approved statements, statements meant to protect the Church. He wanted to talk to people in the parish who would offer candid assessments of Father Joseph, and he knew the parish secretary would know who those persons were.

In addition to parishioners, he wondered about the people outside the church whom the young priest had gotten to know. He remembered Worthy telling him about a cycling club, but he also believed someone as charismatic and handsome as Father Joseph would have made other friends.

It was this vivacity, Father Joseph's ability to attract people to himself, that made it difficult for Nick to believe the young priest was now living somewhere in the shadows. Yet he'd left no trail.

If he committed suicide, why don't I believe that's what happened, he thought.

LENA HAD ASKED WORTHY TO DROP HER OFF at one of the suburban malls out-side Detroit for a couple of hours of shopping before they skyped with Aris' two fiancés. The real reason for the request was that she wanted some time alone to think about the last few days.

While not the type to bemoan the passage of time, she couldn't help but be aware that seven days of her three weeks in the US were already over. She thought back to what her hopes had been for the three weeks in the US and wondered if her personal goals for their being together had any chance of be-ing met.

Over the past year, she and Worthy had been together a total of two months, two or three weeks at a time, alternating between Rome and Detroit. Marriage was not a topic they avoided, neither when they were together nor when they were communicating by phone or email. Yet they acknowledged that their first marriages had failed, even as both knew that second marriages had an even lower rate of success than first ones.

Something that Lena was keenly aware of was that their relationship began under unusual and highly romantic circumstances. To meet and fall in love against a backdrop of murder, international intrigue, and terror at the hands of a megalomaniac meant that in their first days and weeks together, they'd both lived off a heady and regular diet of adrenaline. But that was hardly normal life.

That was why the alternating visits over the past year in their natural sur-roundings were so important. She wanted to know Worthy, the detective who went to work each day to read reports and write memos, the man who drank too much coffee, and the man who could come home grumpy. And she wanted Worthy to know her as the university professor who spent most nights prep-ping for class, grading papers, and complaining about the pettiness of faculty meetings.

Yet, the truth was that their alternating visits over the past year, while lovely and loving, were also artificial. Because they carved out time from their regular lives when the other visited, their weeks together were really more like vaca-tions. That was why, for this visit, she asked Worthy not to take time off work.

Stopping before a women's shop to compare the styles of Midwestern America with those of Italy, she saw her reflection in the window and had to smile. If this visit was meant to experience Worthy's "normal" life, then she had to conclude that his life was anything but normal. Of course, once they found Father Joseph, she knew Worthy would be sitting at a desk to type up the results, but wouldn't another case—one given to him because of its complex-ity—draw him back in?

The question she had to answer was not the one she'd thought about in Rome in the days before her flight—"Do we love each other enough to be bored together?"—but this one: "Can I marry a man with a crazy life like this?" Worthy hadn't failed to explain that his first wife, Susan, wanted a nine-to-five husband, a husband who could leave his work behind, even as she left her work in the ICU at the hospital. The more Worthy's reputation grew as a detective capable of solving the difficult cases, the more Susan resented his being called away for days and weeks on end. Finally, Susan had ended a marriage that she accused Worthy of leaving years before.

But I am not Susan, and maybe Chris isn't the man he was then, Lena thought. She thought it significant that Worthy valued her contribution to the case. If he'd patronized or sidelined her while he was off chasing down clues and witnesses, she'd have a legitimate concern that they didn't have a future together.

Lena felt that before either of them could seriously talk about marriage, they both had to go through something difficult—a genuine difference of opinion, a fight. She was under no illusion that the two of them, both strong-willed and intelligent persons, would always agree. How could she ever forget her mother's wagging finger as she said Lena was too smart *per il tuo bene,* too smart for her own good. So the question for her was not "will we fight?" but rather "how will we treat each other during and after those fights?"

✝

BECAUSE NICK HAD CALLED AHEAD, MRS. Reston, the parish secretary, was waiting with coffee and cookies when he arrived in the afternoon.

"I read the article about you in *USA Today,*" Mrs. Reston said, her voice trembling noticeably as she sat across the coffee table in her office. "Now when was that?"

"Not long enough ago," Nick said with a smile. "And thank you for the cookies. They're homemade?"

"When you called and told me you were coming, I thought, O Lord, what can I give you? Then I remembered I'd just baked a batch of pumpkin spice cookies. My hubby, Jim, bless his heart, dropped them by."

"Then thank your husband for me. To tell you the truth, I wasn't sure how many people in Saginaw would want to talk with me. You must be tired of all the questions."

"I won't lie, Father. At the beginning, it was exhausting. We all wanted to help, but we didn't know anything helpful. But then, as the days turned into weeks and the police and the TV people no longer seemed interested, I think we all . . . well, many of us gave up hope. Some people still think Father Joe had an accident and is lying dead somewhere, while others think we never really knew him. For them, Father Joe just ran off . . . or worse."

"And what do you think, Mrs. Reston?"

Mrs. Reston looked down at her lap and slowly shook her head. "The one thing I've come to accept is that whatever happened to Father Joe, he isn't coming back. I tried not to think that, but eventually, I gave up too." She looked up and offered a weak smile. "But then I got your message and I thought, this is the monk who works with the detective in Detroit. Maybe there's still hope—hope that Father Joe is alive, I mean."

Nick leaned forward and nodded. "It's the not knowing that's so hard, isn't it?"

Mrs. Reston sighed. "Yes, that's it. You know, just like everyone else, I've seen those MIA flags that some people have. I never thought too much about that—having someone you care about who was missing in action. I thought those people would surely prefer someone to be missing than dead. Now I understand. Even if we find out that Father Joe is . . . dead, it's better than never knowing what happened to him."

Nick caught Mrs. Reston's eye. "I'm just grateful that you don't hate him. I'm sure there are some who do, but I can tell that's not how you feel."

Taking a handkerchief from a pocket in her dress, Mrs. Reston dabbed at her eyes. "I prefer to think that people who say they hate him don't really. They're just so hurt, Father."

"Very true, my dear." He waited a moment before continuing. "I've come to Saginaw because I have a few questions that my partner, Lieutenant Worthy, didn't ask, and I thought you would be the best person to start with."

Mrs. Reston raised her hands in protest. "Everyone assumes I knew Father Joe best, and maybe I did, but I don't think I know anything more than I've already told the police."

"Believe me, I know that's how it feels. But so many times people know more than they think they do."

Mrs. Reston nodded slowly. "Of course I want to help, Father."

"I never doubted that. So, for starters, I would like to talk about the weeks just before Father Joseph disappeared. Did you notice any change in him, emotionally or otherwise?"

"I've thought about that so many times, Father. All I can say is that when he didn't come in that first day and then the second, I was as surprised as anyone. No, he seemed his usual self."

"That's helpful. How would you describe Father Joseph's usual self?"

"Well, let me see. He was very considerate. Whenever he asked me to do something out of the ordinary, he'd always say, 'Tell me if that's a problem.' Which it never was. And he was a good listener. Yes, I would definitely say he was a good listener and a patient man."

"Can you give me an example?"

"Well, it sounds minor, but there's a longstanding disagreement in the parish about the fall festival. Some think we need the festival to meet our budget every year. Others think it's too much work for the little profit we make. And then there are others who think it's wrong to ask outsiders to help St. George pay its bills."

"And I suppose all parties wanted Father Joseph to side with them."

"Of course. But he'd listen to them, and then after they were done railing about it, he'd nod and say he understood their position—he was good at summarizing what people said to him, Father—and then he suggested that after this fall's festival, the parish council should offer a survey to the members. I remember him saying, 'We won't be able to please everyone, but at least we'll have a sense of the community.' Well, St. George has never had a survey—not in my time, anyway. Before, the priest and parish council would dictate what the community should do."

"And that was always to stay with the festival," Nick said.

Mrs. Reston nodded. "Nearly everyone in the parish liked the idea of a survey, of having a say, you see."

"Yes, that makes sense. Can you tell me about Father Joseph's sense of humor?"

The secretary shook her head slowly. "No one has asked me that." She paused before saying, "Father Joe was never harsh, if you know what I mean. He'd laugh at jokes that parishioners would tell, but I don't think I ever heard Father Joe tell a joke. That's strange, isn't it?"

Nick shrugged. "Priests are different about how much of themselves they let their parish see. There are some monks at St. Simeon's, my monastery, who I've never heard tell a joke. And as you said, that doesn't mean they are harsh or severe. How about his homilies, Mrs. Reston?"

"Sorry, Father. I'm Baptist. I never heard him give a sermon."

"That's fine. Can you tell me about the cycling club he was a part of?"

"Well, I know when the weather was good, he would ride his bike to the church. And I do remember that the only time I'd see him out of his collar was on those afternoons when he'd change clothes here before biking after work."

"How often would you say that was?"

"Let me see. As I said, it all depended on the weather, but I'd say he'd do that about once every week or ten days."

Nick sat in silence, gathering his thoughts for a moment. "Do you remember if he received any unusual phone calls or mail those last few weeks?"

"No, I don't, but he often picked up the mail before I got here. And I don't know about the emails he received. Of course, the police took his laptop, but I heard they didn't find anything out of the ordinary."

"Ah, you're right. Do you know if he could have had another computer, a tablet perhaps?"

Mrs. Reston shook her head. "I never saw one. I'm sure you know they found his smartphone in his apartment. But then again, I suppose he could have had a second phone."

"Yes, we can't rule that out. How about visitors who came to see him during those last weeks—maybe someone who didn't have an appointment? I imagine you see about anyone who drops by the church."

"No, no, I can't think of anyone, but I don't know about the evenings, Father. I leave at five, you see."

After a pause, Nick said, "You've been really helpful, Mrs. Reston. And I apologize if I ate too many of the cookies."

"I'm happy you liked them, Father."

"Just one final question. Did Father Joseph ever do anything that puzzled you, something you didn't understand?"

Mrs. Reston started to shake her head again but then stopped. "I was going to say no, but a couple weeks before he left, there was something. I can't see how it could be important, but I'll tell you anyway, just in case. For the entire first year, Father Joe had his salary deposited automatically. Then two weeks before he left, he asked me to call the bank and cancel that. All he said was that he wanted to deposit his salary himself."

"But he gave no reason?"

"No. I couldn't believe there was anything fishy at the bank. This is Saginaw, not New York, but he just stopped the automatic deposit."

Nick tried to imagine why Father Joseph made such a change. It seemed a small bit of information, but for reasons he couldn't put into words, even to himself, the priest's decision troubled him.

LENA'S BELIEF THAT PHYLLIDA TISMANAKIS' WOUND, as Aris Kouris' second jilted fiancé, would be deeper than the pain lingering with the first fiancé, determined Worthy's next actions. He thought it best to have an online conversation with Ms. Tismanakis first, and he asked Lena to lead the interview.

"You know better than I do how to have this fiancé open up to us. And we both know what we want to get from the interview—what Aris was like as a person, especially how he made that decision to end the relationship. The truth is, I'm more likely to say something that would upset her and shut her down," he said.

As Worthy cued up the meeting, he positioned himself so Lena's face would be more centered than his on the computer screen. Phyllida Tismanakis' face was bloated, perhaps from crying, Worthy thought, as he congratulated himself on asking Lena to lead.

"Ms. Tismanakis, my name is Dr. Lena Fabriano, and I'm here with Lieutenant Worthy. We appreciate that you're willing to speak with us. We know this isn't a conversation you want to have, but we believe you might help us understand Aris Kouris—now known as Father Joseph."

The dark-haired Phyllida Tismanakis held her arms crossed across her breast. There were dark circles around her eyes, and Worthy wondered if this was how she looked at the end of college, when all her future plans fell through.

"No, you're right. I don't enjoy thinking back on that relationship. But I know he's been missing, so if I can help, I will."

"That's very kind. Let me start by asking if Aris contacted you after college."

Phyllida Tismanakis closed her eyes as if she were blocking something out. When she opened them, she said, "He wrote me a note that first Christmas . . . the first Christmas we were apart. He said he hoped I was well and would have a good Christmas."

"Did you write back?"

The woman shook her head but didn't say anything.

"Was there anything else in the note?" Lena asked.

"He asked me to pray for him. I couldn't believe it."

Little chance of that, Worthy thought.

Lena said, "You must have felt slapped in the face."

Phyllida dried tears as she nodded. "I think it's the cruelest thing anyone has ever written to me. If he'd said that face to face, I'd have been the one slapping him. But it was like he got the last word, and he had the nerve to ask me that."

Lena paused, waiting for Phyllida to regain control. "I'm sorry to bring this all back, but when did you first sense that Aris intended to back out on the engagement?"

Phyllida sighed. "At the time, I didn't sense anything, but ever since then, I've asked myself if I'd ignored some signs. The thing is, to the very end, to that last night we sat on a bench on campus, he was . . . almost considerate. Aris has an unbelievably calm manner. I mean, I left that night with my heart broken but still thinking I had no right to be mad at him. After all, how can a person compete with God?"

"I hope you were mad later," Lena said.

The woman took a deep breath and nodded vigorously. "I'm still mad, more now than I was then. I don't feel I can trust men ever again. And God. . . ? Can you imagine what it's like for me to go to church and see a priest up at the altar? With his back turned, all I can see is Aris."

Lena and Worthy let her cry until she gained control. Worthy then said, "You know, you might not have missed any clues. The more we learn about

Aris, the more I'm thinking he made decisions solely on the basis of himself. Impulsively too, it seems."

Phyllida sat silently, looking down at her hands, even as she slowly nodded. "My college friends and even my family think that I didn't want to see the signs he gave. But for the life of me, I can't remember any signs. Do you think that's important?"

Worthy nodded. "We're trying to establish his habits, and you've helped us with what you've shared. Again, we're sorry we put you through this. The only other question I would ask is if you could recommend whom we might talk to from his college days."

Phyllida Tismanakis looked angry now more than hurt. "Yes, I can. He's the first person I talked to after Aris jilted me. The Orthodox priest in the college town in Maryland, where Aris and I went to church . . . and where we were going to be married. But that would probably be a waste of time. When I went to see him, he refused to tell me if Aris talked with him before he broke off the engagement about becoming a priest. That stupid, stupid confidentiality business," she said.

CHAPTER NINE

---◆---

OCTOBER 12

LOOKING OUT FROM HIS CHURCH OFFICE WINDOW to the sun shining on the Pacific Ocean, Father Elias glanced down at the notes he'd made from his phone call to the Metropolitan-Bishop's office in Detroit. If he were a betting man, he'd have thought the discovery of the Ukrainian woman's identity involved with Father Joseph would have been difficult while the psychologist's name would have been immediately available. But the opposite had happened, and when he recalled his source's explanation, he could see why he'd guessed wrong.

"No, the person I talked to remembered her name very well," his source said, "because she had to ask Father Joseph to spell it. Her name is Natasha Luzinsky."

The opposite was the case with the psychologist. The psychologist's rule in working with the Metropolitan's office was that his name not appear in their files. Elias' source said he asked to be referred to as "the consulting psychologist." Of greater significance, Elias thought, was the phrase the psychologist had used to describe Father Joseph—"clear narcissistic tendencies."

Elias' thoughts returned to Nick as he muttered, "I think Nick will be pleased with my batting one for two." Nick had been one of his closest friends in seminary. Those days had been heady ones, as the seminarians were busy navigating Byzantine theology, history, and liturgics while, on the personal level, were agonizing over the question of marriage. While marriage for Catholic seminarians wasn't a possibility, and never an issue for Protestant seminarians, marriage for Orthodox seminarians was complicated. Any Orthodox candidate for the priesthood who wasn't married before ordination could not be married afterwards. Such a priest would be considered monastic, even if he served in a parish and never set foot in a monastery.

In the midst of all the study and personal questioning, Nick was the seminarian who seemed least concerned about the marriage issue. Yes, he was always a big man physically, but that certainly hadn't precluded marriage. Nick was hardly the class clown, but he was often the life of the parties where women were frequently present. Elias and Nick had become close friends, and eventually Elias had asked Nick about his future.

Nick had surprised his friend by saying, "Unless a woman comes along who convinces me otherwise, I'll be headed to a monastery."

Elias remembered thinking Nick was joking until he saw the expression on his face. "You, a monk in some dank monastery? If anyone belongs in a parish, it's you. Are you forgetting that you won the homiletics prize for best sermon not once but twice? And what about the bishop who said you chanted like an angel?" At the time, Elias hadn't added that he knew no seminarian who listened to more of the struggles of other seminarians—including his own—than Nick Fortis.

Nick had just laughed. "We both know there's more chanting in the monastery than in the parish."

"Look, Nick, my fiancé has three friends who've asked about you. Did you hear me? I said 'three!'"

"And I'm sure they're wonderful women who will make wonderful wives of priests. Elias, you know I don't have a problem with women. I enjoy their company, but that's where it ends."

"But the isolation, Nick, and you being an extrovert. Won't you be claustrophobic?"

"I appreciate your worry, but I think a monastery is what my soul needs."

Now, as Elias recalled that conversation, he realized both Nick and he had been right. While Nick had remained a monk, he was certainly not a monk buried alive in a monastery. From what Elias had read about his friend over the past decade, he knew that Nick had assisted on cases not just in Ohio and Michigan, but also in New Mexico and Italy—twice. *He travels more than I do,* Elias thought.

He smiled as he thought of Nick's unusual journey. Unusual, yes, but somehow a journey that made sense. Who could work better with a homicide detective than a monk so capable of reading the hearts and minds of people?

NICK ENDED THE CALL WITH ELIAS, pleased that his friend had discovered the name of the Ukrainian woman. The task now would be to track her down, for she might know Father Joseph's state of mind better than anyone else. Nick was less convinced of the usefulness of the psychologist's comment about Father

Joseph exhibiting "clear narcissistic tendencies." Yes, Father Joseph never seemed to shy away from what he considered to be the right path, but did that make him a narcissist?

Over a late pancake lunch at a restaurant next to his motel, Nick opened his computer with the intention of going to the University of Thessaloniki site. Instead, he went to "Facebook: Natasha Luzinsky."

He was grateful to find only three women with that name on Facebook, two elderly, so he quickly identified the Natasha Luzinsky he was searching for. He studied her profile photo, which revealed a woman in her late twenties or thirties, with long blond hair and prominent cheekbones.

Thankfully, Natasha posted in both Ukrainian and English, the latter while not being flawless was at least readable. Her profile listed Kiev as her birthplace as well as her two degrees at the university in Ukraine before beginning a PhD program in Thessaloniki in Liturgical Music. Nick didn't expect to find any mention of Father Joseph on her Facebook page, but by scrolling down, he found something else important—her husband's name, Sergei Luzinsky, beneath a photo of the two of them. In the photo, the husband, a foot taller than Natasha, had his arm around her. The gesture, together with the expression on Natasha's face—was she wincing?—caused Nick to wonder if the husband's grasp suggested ownership more than affection.

Below were other photos, some larger family photos in Ukraine while others were from Thessaloniki, and Nick was about to exit Natasha's Facebook page when he noticed the date of the final entry was six months before. His mind raced as he tabulated that the date was eleven months after Father Joseph returned home in disgrace. With no mention of her having finished her doctoral program, the Facebook page presented a mystery of its own. Was she still at the university in Greece, or had she gone back to Ukraine with her husband? Was she still married? And why had she stopped posting on social media?

After another half hour, he found the online address of the office of student services at the university. Because it was still early afternoon in Michigan, however, he knew it was evening in Greece. He shouldn't expect to receive a reply to his request until the next day.

In the meantime, he drove to Mel's Bike and Ski Shop, where an employee directed him downstairs to talk with Dennis Sevreen, the owner of the shop. When Nick introduced himself, Dennis Sevreen stepped back from a partially disassembled bicycle and wiped his hands on a red work towel.

"Joe was a good bloke and not the kind of person I thought would be a priest," he said, his English accent coming through clearly. "To be honest, my first thought was 'You're a priest?' I mean, the guy was an athlete, big shoulders and legs like tree trunks. Yet humble once we got to know him. Definitely not your typical Yank, if you know what I mean. Don't mean to bite the hand that feeds me, but a lot of my customers would rather talk than listen. Not Joe. I don't know if I've met someone who could listen like Joe."

"Tell me about the club," Nick asked.

"Well, I'm the president, but that just means I schedule our weekend rides and send out a newsletter. Most of the rides end up at a pub. Do you mind if I work while we chat?"

"No, not at all. What kind of cyclist was Father Joseph?"

"As I said, the guy was in great shape, I can tell you that. He could ride with the best of us. He must have played sports in college."

"He was All-American in rowing."

"That explains the shoulders and legs. Funny he never mentioned the All-American part."

"And at the pubs, what was he like?"

"He didn't play the priest role, if that's what you're asking. He'd pay for a round like the rest of us. Like I said, Joe was a good bloke."

"Quiet, jovial, what?" Nick pressed.

"It's a bit hard to explain. He didn't sit on the sidelines, mind you, but he mainly listened. I suppose that made him quiet, but then he'd snap out of whatever was on his mind and laugh with the rest of us."

"I suppose there are women in the club."

"Sure, and no, Joe didn't have a problem with them. In fact, I'd say the birds took to him."

"Anyone in particular?"

Dennis Sevreen didn't respond immediately as he turned the crank of the bike and sent the back wheel spinning. "No, the ladies took to him, but he didn't reciprocate."

"Did you notice a difference in Father Joseph in the weeks before he disappeared?"

"Not that I can remember. I believe he did miss the club ride the weekend before whatever happened to him happened."

"And that was unusual?"

"Not really. I mean, he was a priest. Obviously, weddings, funerals, and sick people take priority."

Nick remembered something he'd heard before. "I was told he had more than one bike. Is that true?"

Dennis Sevreen nodded. "He had a nice road bike, a Trek, and he had a used off-road bike. That bike wasn't so nice. He had me work on it several times. Right before he left, I tried to convince him to trade up. We'd gotten a much better off-road in a trade, and I fancied him having it. I gave him the biggest discount that I offer, and I think it would have cost him no more than two hundred bucks. But he said no."

"Did he say why?" Nick asked.

"Not in so many words, but I wondered if money was tight for him. I remember wondering how much priests get paid."

Nick recalled Mrs. Reston's comment about Father Joseph's change in banking, also right before he disappeared.

"You said earlier that he'd take his turn and pay for a round at the pubs. I don't know how many you have on a ride, but that can't be cheap. Did it surprise you then when he passed on the bike?"

Dennis stopped turning the crank and let the back tire glide to a halt. "I hadn't thought about it that way, but you've got a point, mate. He never acted as if money was an issue until the bike became available. Maybe he had some unexpected expenses."

"And how long before he left did you make the bike offer?"

Dennis let out a long sigh. "Can't be certain, but no more than a week. So, I have a question for you, something that's been bugging me about this whole mess."

"If I know the answer, I'll tell you."

"I heard Joe didn't take his car. So I'm wondering if his bike left with him."

Nick thought back to what Freya had told them. "I think they found an older bike in the garage."

"But not the Trek, the road bike?"

"I don't know. It's a good question."

"Indeed it is," Dennis agreed. "We become attached to our favorite bikes, like some people do with their cars or boats. I'd feel a whole lot better about Joe if I knew he took his Trek with him."

LENA AGAIN LED THE ONLINE INTERVIEW, this time with Candace Jakes, Aris Kouris' first fiancé. Her first impression was that this woman could hardly be more different from Phyllida Tismanakis. Phyllida Tismanakis' Mediterranean olive complexion and black hair made Candace's Irish-red hair and fair complexion jump from the computer screen. And while Phyllida spoke in almost a whisper, Candace's voice was forceful.

Something about Candace Jakes' expression told Lena she didn't have to begin the interview by apologizing. Instead, she introduced herself and Worthy before thanking the woman for her help.

"When you first called, I was angry at myself for agreeing to talk," Mrs. Jakes said. "I thought I had nothing more to say. But then yesterday, I found I had some thoughts, new thoughts, about that part of my life."

Realizing that it would be better to let Candace Jakes lead the conversation, Lena waited.

"Originally, I thought that I broke off the engagement because I sensed that Aris was going to jilt me. But after I let that thought tumble around in my brain for the last day or two, I realized the truth was just the opposite. So, here's what I think now. All my girlfriends saw Aris as this great catch. He was incredibly handsome, fit, polite, easy-going. I tried to see him through their eyes and convince myself that I was the luckiest woman on campus. But I now see that what pushed me over the edge was this—Aris and I could be married for fifty years and he'd never fight for us. We'd never be anything other than what we were then because he didn't care enough. Damn it, he was going to be satisfied whether I left him or not."

Lena could see the tears coming down Candace's cheek, but these tears were not like Phyllida's. Candace's tears were those of someone who'd experienced more than one hard lesson in life and who knew that the lessons that brought wisdom came at a price.

After giving Candace a moment, Lena asked how much of Aris' past he had shared with her.

"You mean about the baby?" she replied. "Yeah, he told me about that."

"What was Aris like when he shared that?" Lena asked.

Candace sighed. "Odd; yes, definitely odd. His voice was calm; he could have been telling me about the weather. Oh, shit—"

"What is it?" Lena asked.

Candace shook her head and offered a tight laugh. "I just realized something. When Aris told me about the baby, he wasn't concerned about how I would react at all. Which he should have been, right?"

"I would think so," Lena said. "Maybe he thought you'd loved him too much for it to matter."

"No, that's not it. I don't think he cared one bit about how I'd react. If I'd said that was a deal-breaker for me, I think he would have just shaken his head and walked away. You see, that's what I mean when I said he acted like he could accept whatever happened."

Lena felt Worthy's hand on her arm. She leaned back and let Worthy come into the picture on the screen. "Mrs. Jakes, what did you think when you heard that Aris had become a priest?"

"Please, call me Candace or Candy. Well, I knew Aris was religious. I mean, he took me to that Greek church most Sundays. I'm Catholic, so it wasn't all that confusing, but he never gave me any idea that he was thinking of becoming a priest. What he told me was that after graduation, he was hoping to have an Olympic tryout, then work for some national youth rowing program."

"And when you heard that he'd disappeared, what did you think?" Worthy asked.

"I knew I should have been surprised, but I'm not. I suspect that's my way of admitting that I didn't really know Aris."

Lena leaned into the screen. "After you heard about his disappearance, you didn't have any idea where he might be or what he could be doing?"

Candace looked directly into the computer's camera. "I've thought of nothing. I suppose he could be dead."

The way Candace said that left Lena wondering if she cared one way or another about that possibility.

CHAPTER TEN

---◆---

OCTOBER 13

CHECKING OUT OF THE MOTEL, NICK realized that, before leaving Saginaw, he needed to talk to people who had a different take on Father Joseph. And he thought he knew the right person to direct him.

At St. George, he found Mrs. Reston sitting at her desk listening as a priest explained something for the week's bulletin. For a few seconds, Nick's heart raced as the priest appeared to be young, like Father Joseph. The priest turned and smiled as the parish secretary did the introductions.

Nick shook hands with Father Gregory, a priest who looked as if he were fresh out of seminary. When the young priest spoke, Nick realized he had a French accent.

"I've heard a lot about you, Father," the young priest said. "Is there any progress?"

"I wish I could say 'yes,' but progress is slow. Did you ever meet Father Joseph?"

"Unfortunately, no," Father Gregory said.

"You might still be able to help. Is there anything that parishioners have told you about your predecessor that might help us understand him?"

Father Gregory folded his arms across his chest and looked down. "As my dear mother would say, there's the stone, and then there's the ripple left when the stone hits the water. What I've heard from parishioners is the ripple effect of Father Joe's leaving—their pain, confusion, and yes, sometimes, guilt. They wonder if they did something to drive him away. But Father Joe—the stone himself—no, I can't say I understand him."

"Was there anything out of the ordinary in how he did things, or maybe something you've found in his notes?"

"No, other than the fact that he seemed well-organized. But maybe the credit for that goes to Mrs. Reston."

"No, Father, I agree with you. Father Joe had a system, a schedule, and unless there was an emergency, he stayed faithful to it."

"Mrs. Reston, I hope you won't mind if I ask Father Gregory a couple of candid questions," Nick said.

"No, no, Father. I can give you two some privacy," she said, pushing her chair back.

"Actually, I'd like your opinion on my questions as well, Mrs. Reston."

Father Gregory walked to the office door and closed it. "We're not expecting anyone, are we?"

The secretary looked down at a calendar and shook her head. "No one is scheduled."

Father Gregory offered a chair to Nick, and they both sat down.

"About four years ago, my friend Lieutenant Christopher Worthy and I worked the case of an old priest in Detroit who was strangled."

"I remember it. That was very sad," Mrs. Reston said.

"Yes, it was terrible, but in looking into that, we interviewed a member of the parish who made life difficult for the deceased. The man was a suspect, but, in the end, not the killer. Even so, this man, I'd call him a curmudgeon, shared a perspective on the priest and the parish that helped us. So, I'm wondering who might fit that description here at St. George."

Father Gregory nodded in the direction of Mrs. Reston. "Florence, I think I've been treated fairly well, but then I'm not permanent here. You'd know better than I."

Mrs. Reston looked up at the ceiling. "Oh, my. Well, there were several families who left the parish under our previous priest, but one of them came back when Father Joe arrived. Of those in the parish currently, I feel bad saying it, but Mr. Velonis and his wife, along with their grown son and his family, have a history of being . . . what should I say—prickly? Father Leonites used to say that some families have played the role of 'priest spiders' for decades, going all the way back to the old country."

Father Gregory laughed. "I've never heard of that. What is it?"

Mrs. Reston joined in the laughter. "Father Leonites said that a 'priest spider' is the kind of parishioner who feels his mission is to spin webs—I think he meant spread gossip—to make the priest's life miserable."

"I've never heard the term either," Nick confessed, "but it can be all too true. Do you know if the Velonis family shifted their anger to Father Joseph?"

"That I don't know, but if they did, Father Joe didn't share that with me. I think he would have swallowed the insults."

"And I know who this family is, but they've not targeted me—as far as I know. But now I've been forewarned," Father Gregory said.

"If you could give me the family's address, Mrs. Reston, I think I'll talk with them."

"Of course, Father."

"You said you had another question," Father Gregory said.

"Yes, and this one may be harder to answer. I'm hoping Father Joseph had at least one person, either in the parish or in the community, who he could take his collar off with and just be Joe."

Mrs. Reston frowned. "When you asked that, I thought of my husband's favorite old TV show, *Cheers*. You know, a 'where everyone knows your name' kind of place. I don't think Father Joe had a bar that he went to, at least not locally, but I do know he liked to take his lunch down at Cappy's Diner. It's kind of an historical fixture in Saginaw."

Nick nodded. "It sounds worth a stop, especially because it's nearly lunch time. I'd offer to treat you both, but the three of us asking about Father Joseph might seem a bit intimidating."

"Then I'd suggest the corned beef on rye," Mrs. Reston said. As Nick stood, she added, "You'll let us know when you find out anything?"

He considered how to answer her question. Were there some answers the parishioners of St. George would choose never to know?

CAPPY'S DINER DID LOOK LIKE SOMETHING OUT OF THE 1950S. Having a choice of a booth or a seat at the counter, Nick chose the latter, hoping this would lead to chances to talk with the waitresses. Feeling hungry, he ordered the corned beef as well as macaroni and cheese before asking his waitress if she remembered Father Joseph.

"Oh, yes, he was a regular," she said. "Did you know him?" Nick thought he detected some protectiveness of the priest in her question.

"Not personally, but his family has asked me to look into his disappearance."

The waitress shrugged, but Nick felt she let her guard down. "Good luck with that. Seriously, I mean that. How long has he been gone now—a month?"

Nick read the name "Connie" embroidered on the waitress's uniform. "Yes, about that long. Connie, what was he like as a customer?"

The waitress took the opportunity to wipe the counter with a rag before answering. "I used to say we should let Father Joe eat here for free. We reserved the stool right there," she said, pointing to the one on Nick's left, "on Tuesdays, Thursdays, and Saturdays. He couldn't always make it, but that was his seat."

"People have told me he was a good listener. When he talked, what did he usually talk about?"

"Well, you have to understand, the default conversation around here is sports. Whatever's in season, that's what most folks, especially guys, talk about. Joe could do that. I mean, he kept up on who was winning and losing. I always got the impression he'd been a jock himself."

Nick nodded. "You guessed right. He was quite a rower in college."

"Rowing? Huh, well, there you are, then. But people would talk to Joe about anything—their jobs, their grandkids, their aches and pains. The thing is, he never did the holy-holy thing, like telling people he'd pray for them. That wasn't Joe. But I think we all knew he did that—pray, I mean—without him having to say it."

Tears formed at the corners of Connie's eyes as she wiped more vigorously on the counter.

Father Joseph listened to her as well, Nick thought.

"I wish I'd met him," he said.

Connie's voice quivered as she said, "If you find him, tell him nobody at Cappy's is angry at him. We just miss him."

OCTOBER 14

The next morning, Lena set down her coffee cup in Worthy's kitchen in Detroit and looked across the table at Worthy. "I'm thinking about what Father Joseph's first fiancé said—about him not being willing to fight with her. Do you think that applies to us?"

Worthy stopped spreading raspberry jam on his toast. "You want us to fight?"

Lena shrugged. "I don't know. We sparred a bit when we first met, but that only made you more attractive to me. But we do get along, don't we?"

Now it was Worthy's turn to shrug. "I never thought getting along with someone you love was a problem. Isn't it just the opposite?"

Resting her fork on her plate, Lena said, "But the first fiancé, Candace, has a point. Never fighting, never even disagreeing, that can't be good, can it?"

"Maybe there's fighting and then there's fighting."

"What do you mean?"

"Aren't a lot of fights about one person wanting to change the other person? I mean, when we came into this place, the waitress asked if we wanted a table or booth. I suppose we could have fought about that, each of us trying to change the other's mind."

Lena shook her head. "What would it say if every time we came into a restaurant and were asked that question, you made the decision and never even considered what I'd want? Or, if I did that to you?"

"I'm sure the waitress wouldn't object," Worthy said, smiling.

"Be serious, Chris. Can you see how not fighting might be a bad sign?"

"Are we fighting now?"

Lena sat back and looked at Worthy. "What I'm saying is that we're bound to disagree. No, that's not so likely when we only see each other two or three weeks a couple of times a year and we're on our best behavior. But sparring, like we did when we first met, that might be a good thing."

"Okay with me. But it's not fair to say we could be like Aris and Candace Jakes. Here's what I think about the two of them. She said Aris didn't care enough about their relationship to fight, but think about how he was much the same with the other fiancé. I'm not sure he respected these women enough to . . . to engage with them, to really love them. Remember what Candace said— that it was like he was reading some standard lines from a play? Isn't it possible Aris was so calm, so laid back, because in the end he only cared about himself?"

"You think he's a narcissist?"

Worthy shrugged. "Look at the TV preachers. Aris wouldn't be the first member of the clergy to be all about himself."

THE WOMAN WHO OPENED THE DOOR AT THE VELONIS HOME squinted into the afternoon sun at Nick.

"Do I know you?" she said.

"No, Mrs. Velonis, you don't. My name is Father Nicholas Fortis. I've been asked by Father Joseph's family to look into his disappearance."

Mrs. Velonis made no move to let Nick enter. "We don't know nothing about that." She made a move to close the door but stopped to say, "Who told you to come here?"

Figuring telling the truth was his only chance of being invited inside, Nick said, "Somebody at St. George told me your family has had problems with the priests in the past. I'm wondering what you thought of Father Joseph."

From within the house came a raspy voice, "Let him in, Becky."

Mrs. Velonis stepped to the side and motioned for Nick to enter. She pointed to a parlor and followed Nick into the room, where he saw a man in his late seventies or early eighties sitting in a recliner, connected to an oxygen tank.

"Mr. Velonis, I'm Father Nicholas Fortis."

Mr. Velonis raised his hand to stop Nick. "I'm not deaf. I heard you before." Pausing to inhale slowly, he added, "Somebody tell you we had a problem with Father Joe? If they did, they're goddamn liars."

"May I sit down?"

"Sure, take a seat. We don't bite," Mr. Velonis said, his laugh turning into a cough.

Nick sat on a sofa while Mrs. Velonis brought a dining room chair in for herself. "They're some two-faced hypocrites at St. George, and none of them have ever had a good word to say to us," she said.

"That has to be painful, not to mention not very Christian," Nick said. "I'm hoping you can help me understand Father Joseph. What he was like, I mean."

"I'll tell you one thing. He was too good for that bunch," Mr. Velonis said.

"So you liked him."

"Couldn't help but like him. He'd come by once a week, like clockwork. Over the months he was in Saginaw, he was in this house more than that old fart, Father Leonites, was in his twenty years at St. George. And that new pup, I can't remember his name, has been here only once. Like he's scared of us."

"That's right," Mrs. Velonis seconded.

"Did Father Joseph bring the Eucharist?" Nick asked.

"Of course, never forgot once until the last time he was here."

"But not the last time?"

"No, but then it was on a Monday. He usually came on Thursdays, so we just thought he'd come back later in the week," Mr. Velonis said.

"What do you remember about his last visit?"

"What do you mean? It was like always. We talked about the old country, places we both had visited in Greece. But the last time, he told us he'd studied in Thessaloniki. That's where Becky's family is from, so that's why I remember."

Nick looked at Mrs. Velonis, who nodded. "What did he say about Thessaloniki?"

"He knew my family's neighborhood, and he'd even been to a grocery store run by a cousin," she said. "I showed him photos of our last trip back home. That must have been fifteen years ago."

"So he enjoyed his time in Thessaloniki?"

"He said he loved it. Told us how much he missed being there. Said he wished he could go back someday, didn't he, Angelo?"

"Yep. I told him not to put it off too long," Mr. Velonis said. "So when I heard he'd left—I had to call the parish office three times before they'd tell me— that was my first thought. That he'd gone back to Greece."

And if he had, he'd have taken his passport, Nick thought.

"Do you think he was unhappy in Saginaw?" he asked.

"Didn't I say that Father Joe was too good for this town?" Mr. Velonis said.

"You did, but did he ever say he was unhappy here?"

Neither Mr. nor Mrs. Velonis said anything for a moment. Finally, Mrs. Velonis said, "No, but he never came out and said he wasn't. But I'll tell you this.

He told us one of his goals was for Angelo and me to come back to the church. He said he wanted us to be happy at St. George."

"Nobody ever said that to us," Mr. Velonis said.

IT WAS AFTER NINE THAT EVENING BEFORE NICK ARRIVED at Worthy's apartment. Though he was usually in bed by that time, Nick was eager to hear and share with Worthy and Lena what they all had discovered.

Perhaps in anticipation of a long night, Lena had found a wine shop that carried Italian wines, white and red, that she approved of. After pouring three glasses and setting out some sandwiches and veggies, she turned to Nick and Worthy and said, "You're the detectives. Are we closer to finding Father Joseph?"

"Finding him?" Worthy asked. "I'd be happy if we were closer to understanding him. Nick, what did you learn in Saginaw?"

Nick thought to himself, *what did I learn?* After a moment, he said, "I remembered something we did years ago on another case, Christopher. So I did the same in Saginaw. I talked to some folks in the parish who were known to be thorns in the priest's side."

"Ah, and did it pay off?"

"I think so. There's a crusty older couple who are notorious in the parish. Instead of battling them, Father Joseph reached out; he made a connection."

"Maybe he took them as a challenge," Worthy said.

"Could be, but I had the feeling Father Joseph was concerned about them. He'd visit them weekly, and the last time he was there, he told them how much he loved Thessaloniki. The wife of the couple has family from there, so maybe it just came up in conversation."

"He said he loved Thessaloniki?" Worthy asked.

"According to them, he also said he hoped to go back there sometime. So the couple's first thought, when he disappeared, was that he'd gone back there."

"If it weren't for his need for a passport, they could be right," Worthy acknowledged.

"Would it be that hard for him to get a false one?" Lena asked.

"Unless he's more connected to the crime world than I can imagine, I think it would be," Worthy said.

"I have to say, the more people in Saginaw tell me about Father Joseph, the more I respect him as a priest," Nick said. "That's despite what the Metropolitan-Bishop's psychologist said about him. According to what my friend Elias gained from his source, the psychologist wrote down that he had clear narcissistic tendencies."

Nick saw Lena glance at Worthy. "What?" he asked.

Worthy shrugged. "Let's wait on that a bit. Nick, you said you were left with two impressions. What was the other?"

"I'm not saying it was something factual—just a gut feeling. I don't think Father Joseph was the reckless priest that the one brother in Lansing and the church hierarchy in Detroit believe he was."

After a pause, Lena said, "We received a much different impression of Father Joseph, or Aris, from his two fiancés. That's not all that surprising. The one ex-fiancé, the most wounded one, sees him as someone who ends relationships easily—obviously the one with her—but I think she'd also see him leaving the parish in Saginaw as another betrayal. She'd certainly agree with the psychologist on the narcissism score. To her, he's what we used to call a 'running man.'"

"Hmm. And the other fiancé?" Nick asked.

"She's the first one, and she broke off the engagement," Worthy replied. "She clearly has no regrets about her decision. She described Aris as saying all the right things, but they sounded like he was reading from a script."

Lena poured more wine in the three glasses before saying, "Chris, I think it's time for you to share your own conclusions about Father Joseph with Nick."

"It's too early to say I've come to any conclusions, but the feeling I got from the second fiancé, the one whose heart is still broken, is that Aris Kouris is a self-absorbed prick. And I see her point. On the first Christmas after he'd told her he intended to be a celibate priest, he sent her a Christmas card. That's only seven months after he broke up with her. Now, it would have been condescending but also at least caring if he'd written that he hoped she was healing and that he was praying that she'd forgive him. But get this, Nick. In the card, he wished her a good Christmas and then asked her to pray for *him*."

Nick winced.

"It was so unfeeling, so all about him," Worthy said. "So yes, the narcissist label fits for me."

The room was quiet until Nick asked, "Lena, do you agree with Christopher?"

Shrugging, Lena said, "I don't think we should assume Father Joseph is either a wonderful priest or a narcissist."

"Okay, but what is he then?" Worthy asked.

"I'm not sure, but I will say this. Nick, I don't think Father Joseph and you are much alike as priests. I see you as someone who knows himself and knows who he is as a priest and why he's a priest. I don't think that describes Father Joseph. He seems to be in search of himself. But that doesn't mean he's a narcissist. Does he exhibit narcissistic tendencies? Sure, but most people do. I want to keep the possibility open that Father Joseph is someone we don't understand yet. Now, unless either of you has something more to say, I think it's time I go to bed."

Nick took a sip of wine before his hands flew up. "Good Lord, I almost forgot. Elias' source in the Metropolitan's came up with the name of the Ukrainian woman. It's Natasha Luzinsky."

"Does that help us? We know Aris hasn't left the country," Worthy said.

"She might help us understand Father Joseph," Lena said, "if she can shed light on what really happened in Greece."

Worthy sat back on the sofa and sighed. "Would we understand what really happened or hear yet another version of the man?"

CHAPTER ELEVEN

———— ◆ ————

OCTOBER 15

AFTER USING THE SPARE ROOM IN WORTHY'S APARTMENT, Nick rose early to offer his morning prayers before sunrise. He had a slight headache that he attributed to the late evening and the wine, but that wasn't what was uppermost on his mind.

How could I forget to mention Father Joseph's banking decision to Christopher and Lena? he asked himself. He couldn't think of a reason why Father Joseph's decision to change how he deposited his salary would be important, but he was interested in Worthy's take. Looking at his watch, he realized that neither Worthy nor Lena would be up for perhaps an hour. Opting for a walk, he left a note on the kitchen table and set off.

Worthy's apartment was less than a mile from Detroit's airport, and as he walked the sidewalks of the subdivision, he watched as one early-morning flight after another took off. He pictured Father Joseph boarding one of those flights, but immediately remembered that all passengers would have to show an ID. And certainly, he reasoned, checking airport records at the Saginaw and Detroit airports would have been one of Freya's first steps on the case.

That meant that unless Father Joseph had used a false ID, he hadn't flown anywhere the day he disappeared. And he'd left his car in the garage. So how had he left Saginaw? Was the answer as simple as him taking his bike out for a ride through the nearby forests and having a fatal accident? But if that were the case, why hadn't his body been found? Nick walked another block, his mind blank, until a new thought struck him. *Of course*, he thought, *why haven't we thought of this before? Father Joseph must have had an accomplice.*

Nick turned around and headed back to Worthy's apartment, and, as he did so, he thought of all whom he interviewed in Saginaw. One of them could have been his accomplice, but who? Immediately, he ruled out anyone from St. George. That left Dennis Sevreen from the bike shop or the waitress Connie at Cappy's Diner. But then he remembered the waitress saying Father Joseph was so popular at the diner that he had a reserved seat at the counter. The accomplice could just as easily be someone who spilled his or her troubles to Father Joseph.

He groaned, wondering if they would have to return to Saginaw and interview everyone who frequented Cappy's Diner as well as the other members of the cycling club. Even if they could manage to conduct all those interviews, there was no guarantee that the accomplice was from either of those groups. Father Joseph might have met and recruited that person from anywhere in Saginaw—or elsewhere.

Yet, he couldn't deny that the thought of an accomplice excited him. *Someone knows how he left Saginaw and maybe even where he is right now,* he thought.

"NICK WENT FOR A WALK," LENA SAID OVER COFFEE, as Worthy entered the kitchen.

"No doubt trying to clear his head," Worthy said, bending down to kiss Lena. "I'm going to need some of that coffee to clear mine."

"I hate to bring this up, but you know what day this is, don't you?" she said.

"If you're talking about how many seconds, hours, and days until you fly back to Rome, no, I don't know, and I haven't thought about it at all."

Lena put her arms around Worthy's neck, kissed him again, and sighed.

"Are you sorry I dragged you into this?" he asked.

"You didn't drag me into anything, and no, I'm not sorry. I'm just saying that we'd better hurry up and find Father Joseph. I don't like leaving in the middle of the story. I have more than one question I want to ask him."

Worthy stepped back to lean against the kitchen counter. "No chance you could stay longer?"

"Are you asking me about my chances of staying or telling me that's what you want?"

"What if I write a letter to your university saying you're an indispensable part of a missing person's investigation?"

"Indispensable? Am I?"

Behind them, the apartment door closed. "Yes, you are indispensable, Lena. That's exactly what you are," Nick said as he entered the room.

"Nice walk, Nick?" Worthy asked.

"No, but thanks for asking. A couple of new thoughts about Father Joseph—not all encouraging—came to mind, but before I get into that, I need a cup of tea. Would you happen to have spiced chai, Christopher?"

"He does now, because I bought some yesterday, Nick," Lena said. "I'll switch from coffee and have a cup with you. What will you have, Chris?"

"Would anyone mind if I make myself a milkshake?"

Lena asked, "For breakfast?"

"Don't you remember the last time I was in Rome?"

"You mean stopping four times in one day for gelato? Of course, I remember."

Nick put an arm around Worthy's shoulder. "And the worst thing is that Christopher won't gain a pound. It's just not fair."

When the tea and the milkshake were ready, the three returned to where they'd sat the night before.

Nick began. "I forgot to tell you something last night, something else I learned from the parish secretary. Maybe I forgot because I can't see how it's important, but something tells me it is."

"Ooh, I like the sound of this," Lena said.

"Hold on, Lena, it may mean nothing. But here is it. Shortly before Father Joseph disappeared, he asked Mrs. Reston to cancel the automatic deposit of his paycheck in the bank. I asked her if he could have simply changed banks, but she said if he did, he did that without telling her."

Nobody said anything until Worthy asked, "Would that mean the paycheck went directly to him?"

"That's what I assume," Nick replied.

"But he still could have deposited it, right?" Lena asked.

"Of course, at the same bank or at another. I just can't figure out why he changed."

"The most logical reason would be that Father Joseph didn't trust someone at the bank," Worthy said. "Hang on a minute." After a moment, he asked, "What if . . . what if he was putting cash aside? And to do that, wouldn't he want to cash his check rather than have it automatically deposited?"

Nick sat forward in the chair. "Traveling money! Good heavens, Christopher, he was saving up."

Lena exhaled slowly. "You do know what you're saying. Father Joseph didn't disappear on a whim. He had it planned."

"For at least a few days," Nick added. "Of course, we could be completely wrong. He might have opened an account in another bank."

"I think I know how we can find out. Freya should be able to see if he used other banks toward the end," Worthy said. "And as I've said before, Nick, always trust your intuition. This could be a breakthrough for us."

"I hope so, but there's something else that I thought about on my walk," Nick said. "And if I'm right about it, we have a problem."

Before Nick could explain what that problem was, Lena suggested they take a few minutes and have another cup of tea.

"Before either of you chide me about the milkshake, I'll make the tea and bring it in," Worthy said. "And as long as we're taking a break, I'll call Freya and ask her to call around to the banks in Saginaw. Unless she's tied up with another case, we might know something by the end of the day."

While Worthy was on the phone, Lena asked Nick, "Is it unusual to go this long on an investigation and be so confused about the missing person?"

"It always seems longer on a missing person's case. When I've worked with Christopher on a homicide, we had the victim to work off of. But with missing persons, you have this void and uncertainty. Is Father Joseph alive or dead? If he's alive, where could he be? And why haven't the authorities been able to find a trace of him? In other words, he's elusive."

"But you do think we'll find him?" she asked.

"There are no guarantees in missing persons cases, but what I do know is that if Christopher doesn't find him, he probably won't be found."

"Not just me," Worthy said. "I'd say if the three of us can't find him, then he's in the wind."

"Why did I just feel a ton of pressure descend on us?" Lena said. "Are you saying we're the last chance to find him?"

"There's always the chance that sometime down the road, Aris will break cover and come out of hiding," Worthy said.

"Why would he do that?" Lena asked.

"I have a thought," Nick said. "If he ran away to solve some problem—his own or someone else's—then he might reappear if he accomplishes the goal."

"Okay, Nick, I think it's time you shared the bad news," Worthy said.

"It hit me while I was watching planes take off from the airport. I couldn't help wondering how Father Joseph left Saginaw. He didn't take his car, and if he took one of his bikes, how far could he have gotten on that? Then I considered a taxi or bus, but Freya would know if he had taken one of those. So how did he leave? That's when something dawned on me. He had to have an accomplice."

The room was quiet until Worthy said, "Talk about forgetting Missing Persons 101. We've been focusing so much on where he might have gone and when he was last seen that we forgot about how he got away so cleanly."

"It's like there are two missing persons," Lena said. "I don't mean that an accomplice—if he did have one—is physically missing, but missing in another sense."

"Yes, missing from view. Whoever that might be is also hiding," Worthy added.

"I was hoping I'd just forgotten something obvious," Nick said. "Where would we even begin to find such a person?"

The question hung over the room until Nick said, "It's definitely one of those times when I wish I were wrong."

"But is this bad news?" Worthy asked.

"How is it not?" Lena posed. "An accomplice could be anywhere."

"I'm afraid I agree with Lena, Christopher."

"Nick, you know I'm not normally prone to optimism, but this might actually be a break. If there's an accomplice, that person has been sitting on a secret for two months. That person must know the grief Aris' . . . Father Joseph's leaving has caused. Perhaps the accomplice has had second thoughts; maybe, he or she has even considered telling someone in authority, especially if that person doesn't know where Aris is right now. I'm thinking we might be able to put some pressure on this person and smoke the answer out."

"I'd like to believe you're right, Christopher, but how would we do that?"

"Freya is the one to do that, if she can convince her captain to dangle something in the press, something addressed to the accomplice," Worthy said.

"What are you thinking of, a carrot or a stick?" Lena asked.

"I'm leaning toward a 'stick,'" Worthy replied, "something like having have the local police put out a statement that evidence has come to light that Father Joseph had an accomplice and that this person could be charged with withholding vital information on a missing person's case."

"Of course, we have no concrete evidence that there is an accomplice," Nick said.

"Am I wrong to think that bluffing couldn't hurt?" Lena asked. "If there is no accomplice, we lose nothing. If there is an accomplice and that person is, as you say, Chris, rethinking the help he or she gave, the threat might work."

"I tell you what I like about this idea," Worthy said. "To this point, the police and even the three of us have been hitting a brick wall. But now, we have Aris' odd banking decision and we're pretty certain that he had an accomplice. If we can scare that person into coming forward, we move from being passive to active players."

After a pause, Lena said, "I don't mean to pour cold water on this, but what if the accomplice lets Father Joseph know that the police are putting the squeeze on him or her? Might Father Joseph take off again and end up being even harder to find?"

"Don't feel bad, Lena. Every strategy has drawbacks. That means that we have to ask if the risk is worth it."

Nick looked from Worthy to Lena. "I say we take the risk."

"Then, I agree," Lena said. "In Italian, that's 'Chi non risica, non rosica.' 'Nothing ventured; nothing gained.'"

LATER THAT DAY, SERGEANT FREYA MAAKI LAUGHED when Worthy called to ask for her help. "You asked me to do something similar two years ago."

"I remember, but this time I'm not asking you to go over your captain's head."

"No, you're not. It makes sense that Father Joseph had an accomplice, and it's true that this person is withholding key evidence. Putting a piece in the local paper is a lot better than doing nothing."

"Speaking of doing something," Worthy said. "Would you also check into the priest's bank accounts?"

"We already did that and found nothing irregular. He left a little over one thousand at his bank."

After Worthy explained Father Joseph's decision to change his checking routine, Freya agreed that this new bit of information changed matters.

"I'll check all the banks in Saginaw and the rest of the county. Is tomorrow soon enough?"

"Of course," Worthy said as Nick came into the kitchen.

"I believe, my friend, today could be a breakthrough day."

From down the hallway, Lena called out, "Wait; I'll be there in a minute."

After Lena came into the kitchen, Nick said, "I contacted the university in Thessaloniki and learned something about Natasha Luzinsky that I think you'll both agree is important. Where to start?" he said, selecting a pastry from the kitchen counter before sitting at the table.

"First of all, Natasha Luzinsky gave birth to a baby boy in Thessaloniki two months ago. That was the first surprise. The second is that she withdrew from her doctoral program a week later. The university doesn't know if she's still in Greece, but without a valid student visa, she could be back in Ukraine."

"That's understandable," Lena said. "When I was in my doctoral studies, I saw others in the program trying to juggle their studies with being a parent. It rarely worked."

"I thought of that as well," Nick said. "But there's more. Think of the calculations. Natasha has a baby, and a week later she withdraws from her studies. A month later, Father Joseph disappears from Saginaw."

"You're certainly not thinking Father Joseph can be the father, Nick," Lena said.

"No, he left Thessaloniki long before the baby was conceived. You're probably right, Christopher. I was seeing a connection where there isn't one."

"As with any case, we have to work with the facts. And the key fact is that the police have his passport, so Aris Kouris hasn't left the country," Worthy said. "Another fact is that Aris' computer doesn't have any emails from the Luzinsky woman. I suppose he could have deleted them, but there are too many 'ifs' with that line of thinking."

"Then, the second thing I learned might not mean anything either," Nick said.

"No, let's hear it," Lena said.

"Are you interested as well, Christopher?"

Nick's question surprised Worthy. "Of course, Nick."

"The university gave me the phone number of the house—apparently it's an old manor house—that the Luzinskys shared with six other married couples. I called the number, and the housemother confirmed that the Luzinskys had moved out. But here's what I found interesting. In the months before the baby was born, other couples in the house complained of Sergei Luzinsky, the husband, shouting a lot. Because the shouting was in Ukrainian or Russian, no one knew what the fighting was about. It was only a week after Natasha came out of hospital with the baby that the Luzinskys left."

"So they did go back to Ukraine or Russia," Lena said.

Nick shrugged. "I don't know that for certain, but I don't know what other options the Luzinskys had."

Worthy took a sip of his tea. "Even if we did think the Luzinsky woman might know something, it'd be difficult tracking her back in Ukraine or in Russia, given the hostilities between the two countries."

"If there's even the slightest chance of contacting Natasha," Lena said, "I want us to try. And there's one person we should talk to. If Natasha was a doctoral candidate, the person who knew her best would be her academic advisor. When I was in grad school, I told my advisor everything. Not just about my thesis or my classes, but because she was a woman, I even told her about my love life."

Worthy nodded. "Well, there's nothing else we're doing now, so I don't see how it would hurt for you, Nick, to call the university again."

OCTOBER 16

IT DIDN'T TAKE NICK LONG TO REALIZE THAT PROFESSOR BAMBRIS wasn't the type of advisor with whom a woman would share personal matters. When he mentioned the name Natasha Luzinsky, the professor set off on an angry screed about the lack of perseverance among contemporary students.

Nick broke into the diatribe to say, "She was a capable student, then."

"I just told you she didn't have the perseverance. Of course, she wasn't a capable student."

"Intellectually, I mean. Was she making progress in the program before she withdrew?"

Professor Bambris paused for a moment before grudgingly agreeing. "When she first came to us, I felt confident she would finish. That's what makes it so frustrating. Students these days don't value the time we invest in them."

"I'm sure you're right," Nick said, trying another approach. "Was it because she had a baby?"

"Women pursuing graduate studies must decide what is important. I asked Natasha when we first met if she planned to have children while pursuing the doctorate. She assured me—no, she promised me—that her husband and she had agreed to wait to start a family until she completed her degree. I trusted her, but she betrayed that trust."

Nick tried to imagine an academic advisor in the States intruding on the privacy of a student as Dr. Bambris had done.

"When she got pregnant, the quality of her work dropped off. I reminded her of her earlier promise and warned her several times that my patience was running thin," Dr. Bambris said.

"Did you ever meet her husband?"

"Once, at a Greek Independence Day party at my house. I didn't care for him. He was boorish and rude, a typical Russian. His Greek was horrendous."

I can't see you making much of an effort, Nick thought. "Do you know where Ms. Luzinsky went after she dropped out of the program?"

"I assume she returned to Ukraine. Our country has more than enough refugees."

Nick was about to end the call when he thought of a final question. "Was she close to anyone else in her program? A fellow student, perhaps?"

Dr. Bambris sighed. "I was her advisor, not her social worker. But yes, she was close to Irene Nestoris."

"And is Ms. Nestoris still in your program?"

"Look, I have a meeting . . ., but yes, Irene is disciplined. Unlike Natasha, she will finish the program."

After the call ended, Nick called the university's student services office again. He was grateful to reach the same helpful administrator with whom he'd spoken earlier that day. Nick knew that a student's contact information would hardly be given out by a US college or university, but Greece was not the US, and his being an Orthodox priest had clout with the college official.

Receiving the number for Irene Nestoris, Nick offered a prayer before dialing. The conversation with Natasha's friend might provide Natasha's present location, and he agreed with Lena that Natasha might help them understand Father Joseph.

Unfortunately, he reached Irene Nestoris' answering machine. Leaving his name and number, he asked her to return his call no matter the time of day or night.

Disconnecting, he offered another prayer—this one for patience.

✠

DRIVING BACK FROM A POLICE SUBSTATION IN SAGINAW, Freya Maaki passed the First National Bank of Michigan where Father Joseph's checks had, until recently, been deposited automatically. Inside the bank, a teller directed Freya to the manager's office, where she explained her errand.

"When I was told Father Joseph no longer wanted direct deposit of his salary, I called him immediately. I wanted to know if he was dissatisfied with our service. We don't like to lose any customers, but it is particularly worrisome when a member of the clergy ends a relationship," the bank manager explained. "Father Joseph assured me that the bank had done nothing wrong, but when I asked if one of our competitors had stolen him away, he was evasive. He said he planned to leave his savings account with us, which he did, but was taking his checking elsewhere."

Returning to the police station, Freya opened the yellow pages to a list of the banks of Saginaw. Along with credit unions, she counted eighteen. For each, she brought up the bank's website, hoping to narrow the number to investigate further by isolating those with tempting offers for checking accounts. After forty-five minutes, she realized it would take an accountant to compare the offers—some offering free checking, some offering a small percentage point of savings for a checking balance over a $500, and others offering a $100 to $200 gift card for new customers.

On the tenth call, she discovered that Father Joseph had opened a checking account at Midwest Savings and Loan, a small financial institution of the city. And no, a bank official informed her, there wasn't an incentive offered by the bank that could explain the priest's decision. Father Joseph had made just the one deposit before he disappeared.

Just before she ended the call with the bank official, Freya asked, "Can you tell me the amount that Father Joseph deposited?"

"Ordinarily, we don't give out that information, but because you're asking about the missing priest, I'll make an exception. He deposited $3500."

Freya felt her heart begin to race. "How much did he take in cash?"

The bank official paused a moment. "It looks like a little over $2000."

"That seems quite a bit. Is keeping back that amount of cash normal?" she asked.

"It can be if someone is saving up for something out of the ordinary," he said.

AFTER WORTHY LEFT FOR HIS OFFICE at the police station, Lena went for a walk to think about what Nick had told her.

"I feel I must warn you, Lena, about something that tends to happen at this part of a case. I'm talking about the waiting part." Somehow, the way Nick said that made her catch her breath, as if she might not want to hear what he would say next.

"Christopher has his own way of dealing with the waiting, you see," he said.

"Why so vague, Nick, and why do I have the feeling that you're trying to shield me from something?"

"Am I that obvious? It's just that I don't want you to misunderstand. Christopher wouldn't mean to shut you or me out, especially you."

"But he will, is that what you're saying?" she'd asked. Now, as she turned a corner and walked toward what looked like a school, she recalled that Worthy's kiss when he left for his office had been more a brush on her lips. Hadn't she already sensed what Nick was telling her?

Nick had nodded and smiled weakly. "He tends to go into himself, you see, and he can be a bit crusty. It's like a 'No Trespassing' sign goes up. I'm sure he's told you about his problems with partners on previous cases. When he withdrew into himself, his partners found him aloof, as if he didn't trust them. It doesn't help that Christopher tends to have his breakthroughs after his quiet periods."

"I suppose this also happens with you, Nick."

"Oh, yes. The first time it happened, I thought it was something I'd done. But when it happened again on other cases, I accepted that this is something Christopher needs to do."

As she came to the school and its quiet playground, she realized the building was boarded up. *One of Detroit's other victims,* she thought. She stared through the metal fence at weeds growing up around a set of swings, remembering that the case they'd shared before in Rome had progressed so rapidly—almost insanely so—that there had never been an opportunity to see this other side of Worthy. *The question is,* she thought, *what does this new information mean for the two of us? What does it mean for me?*

She was shocked by how much the thought of Worthy shutting her out troubled her. Hadn't he thanked her for how she conducted the interviews with the fiancés? And hadn't she just that morning decided to extend her stay to see the case through to the end? But after what Nick said, she now thought about leaving for Rome a few days early. How she hated that possibility. If she returned to Rome now, wasn't she as good as admitting that their relationship would also end? She sighed heavily, realizing she was dreading returning to the apartment and waiting for the man she loved to walk through the door.

Worthy returned with Chinese for lunch to find Lena sitting with her feet up on the couch.

"Where's Nick?" he asked.

"I asked him to give us some time to talk," Lena asked, patting the cushion next to her.

Worthy's heart skipped a beat as he realized Lena had been crying. "What is it?"

"I need you to be honest with me, Chris," she said looking down.

"Of course. When haven't I been honest?"

Looking up to meet his eyes, Lena said, "Nick told me about how you change on a case, how you need to withdraw. This morning when you left, I felt you'd already started doing that. Please understand that I'm not checking up on you—I hate when people do that to me—but I need to know if you went to your office this morning to get away from Nick and me. Actually, I need to know if you left to get away from me."

"I . . . I know I do that, but you have to believe me when I say it's not something that I do consciously. At least, not until someone points it out to me."

"Like your partners on previous cases?"

"Yeah, like them. I haven't had the best luck with partners."

"Except for Nick?"

"Okay, except for Nick."

They sat silently for a moment before Lena whispered, "But I'm not Nick."

Worthy rose from the sofa and walked to the front window. He felt panic rising within him. The last thing he wanted to do was turn around and face Lena's tearful face. "Lena, would you go somewhere with me without asking why?"

Lena didn't respond for a moment.

"Please," Worthy said.

Lena came to stand behind Worthy and hugged him. He felt she was holding onto him for dear life. "Where are we going?" she asked.

"Someplace special. Someplace that I hope will help you understand me."

For a moment, Lena didn't say anything. Then, she said, "Of course I'll come."

"We'll probably stay overnight, so you'll need to pack a bag."

"What about Nick?"

"I'll phone him while you're packing and let him know where I'm hiding the key. He'll understand."

"Don't you need to pack a bag?" Lena asked.

"No, everything I need is already there."

The car ride took five hours, and Worthy would remember them as the longest and tensest hours that he'd spent with Lena. He tried to think of how to explain why he withdrew on cases, only to end up asking himself a question: *When did I start doing this?* By the time they arrived at a cabin on Lake Skoglund near Traverse City, Worthy was mentally exhausted.

"Where are we?" Lena asked.

Worthy turned off the car and looked over at Lena. "At my cabin. Actually, I still share it with my ex-wife, Susan."

Lena looked out the side window at the old log cabin and to the sunset on the lake beyond. "And why are we here?"

Worthy opened his car door, got out to stretch, and thought, *That's a good question.*

"If you're ever going to understand me . . . no, that's not it. If I'm ever going to explain why I am the way I am on a case, I need to be here to do that," he said.

Lena exited the car and gazed at the lake. "It's been a long drive. I think we should wait until the morning to do any more talking. Other than showing where we're going to sleep."

Worthy felt the tension that had built up all day begin to fade. It was a small thing, but the fact that Lena hadn't asked to sleep in a separate room felt like a gift. He took it as her way of saying she wanted to understand him as much as he wanted to understand himself.

Her gift did not mean Worthy slept well, but when he awoke in the night, he was relieved all over again that Lena remained curled up next to him.

✠

OCTOBER 17

FOR THE THIRD TIME, NICK READ THE NOTE LEFT BY WORTHY. "Lena has asked me a question I'm not sure I know how to answer. So, I'm taking her to my cabin for a day or two, because this is the place where I'm most myself. I hope it's where I'll make sense to Lena. Call me only if something important happens on the case. Otherwise, we'll see you late tomorrow."

Good Lord, what have I done? Nick asked, also for the third time. He'd talked openly to Lena about Worthy's tendency to withdraw on cases, but he hoped that Lena would follow his example and let Worthy be Worthy.

The more he thought about the matter, the more he realized his mistake. Lena would surely recognize the connection between turning inward on cases and his failed first marriage.

Having no appetite, a rarity for him, Nick paced Worthy's apartment and tried not to fixate on all the ways he might have jeopardized Lena and Worthy's relationship. He'd just finished praying for God's mercy on his two friends when his phone rang. He jumped, hoping the call was from Natasha's friend in Thessaloniki.

"Nick, It's Freya."

"Oh, Freya. Yes," He fumbled to hide his disappointment.

"Am I interrupting something, Nick?"

"No, no, sorry. Do you have news?"

"I think I might. I tried Worthy, but he isn't answering his phone."

"No, I don't suppose he is. But I'm at your service."

"Good. I was about to contact the local paper and our local NBC station about having them put out the feeler to Father Joseph's accomplice. But then I realized it might take days or more for us to hear anything."

"Yes, I agree. And the waiting is hard, isn't it?"

"That's what I'm calling about. I don't think we have to wait."

"If you're right, I know we'd all be happy," Nick said.

"Here's what I'm thinking. If Father Joseph had an accomplice, I think it's likely that person is from here in Saginaw. I think it's even possible one of us has already interviewed him or her."

"Certainly possible, my dear."

"The next thing I asked myself was what kind of person Father Joseph would approach. Obviously, the person must be someone he trusts. I mean, he confided in this person, explained why it was necessary for him to leave, and asked him or her to say nothing."

"I'm with you so far," Nick said.

"That's when I went back and looked through the list of everyone I interviewed before. First, I looked at everyone from the parish. But I couldn't see a good parishioner helping a priest shirk his duties and betray his vocation."

Nick thought for a moment. As he had been on their previous case together, he was impressed with Freya's logical thinking. "While it's possible the accomplice is one of Father Joseph's flock, I agree it's unlikely. So where does that leave us?"

"I think there are two possibilities. The accomplice could either be someone Father Joseph met through the cycling club or someone he befriended at the diner."

"Does anyone come to mind?" he asked.

"Yes and no. If the accomplice is someone from the cycling club, that person will likely be young. A young person might have helped him out, thinking he or she was in on his adventure. If that's the case, the threat of being charged with a crime could sober that person up pretty quickly. But if the accomplice is someone from the diner, then that person, given the clientele of the diner, would more likely be older."

"And an older person might not scare so easily," Nick said.

"That's my thinking too. But that's when another thought struck me. What if the accomplice is someone who works at the diner, like one of the waitresses or cooks?"

Nick could hear the excitement in Freya's voice and was beginning to share the same feeling. Instead of waiting for the accomplice to respond to the publicized warning, something an accomplice might choose to ignore, they might be able to confront the most likely suspects and take them off guard.

"But there's more," Freya said. "I think I know where we should start looking. I'm going to check with the diner's owner, Cappy, to find out who was scheduled to be off on the day Father Joseph disappeared."

"I think you're on to something, Freya."

"Phew, good. I'll call Cappy now. And Nick, if you want to do the interviews with me, I'll wait until you get here from Detroit."

"Absolutely, my dear. Call me back when you find out anything. I have a good feeling that I'll be driving up tonight."

CHAPTER TWELVE

---◆---

OCTOBER 17

"SOME OF THE BEST ADVICE I EVER GOT AS A COP didn't come from a fellow officer but from an old fisherman on this lake," Worthy said, as Lena and he sat out on the deck.

Lena had slept better than she expected, and she'd risen to the smell of coffee in the old cabin. The logs and the faded photos of fish on the walls gave evidence to the place's age. Sometime while they were there, she'd ask Worthy how and why he'd bought the place, but now she waited for him to say what he'd taken her to his cabin to say.

As they looked out at the lake, Worthy said, "There's a time in the fall when lakes do something called 'rolling over.' In the summer, the water warms at the surface while the deeper holes are colder. But in late-September to mid-October when temps drop, the surface water gets colder, even colder than the deeper water. The lake water literally rolls over, the warmer water rushing to the surface. But here's the important part. In the days before that happens, the fish become disoriented. My old fishing buddy told me that the fish seem to know that their world is going to be literally turned upside down."

Worthy paused, and Lena tried to fathom what Worthy was trying to explain.

"Homicide cases can be a lot like lakes, when they roll over, I mean," Worthy continued. "What everyone has been taking for granted is about to be replaced by what's coming up from down below. And just before that happens, I'm like those disoriented fish. I know something important is about to happen, something none of us has considered."

Lena glanced at Worthy and saw him studying his cup of coffee.

"But this is a missing person's case, not a homicide," Lena said. "Or am I wrong?"

"Not just you, Lena. Yesterday, I woke with that same feeling—of being disoriented—about this case. It's just a feeling, but it always hits me hard. I'm so dizzy that I even feel a bit nauseated."

"And that's when you begin to withdraw," Lena said.

"It's the moment when talking is the last thing I want to do. No, it's fairer to say talking is the last thing I *can* do. But here's the worst part. The feeling only intensifies. It's like I'm one of those confused fish in the days before the lake rolls over. I just seem to go down and down."

Hearing a thickness in Worthy's voice, Lena understood that he was feeling what he was describing.

"It's like I know that something is down there," he said, "something that doesn't want to come up to the light. I have to dive down to find it or else . . ."

"Or else what?" Lena asked.

"I don't know. Ever since the first time this happened, I've always given in to that feeling and descended. It's like I don't have a choice."

"This must have been hell for your family."

"Oh, yeah. It's hell for everyone. Partners complain they've been shut out, and I can't say they're wrong. If what I've found down there didn't end up being important, I'd have been fired long ago."

"Do you ever wish this didn't happen to you?"

Worthy nodded, but then stopped. "I was a decent cop before this all started. 'Decent' means I was a little better than average. The cases I couldn't solve became cold cases. After this 'rolling over' sensation began to happen to me, I became the one who was given those cold cases. Families who'd given up hope got some answers. I became a kind of wonder-cop." He lapsed into silence again before adding, "No, I don't have a choice. I wouldn't be able to stop this happening to me even if I wanted to."

They sat together without saying anything. Finally, Worthy rose. "Can I get you some more coffee?"

Lena nodded and watched him enter the cabin. She figured Worthy had only begun to explain what had happened to change his life as a detective and cost him his family. The question facing her was if she could live with what Worthy was describing.

When he returned to the front deck with more coffee, Lena said, "I'm still wondering how what you're describing pertains to this case. What do you think you'll find this time?"

Worthy sat down and sighed heavily. "I can't see it clearly yet. But I know this case is about more than a missing priest."

✝

NICK HAD ALREADY SHED HIS MONASTIC ROBES and donned a simple clerical collar and dark sport coat, in hopes that Freya would call back with encouraging news. He had to laugh as he looked at his reflection in the mirror. If it hadn't been for the clerical collar, his long beard and ponytail made him look like a leftover hippie. The humorous sight offered a welcome break from his worries about Lena and Worthy.

From the first time he met Worthy, he understood that Worthy was an introvert with many of the same needs as his fellow monks. Consequently, when Worthy described his cabin in northern Michigan, Nick thought it sounded like a hermitage. That impression was confirmed when Worthy, after they'd solved the murder of an elderly priest in Detroit, had taken him to the isolated cabin. Because the cabin had no TV or internet, the only sounds at night were from the loons on the lake.

Nick knew that the cabin was more than a retreat for Worthy. The photos on the wall of his daughters as young girls, smiling as the camera caught them fishing or swimming, didn't surprise him. What did surprise him was the photos of Worthy with his first wife, Susan, from the happier days of their marriage. He initially thought the photos were there because Susan and Worthy owned the cabin jointly. But such an arrangement didn't preclude Worthy storing those painful photos away when he used the cabin. Later, when Nick knew Worthy better, he understood the photos to be something Worthy hung on to, proof that he'd once been a beloved husband and father.

With Worthy and Lena having known each other for nearly a year, Nick hoped his friend no longer needed to look back to experience happiness. But he trembled at the thought that Worthy's relationship with Lena could founder on the same rock that destroyed his marriage to Susan.

Blessedly, Freya called at that moment. "Nick, you won't believe what I found out. I can't believe this clue has been there all this time. Really, I just can't believe it."

"The suspense is killing me, Freya. What is it?" Nick replied, grabbing the keys to the monastery car and heading for the door.

"Do you remember Connie Ferwerda?"

"I don't recognize the last name, but isn't Connie one of the waitresses as the diner?"

"Yes, yes, yes," Freya replied. "When the owner looked back in his records, he found that Connie called in sick the day Father Joseph went missing, as well as the next day."

"Two days. Good Lord, Freya, if Connie helped Father Joseph disappear and didn't come back for two days, she could have taken him far away from Michigan."

"Which would be considerably beyond where we were looking at the time. Oh, and here's something else. I asked Cappy if it was unusual for Connie to call in sick. He said Connie is his best waitress. She almost never calls in sick. Plus, she's a single mom with two kids."

"I'm on my way, Freya. I should be in Saginaw by about six or seven this evening. Should we meet at the diner?"

"No, come to the police station, Nick. When we go to the diner, I want Connie to see both of us at the same moment."

CONNIE FERWERDA GLANCED UP AT FREYA AND NICK as they sat on stools at the counter. "What can I get you?" she asked.

Nick thought the waitress looked guarded, as if she were pretending that she didn't remember speaking with him just days before.

"When do you go on break, Connie?" Freya asked. "We need to talk with you."

Connie busied herself with wiping down the counter. "I've had my break. What's this about?"

The way Connie said that gave Nick the impression that she'd dealt with the police before and knew the safest course was for her to ask the questions.

"We have a few follow-up questions about Father Joseph," Freya replied.

Connie shook her head without looking up. "I've told you all I remember. Nothing more to be said."

"Nick and I will have coffee, then, and wait until your shift is over. I've already talked to Cappy. He told me you're off at eight. Nick, would you like something else?"

Connie met Nick's eye, looking as if she were a cornered animal. "Connie, we think you can help us," he said, trying to break the tension. "But if you have any more of that apple pie I had last time, I'd love a piece."

From the other end of the counter, one of two old men sitting together called down to Connie for another cup of coffee. Connie moved rapidly to fulfill his request, taking a few moments to open a glass case behind her to find the apple pie and bring Nick a generous slice.

"Would you like a scoop of ice cream on that?" she asked.

"I'd love that," he said with a smile.

With twenty-five minutes to wait, Nick enjoyed the pie and made small talk with Freya. He noted since his last time in the diner that Halloween decorations had appeared, a string of paper jack-o-lanterns and black cats hanging above the windows.

He could see that Connie was doing her best to ignore them by chatting with other customers. He stole glances at her, trying to understand why she might have agreed to be Father Joseph's accomplice. Connie could have been in her mid-thirties, but her face belonged to someone who found life to be mostly uphill. Rings glistened from fingers on both hands, but there was no ring on her left hand indicating marriage. He pictured Connie in twenty or thirty years, working behind this same counter, and he wondered if she saw the same future for herself. Nick sensed Father Joseph might have found Connie to be a willing accomplice, as maybe she hoped that someone would help her escape her life in Saginaw someday.

Eight o'clock came and went, and Nick realized Connie was deliberately stalling by going back into the kitchen to talk with one of the cooks.

"I assume you have a plan for how this is going to go," he said.

Freya nodded and said in a whisper, "Oh, yes. She's made it easy. She's as much as giving herself away."

Finally, at a quarter past eight, Connie seemed to give up. Coming out to the customer side of the counter, she said, "Where do you want to do this?"

"We can go back to the station, where it's warm, or we can talk in my car," Freya said.

"The car," Connie said as she put on her parka and led the way out into the parking lot.

Getting into the unmarked Dodge, they sat in silence while Freya started the car and turned the heat on high. Despite the vehicle warming up rapidly, Connie's arms gripped the collar of her coat tightly as she sat in the front seat with Freya.

Connie looked out the car window. "Have you found him, then?"

"No, but we think he had an accomplice, someone who helped him leave Saginaw. That person could face charges of obstructing a police inquiry."

Although Connie didn't say anything, Nick saw her flinch. Finally, she said, "Why are you telling me this?"

"We think you know, Connie," Nick said. "There are a lot of people worried about Father Joseph, wondering what happened to him, if he's still alive. I'm sure you can understand that. What did he tell you about where he was going?"

She turned around, her eyes flashing. "Why can't people trust that Joe knows what he's doing? If I left Saginaw tomorrow—and if I didn't have two kids, don't think I wouldn't do that—if I left to take a job in Detroit or Chicago, people would just let me do that. They'd say 'Good luck, Connie. It's about time.'"

"But he's a priest, Connie—" Nick began.

"No, he's a damn adult. Last time I checked, he's an American with free will."

Nick wondered if Connie appreciated the priestly vow that Father Joseph had taken. "Except he didn't leave for another job, did he?" he said. "A priest is like a shepherd. Father Joseph left his flock, his community that counted on him, trusted him with their problems and hopes. And he left you."

Connie bowed her head and started to cry. Speaking through her tears, she said, "He said he hoped to come back someday and explain. But he couldn't say when that might be."

"What did he tell you about why he needed to leave?" Freya asked, offering Connie a tissue.

After she blew her nose and wiped her eyes, Connie said, "He told me someone needed his help. He said it could be a matter of life and death. Then he said something that surprised me. In fact, I wasn't sure I heard him right. But then he repeated it. He said that what he had to do would be the only worthwhile thing he'd ever do in his life. I never thought anyone who's smart and popular like Father Joe ever felt that way. It was like something I would say."

"Did he say whose life was in danger?" Freya asked.

Connie shook her head. "No, he just asked me to trust him . . . and I did."

No one said anything for a moment. "Has he contacted you since he left?" Freya asked.

Connie shook her head. "I don't know anything but what I've told you."

Nick glanced at Freya before saying, "There is one more thing you can do to help us. You mentioned Detroit and Chicago before. Did he ask you to drive him south?"

"No, he asked me to take him to the Upper Peninsula. I took him north."

Connie's answer made no sense at all to Nick. All of Father Joseph's life until the past year had been spent in eastern states. Why would he head north?

"Where did you leave him?" Nick asked.

"I told him I couldn't be gone for more than two days. You see, my babysitter thought I was going to meet some guy at a casino. An overnight. Joe said it was fine if I dropped him outside Marquette."

So he went not only north but west, Nick thought, now further puzzled.

"Did you get the idea that he knew someone in Marquette?" Freya asked.

"Not really. I dropped him at a truck stop outside the city. The last I saw of him, he looked like he was going to hitch a ride."

Nick sat quietly, trying to picture a scenario that made little sense. "What was he like on the trip up there? Was he talkative? Did he seem to be in a good mood?" he asked.

"He didn't say much. When it got dark, we stopped along a country road. He told me I could sleep in the back. He stayed up front, but I don't think he slept."

"Did he ever give you the feeling he might change his mind and ask you to drive him back?"

Connie shook her head. "When I woke up next morning, I asked him if he still wanted to keep going. He said it was something he had to do. The only thing he said after that was that he hoped he wasn't too late."

✝

LENA ACCEPTED THE CUP OF HOT CHOCOLATE FROM WORTHY as they sat before the warming fire in the cabin. They'd taken a break from the heavy talk of that afternoon, and while she was on a walk alone to an overlook above the lake, a thought struck her that flooded her with relief. But would Worthy understand what she'd realized?

"I want to tell you something about my family," she said.

Worthy sat forward in his chair but said nothing.

"I come from a typical Italian family, if living through Fascism can be described as typical. I was fortunate to have both grandfathers survive the war, but there the good fortune ended. My mother's parents fell in line with Mussolini—the rebirth of the mighty Roman Empire, the right to invade Ethiopia, everything Il Duce said was gospel to them. I didn't know the full extent of their involvement until I was in secondary school. But it shook me. I love Papa and Nonna, and they love me. I'd go to Mass with them every week. It was hard for me to picture them in the mobs you see in the newsreels, but they were there. I hope the US avoids that madness, but your country worries me.

"Anyway, my other grandparents were active in the resistance. I suppose if my two grandfathers had met during the war, one of them would have killed the other, and I wouldn't be here. I was younger when I heard what these other grandparents did during the war, so I didn't know until much later that papa killed German sympathizers."

"I assume your two grandfathers have met. Do they ever talk about it?" Worthy asked.

"Like most Italians of that era, they choose not to talk about the war, and my parents' generation, in order to keep the peace, honors that. But that wasn't good enough for me. By the time I entered university, I was aware that I had these stories warring within me. I have no doubt that's why I turned to psychology."

"I'm trying to see how your specialty on mystics relates to what your grandparents lived through."

Lena took a sip of the hot chocolate. "My interest in mystics and mystic pretenders came later. Where I started was trying to understand how mobs work, how they lure decent people—like my one set of grandparents—into doing horrible things. That led me to study how Mussolini and his top officers not only manipulated mobs but also were created by those mobs. What I came to understand is that there's something within most people that's keen on being part of something big, so keen that they'll turn off their consciences. In one of my essays, I called it the human desire to be historical, to participate in something so important that you feel immortal."

"I think Nick might call that the need for 'transcendence,'" Worthy said. "A person rises above being a mere individual."

"If it is, it's demonic transcendence. But I'm not talking about demons with pitchforks and tails. I meant it when I said that Mussolini and the other fascist leaders manipulated the mobs and at the same time were created by them. It's like a circle of energy that builds and builds. Ordinarily decent people become energized by charismatic leaders like Mussolini and Hitler. But I'm convinced that Mussolini and Hitler were energized by the mobs. The mobs my grandparents were part of *made* Mussolini, recreating him in a more extreme form with every rally. The energy flowed back and forth between Mussolini and people like my grandparents, and as it flowed, it also grew in strength. For me, that energy is the demonic."

The two sat silently for a few moments as the wood in the fireplace crackled and hissed.

"After I understood that, I wanted to understand my other grandparents and people who joined the resistance. That couldn't have been an easy decision, given that almost the whole country was caught up in fascism. I discovered that a lot of the research credited everyone in the resistance with having a stronger will or conscience. I wasn't so sure about that. I began to think their decision had more to do with what informed their wills and consciences. Does that make sense?"

"It does, and I understand why you couldn't ask your one set of grandparents why they joined the mobs. But did you ever ask your other grandparents why they didn't?"

"I did. In fact, I interviewed them for another paper I wrote. At first, my grandfather credited his decision to his own parents' Communist leanings, even though he said he was never tempted by that ideology. Then he said that resistance seemed the only sane stance to take with Mussolini. When I asked them both why so few saw the fascists as insane while the majority saw them as the sane ones, my grandmother said something that helped me the most. She was a poet at heart, and she said being a fascist in those years was like being caught in a fast-flowing stream, a stream that at the beginning seemed full of glory and excitement. Those in the resistance, she said, were those who knew from the beginning that they had to somehow get out of that stream and make their way to the shore. From the shore, people in the resistance could see that the stream was going to destroy everything in its path. And that's when they decided to do whatever they could to stop it—to stop the river."

"And now your research centers on mystics. I'm still not sure how you came to that."

"To be honest, I backed into my interest in mystics from my earlier interest in resisters. I kept thinking of my grandmother's metaphor of the stream. Mussolini promised national glory and power, and people jumped at the chance to escape their small, individual lives."

"Sounds a lot like 'Make America Great Again.'"

"You're the American, but I don't disagree. Anyway, I discovered mystics when I studied the earlier resisters. The further I went back in time, the more I discovered that the earliest resisters were the mystics."

"That's quite a jump, isn't it?" Worthy asked.

"Is it? If mobs take people out of themselves, resisters and mystics—real mystics—go deeper into themselves. For resisters and mystics, the inner life is everything, a place where they're listening for something—or someone. It's where they make sense of life. That's why true mystics never join mobs. At best, a genuine mystic, such as St. Francis, will inspire a few others who inspire others who then inspire others to take the inward journey."

"But mobs are all over history," Worthy said. "And didn't you tell me last year that genuine mystics are rare? It hardly seems a fair balance."

"All the more reason to study them. A theologian recently predicted that the future of humanity would see the rise of mystics. I don't know if he's right, but I'm intrigued. A mystic like St. Francis has a greater long-term impact on history than a hundred mobs."

Lena took a deep breath, feeling exhausted. What she'd said so far was prologue, which she knew Worthy could hold at arm's length. Now she would see if he could accept that she was also talking about him.

Worthy interrupted her thoughts by saying, "Can I get you some more hot chocolate?"

"No, but I suddenly have a chill. Could you get me a blanket or something?"

Rising from his chair, Worthy said, "I'm not surprised. This old fireplace can't keep up with the temps in the fall after sunset. But maybe another log or two will help."

Lena watched as he carefully stacked two logs on the coals before opening a closet door and coming back with a wool blanket. "It's been in that cold closet since last spring, so it might take a few minutes to warm up."

"No, I feel better already."

As the flames danced in the fireplace, neither spoke. Finally, Worthy said, "So tell me about your infatuation with mystics."

Taking a deep breath and looking at Worthy, Lena replied, "Infatuation? I don't know if that's the right word. But I became infatuated with you."

A puzzled look crossed Worthy's face. "Well, I'm hardly . . ."

"What I mean is that what you described this morning, your impulse to go down into yourself on a case, well, that has clear similarities with mystics."

Worthy shook his head. "I don't see that at all. I have to go into a very dark space. And what I find, if I'm successful, is clues that I—and others—have overlooked about a case."

"Okay, put the mystic comparison aside for a moment. How about if I say that what you do when you descend into yourself is similar to what resisters did in the war?"

"Hmm."

Lena waited for more from Worthy, but he said nothing.

"Chris, think about the problems you've had with partners. Doesn't that happen when you disagree, or what I would say when you resist, their overly simplistic approaches to a case?"

A log in the fire collapsed, sending sparks into the air.

"And think about that 'lake rolling over' metaphor. I believe every fighter in the resistance had something like that happen to them. Instead of getting swept up in the crowds, they turned inward, were listening for something—truth, I imagine—and their sense of reality 'rolled over' for them. They saw what the mobs were doing as insane. Mass insanity, but insanity."

"But all I'm looking for in that darkness is clues."

"No, what you are looking for is just what resisters and mystics have always looked for. You're looking for that deeper truth."

Worthy coughed and looked away. When he spoke, his voice was little louder than a whisper. "Ever since we met, part of me has dreaded you witnessing one of my 'spells.' I thought if you ever saw one, you might decide we don't have a future together . . . like Susan and my daughter, Allyson, did. But now . . ."

Lena rose from the rocking chair and wrapped the blanket tightly around her as she came and stood in front of Worthy. She reached down and lifted his face. "But now what?"

Worthy closed his eyes as he shook his head. "I never expected anyone, not counting Nick, to care enough to understand me. And I'm not sure even Nick understands me. He just knows that my silences are part of what has to happen to me on a case."

"Chris, what you need to know is that neither of us is ever going to understand everything about what happens to you when you descend. But I understand enough. And maybe, just maybe, I'm the one person who can help you do just that—go down as deep as you need to."

CHAPTER THIRTEEN

───────◆───────

OCTOBER 18

"I RENE, CAN I PUT YOU ON HOLD A MOMENT?" Nick said in Greek to Natasha's closest grad school friend, Irene Nestoris. "I need to try to bring somebody else into this . . . this . . ."

"What? I don't understand."

"Please, I know it's early morning in Thessaloniki, but it's late night here. And I apologize if I'm not making much sense. An American policeman and an Italian professor need to hear what you just said."

"An American policeman and an Italian professor speak Greek?"

"No, no; I'll translate. Please, just stay on the line for a moment?"

There was silence on the other end of the line, and Nick feared that Irene thought he was a madman and hung up.

"Irene, are you still there?"

"Yes, but I'm very confused."

"Everything will become clear, I promise. Just give me a minute."

Again, there was no response from Irene, and Nick offered a pleading prayer as he hit a button on his phone and called Worthy's number. As he waited, he also prayed that Worthy's hopes in bringing Lena to the cabin had been realized.

"Nick, what is it?" Worthy said.

"Thank God. Christopher, I know it's late, but Irene Nestoris is on another line. What she told me is . . . it's important. But she speaks only Greek, so I'll translate. Can you put your phone on speaker so Lena can hear?"

There was a pause before Lena said, "I'm here, Nick. Go ahead."

Nick felt a wave of relief pass through him. Until that moment, he hadn't admitted his fear that Lena and Worthy might not be on speaking terms. So he hoped it wasn't his imagination that her voice sounded normal, not strained. Offering another prayer for the conference call to work, he hit a button and said, "Irene, my colleagues are on the line now. Please repeat what you told me about Natasha."

Instead of doing that, Irene Nestoris asked, "Is there more bad news about Natasha? Is that why a policeman is involved?"

In Greek, Nick replied, "No, she's not in any trouble, but she might be able to help us on a case here in the U.S. It's one involving Father Joseph Kouris."

"Father Joseph? Is he all right?"

"He's missing," Nick explained.

"Oh, my God. Oh, my God."

Nick could hear the woman begin to whimper. "Irene, please repeat what you told me about Natasha. It could be very important."

"And you swear you are a priest?"

"As God is my witness—yes, I am a priest."

When Irene didn't say anything, he thought she might not have believed him. But then she said, "You told me that you knew Natasha had a baby. But that isn't the reason she quit her degree program. Her husband, that bastard, made her quit. He wanted to take her back to his family in Russia."

"Tell my friends what you told me about her pregnancy," Nick said.

"Must I? It's so painful."

"Yes, it's vital."

Irene sighed. "It's so sad. Natasha told me she was raped in one of the university parking lots after one of her night classes. Her husband, Sergei, he is a crazy man. He demanded she get an abortion, but Natasha doesn't believe in abortion, so she said she would keep the baby. That's when Sergei accused her, saying she wasn't raped but slept with other men, just as she slept with Father Joseph."

Nick heard Lena gasp when he translated what the woman said. "Nick, is she saying Father Joseph slept with Natasha?"

Nick put Lena's question to Irene. "No, no, it's what Sergei said. I say again, he is a crazy man. Father Joseph only protected her. Nothing more," Irene explained.

"Nick, did Natasha's husband take her back to Russia or not?" Worthy asked.

After Nick translated the question, Irene said, "After the baby was born, Sergei became crazier. She told me he started beating her again. Natasha said she was afraid he would harm the baby. But Natasha, she thinks of a way to protect the baby, Mitya. Her husband, he had business in Greece, so he wanted to send her and the baby back to his family in Russia."

"You said that Natasha had a plan. What did she do?" Nick asked.

"Natasha told me she was certain, when Sergei's family heard about the rape, that she and the baby would be killed. I asked her if she is sure about this.

That made her mad. But then she told me her plan to fool Sergei. Her flight would have a stopover in Munich. That's where she'd change her ticket from Moscow to Kiev in Ukraine where her family would be waiting. She said they would protect her."

"Was she intending to leave Sergei?" Lena asked.

When Irene heard the question, she said, "Yes, that is what she said."

"Have you spoken to her since she returned home?" Nick asked.

"I tried the number she left me. At first, a man answered. He said I had the wrong number. His English wasn't very good, and neither is mine. But I knew that it wasn't the wrong number. I tried every day for a week. Finally, a woman with better English answered and said that Natasha couldn't come to the phone and for me to stop calling. I asked if she was all right, and the woman said, 'Don't call any more. It isn't safe.' Sorry, that's all I know. Please, if you find Natasha, tell her I light a candle for her and the baby when I go to church."

✝

OCTOBER 19

EARLY THE NEXT MORNING, WORTHY AND LENA LEFT the cabin to meet with Freya Maaki and Nick in Saginaw. The trip back bore little resemblance to the drive up two days before. The silences were still there, but they weren't filled with tension. Although the last forty-eight hours seemed like a month, he felt certain that Lena and he had done more than weather a crisis. Their relationship had changed for the better. His greatest fear—that Lena would react like Susan to his methods of doing his job—hadn't materialized.

The miles slipped away rapidly as the two discussed what they learned from the phone call with Irene Nestoris and what Nick and Freya had gleaned from their encounter with Connie Ferwerda. Father Joseph had fled north, while Natasha had fled from her husband. Two people fleeing, but no connection.

"I was thinking more about resisters," Lena said. "Could that also describe Father Joseph?"

"What do you mean?"

"Well, most of his family thinks he's made one bizarre decision after another. That's similar to the reaction mystics and people who join resistance movements face from their families. St. Francis' father never did accept what his son had done with his life, and this was after most of Italy, as well as other parts of Europe, already considered him a saint."

"But in Aris' case, it isn't just his family. The church authorities and a lot of others view him the same way," Worthy said.

"Again, that's not uncommon for mystics and resisters. There was an Austrian Catholic named Franz Jägerstätter, who refused to fight during the

Second World War. It wasn't because he was a pacifist. Somehow, despite the attitude of everyone around him in Austria, he saw through Nazism. I bet you can guess what his parish priest and his bishop told him to do."

"I suppose they told him to get on the bandwagon."

Lena sighed. "That's close. They told him how noble it was to fight for his country. Even after he was executed and the war ended, his neighbors thought he was a coward and a crazy man. It's only been in the last couple decades that the Catholic Church has recognized him as a possible saint. I have no opinion about that, but what's clear from Jägerstätter's diary is that he looked inward."

"And you think Aris Kouris is like him?" Worthy asked.

"Do you?"

"You know the guy troubles me. Half of those who know him think he's saint. The other half, and that includes some of his family and the two fiancés, see him as a self-centered egotist. A narcissist would also turn inward, wouldn't he?"

"That's exactly how Jägerstätter's friends and neighbors saw him—a narcissist who was convinced he was right and everyone else was wrong. They thought it was selfish for him to die without thinking about who would take care of his family," Lena said.

For a few moments, Worthy drove without talking. Finally, he said, "What makes someone a saint or a genuine resister and another a narcissist? I have colleagues who've told me to my face that I'm a narcissist. Sometimes, I wonder if they could be right."

FREYA NOTICED HER COLLEAGUES IN THE POLICE STATION stealing glances her way as she led Lena, Worthy, and Nick into her office. Some of them, she imagined, recognized Worthy from their training at the police academy, and men never missed attractive women like Lena coming into the station. Even Nick in his robes might be known by some from the media.

When Freya first met Worthy and Nick two years before, she was a green sergeant in the Houghton police station in the Upper Peninsula. More than once, she compared the Houghton Police Department to one of the lower rings of Dante's hell. Most of her co-workers there never became colleagues, resenting her from day one, but that feeling rose to the level of hatred after she embarrassed them by helping Worthy and Nick solve one of the toughest homicide cases in Upper Peninsula memory.

Transferring anywhere after Houghton would have been an improvement, but her last sixteen months in the Saginaw Police Department had been more than just a bit better. Her captain was a woman who seemed to value Freya's style of investigation, a style she learned both from Worthy's lectures at the police academy and from their case together.

As her colleagues in the Saginaw office stared at her visitors, she knew their stares showed curiosity, not resentment. They would likely ask her later what was going on, but she also knew that she wouldn't face any criticism or jealousy for inviting Lena, Worthy, and Nick to help with her missing person's case.

Freya wasn't surprised that Worthy asked her to lead the meeting; he'd done the same thing two years before. And she was prepared. From her computer, she projected onto the wall what Nick and she had learned from Connie Ferwerda.

Date and time of Father J's departure from Saginaw: 11:00 a.m. September 10

FJ's attire: blue sweatshirt (without logo), jeans, Nike shoes.

Direction taken: North to Mackinac Bridge; northwest to Marquette.

Where accomplice left FJ: truck stop on bypass around Marquette.

FJ's ultimate destination: Unknown. Seemed to be heading west.

Statements by FJ to accomplice: "Someone I know needs my help." "I hope I'm not too late." "He said that what he had to do would be the only worthwhile thing he'd ever do in his life."

Further contact by FJ with accomplice: None, assuming she is telling the truth.

Looking up from her computer, Freya said, "Anything I missed, Nick?"

"No, that seems very well organized, much better than my report about what we learned from Natasha's friend, Irene Nestoris, in Greece. I think the first thing we learned that's important is that Natasha was raped. Then she refused to have an abortion, which was what her husband, Sergei, demanded. She gave birth to a baby boy, Mitya. The next thing we learned was that as soon as Mitya was born, her husband made her quit her graduate studies. According to Irene, his plan was to send Natasha back to Russia to stay with his family. That leads to the last thing. Again according to Irene, Natasha was convinced that her life and the life of the baby would be in danger if she went to Sergei's family in Russia, so she intended to fool her husband by flying to her family in Ukraine."

"It sounded to me like her husband is a royal shit, maybe even psychotic," Lena added.

"Her husband didn't fly back with her?" Freya asked.

"No, he apparently stayed in Greece to finish some business. Irene insinuated it was probably something illegal," Nick replied. "What am I forgetting, Lena?"

"Only what Irene did after Natasha left Greece. She tried to call Natasha's family in Ukraine several times. Finally, a woman told her it wasn't safe for Irene to keep trying to reach Natasha. That made me catch my breath."

Freya nodded. "Yes, me too. It means Natasha managed to fool her husband, but it also means her life might still be in danger." She looked at Worthy, aware that he hadn't said anything.

Nick spoke next. "If Father Joseph had taken his passport with him, wouldn't we all be thinking he'd flown to Ukraine to protect Natasha and the baby?"

The question hung in the room until Lena said, "I'm not sure Chris views it that way."

Worthy exhaled slowly before saying, "I have no proof, but I have this . . . this feeling that there's something not right about this whole case."

"Come on, Christopher, tell us what you're thinking," Nick said.

Worthy rubbed his forehead. "Nick, you know better than anyone that my instincts are sometimes wrong."

"But not two years ago," Freya said. "You guessed right."

Worthy looked down at his hands. "I warn you, what I'm thinking makes both Aris and Natasha Luzinsky look pretty bad." Clearing his throat, he said, "Okay, here goes. Let's go back to how the two fiancés and some of Aris' own family describe him. To them, he's someone who doesn't care what pain he causes. For all we know, he's been like this since high school, or maybe even earlier."

Freya cleared her throat and said, "It looks like I'm the only one who doesn't know what Father Joseph was like when he was younger."

Worthy apologized for the oversight before describing the details of Aris Kouris' past: his fathering a child, the adoption and death of that child, his obsession with rowing, his two broken engagements, and his decision on the day of his college graduation to enter the seminary, a decision that broke his fiancé's and his father's hearts.

"Hmm," Freya muttered. Well, I can see how that makes Father Joseph look pretty bad. But you said what you're thinking makes Natasha look bad too."

Worthy nodded. "It's important to remember that everything Irene told us was something Natasha had told her. Irene witnessed none of what Natasha told her—the abuse of the husband, her claim that he demanded an abortion, and her notion that her life and the baby's were in danger if she went to Sergei's relatives. It's all hearsay."

Freya saw Nick's brow furrow as he stroked his beard. "What about the house-mother who told us everyone in the house could hear Sergei yelling at Natasha?"

"Remember, the housekeeper said the yelling was in Russian or Ukrainian, so we don't know what he was angry about."

"Ok," Nick said. "What about the comment by Natasha's academic advisor?"

"As I remember, Nick, all he said was that he didn't like Sergei. But he didn't like Natasha either," Worthy said.

"Putting Father Joseph aside for a moment, why would Natasha make up all those stories?" Freya asked.

"Lena thinks I'm seeing Aris . . . Father Joseph as a narcissist. What if Natasha is just as much a narcissist as him? What if they fed off each other?"

"Really? Do narcissists do that?" Nick asked.

"Lena, you're the expert in abnormal psychology. I'll let you handle that question."

Lena shrugged. "I've been quiet because I'm trying to find evidence to prove you're wrong, Chris. But I have to concede that what you're saying is possible. Narcissists imagine their lives are special, that they're living out a drama. They're always the lead characters, with those around them just minor characters in their stories. What you're suggesting is that Father Joseph and Natasha, maybe unconsciously, are living out a romantic tale—she's the damsel in distress, he's the knight in shining armor who she runs to, and Sergei is the menacing dragon. It's a myth they invented, but it's a myth that they undoubtedly believe. That is, if you're right."

Nick put his head in his hands. "Oh, now I don't know what to believe. Father Joseph's brother Paulus said when Aris was younger, reminded him of a medieval knight. Those were his very words. Good Lord, have I been completely duped?"

"We don't know yet, Nick. Remember, we're not going to know the whole truth about Father Joseph until we find him," Lena said.

Freya shook her head. "There's something we can do in the meantime. If we can contact Natasha back in Ukraine, we'll know if she's in real danger. And that will tell us a lot about Father Joseph."

WORTHY COULD TELL THAT NICK WAS JUST AS UNCOMFORTABLE as he with their different views of Father Joseph. They'd disagreed on other cases but never to this extent. Hoping to close the gap, Worthy took Freya aside to ask if Nick and he could look over the priest's apartment.

"Of course," Freya said, "although I can show you a list of what we found—mainly clothes in the bedroom closet, quite a few books on a shelf, and food in his fridge."

"I'm not doubting that, Freya," Worthy whispered, "but it would be good if Nick and I could work together on something, don't you think?"

A half-hour later, Worthy and Nick drove to Father Joseph's apartment, neither of them bringing up the issue that divided them. Opening the door of the priest's apartment, Worthy was happy to see that Freya had kept the owner from cleaning the rooms.

After they both did a quick walkthrough of the two-bedroom apartment, Nick said, "It looks pretty bare. Do you really think he would have left something incriminating?"

Worthy suspected that Nick saw through his ploy but was happy that Nick was going along with it.

"We're not going to find a diary or anything like that, but you know as well as I do, Nick, that what people assume isn't important can turn out to be vital."

"Agreed, my friend. Where would you like me to start?"

Worthy thought for a moment, trying to determine in which rooms Nick would be more likely to find something. "Why don't you take the kitchen and his bedroom, and I'll take the main room and the bathroom. If we don't find anything there, we can tackle the spare room together."

Worthy began in the bathroom. As expected, he found neither toothbrush nor toothpaste. The shower area was also missing soap and clean towels, suggesting that Father Joseph had taken those items with him. In the wastebasket, he did find an empty box that had held bandages, leading Worthy to conclude that Father Joseph had packed those as well.

In the main sitting room, he scanned the used sofa, coffee table, writing table, shelf of books, and a TV. Lifting off the sofa cushions, he found the usual stray pencil and paper clips, as well as some paper, which gave him a brief moment of hope. But when he unfolded it, he realized it was nothing more than a receipt from Cappy's Diner for a breakfast of corned-beef hash and eggs, sunny side up.

He could hear the sound of Nick opening and closing drawers in the bedroom, but then he became aware of sudden silence.

"Christopher, I might have found something."

Entering the bedroom, Worthy saw a pillow and pillowcase lying on the bed, with Nick studying something in his hand.

"Look at what was in the pillowcase."

Worthy stood next to Nick and looked at an official-looking document. From the embossed heading, he realized he was looking at a formal letter of some sort, dated in April eight years before. At the bottom, he saw Aris Kouris' signature. Reading the document's small print more carefully, Worthy realized he was looking at an invitation from the US Olympic Committee, inviting Aris Kouris to a tryout in rowing for the upcoming Summer Olympics.

"I don't understand. I can see that he signed it, but Father Joseph didn't go to a tryout, did he?" Nick asked.

"No, he did not."

"Then why keep the invitation and hide it in a pillowcase? I'd understand if Father Joseph's Papa had kept it and used it to harangue his son, but why would Father Joseph keep it?"

"I'm not sure, Nick, but the date suggests that Aris Kouris received this letter a month before his college graduation."

"Ah, I think I see what you're getting at, my friend," Nick said. "That was the same month he told his fiancé and his family that he was passing on the Olympic tryout, passing on marriage, and heading for the seminary and the priesthood. But I still don't understand why he would keep this letter. Wouldn't it cause him pain?"

Worthy looked at the well-worn edges of the invitation, trying to imagine Aris Kouris sitting on the bed and rereading the Olympic committee's invitation. "Nick, I think this letter does tell us something important. Aris didn't ponder becoming a celibate priest for months. He was thinking of becoming an Olympian. But then something must have caused him to change his mind in a hurry."

"It must have been something big," Nick added.

"Yes, without a doubt. Now all we have to figure out is what that something was."

CHAPTER FOURTEEN

THE NEXT MORNING, WITH NOW EVEN MORE QUESTIONS about Father Joseph, the group returned to Freya's office to consider their next moves. Even Nick, normally the optimist, was sure he'd never felt lower on a case. It wasn't all because Worthy could be right about Father Joseph. It was more that Worthy and he, on all their cases together, had never been so far apart.

Oddly, the person who seemed most committed to pushing back against the lethargy in the room was Worthy. More than once he reminded them that though the priest was still a mystery, they were making progress in understanding him. But it was clear to Nick that Worthy's argument for Father Joseph and Natasha being both narcissists was sapping the energy of the rest of them. There was a clear possibility that the wayward priest and Ukrainian woman had had taken them all into their shared delusion. Finding Father Joseph—if they found him—could be the bitter end to a wild goose chase.

It wasn't Worthy but Freya, with an offhand and flippant comment, who broke the dark spell in the room.

"There's something about your version of the story, Chris, that didn't come to me until I tried to fall asleep last night. For you, Father Joseph and Natasha are living in the same fantasy world, and that's what connects the two of them. For the rest of us, we thought—and maybe still want to believe—that Father Joseph was forced to leave Greece in disgrace because he truly cared for Natasha, a woman who really was being abused by her husband."

"I still believe that," Lena said. "If Father Joseph had taken his passport, I think we'd be looking for him in Kiev. That's just as true if your view is right, Chris. But what doesn't make sense to me is Father Joseph asking his accomplice to drive him north and west. I mean, I'm not an American, but isn't the Upper Peninsula mainly forests and lakes? And what's beyond that but Canada?"

Freya laughed. "Do you want to know how crazy my mind works when I'm tired? Just as I was drifting off to sleep, I had this crazy image of Father Joseph, the potential Olympic athlete, rowing his way across the Atlantic."

Lena and Nick joined in the rare moment of laughter, but they all stopped when they saw the expression on Worthy's face.

Blushing, Freya said, "Sorry, I was just trying to lighten the mood."

"No, no, I'm not angry," Worthy replied. "Repeat what you said about rowing."

"It's just an image that came to my mind. According to what you told me, both brothers described Father Joseph as being obsessed with rowing. That's all."

"And you said something about Canada, Lena," Worthy added.

"Yes . . ., but I didn't mean it seriously."

Staring at Freya, Worthy said in a low voice, "Do you have a map?"

"A map? What kind of map?"

"A plat map of the Upper Peninsula, Freya."

Freya went to a bookcase, brought back a detailed map of Michigan, and opened it to the Upper Peninsula. Worthy's finger moved from Marquette to the west, leaving Freya, and she assumed Lena and Nick, to guess what he was thinking.

After a moment, Worthy looked up and asked, "How about a plat map of Wisconsin . . . and one of Minnesota too."

"I'll have to ask somebody out there," she said, nodding toward the squad room.

"Fine, it's not a secret."

After a phone call, a tall, uniformed officer who appeared to be in his twenties brought two atlases. Freya thanked him and nodded for him to leave. When he didn't, the four gazed at him.

"Maybe I could stay and learn something?" he mumbled. Looking at Worthy, he added, "You talked to my class at the academy, sir."

"It's up to Sergeant Maaki," Worthy said.

"Okay. Everyone, this is Henry. You can stay," she said.

Worthy opened the Wisconsin plat map to the page with the state's northwest corner, but after a moment, he closed it and opened the Minnesota to the page showing the state's most northern counties.

"Ah, maybe . . ." he said.

"Maybe what, Christopher?" Nick asked.

"What did he do in high school after the baby was born and then died? Freya just said it. He became obsessed with rowing. Now, look at all the lakes up here in the north of Minnesota that run into Canada. Maybe the reason we haven't been able to track him is—"

Freya finished the sentence. "You think he rowed into Canada?" She laughed before saying, "But why would he do that, and we know he doesn't have his passport."

"What if the person he thinks needs his help is in Canada? Look at the map of Minnesota. In the north, it's like there are a thousand lakes. Couldn't he cross into Canada without ever showing a passport?"

Henry, the uniformed officer, cleared his throat. "That area is called the Boundary Waters. I've canoed up that way. You're supposed to check in with Canadian authorities if you come ashore up there."

"You said the key words. 'Supposed to.'" Worthy said.

"But if he did that, he'd be breaking the law," Henry objected.

"I don't think Father Joseph would care about that," Lena said.

It was Nick who noted the obvious. "So, everything we've discovered about Natasha Luzinsky is what—beside the point?"

No one said anything until Worthy replied. "Not necessarily. In Greece, Father Joseph was willing to throw away his vocation to help Natasha. I think it's possible that he sees himself doing something similar this time. It's not Natasha he needs to save, but someone else who is, or who he thinks is in a great deal of trouble."

Everyone was quiet, thinking about what Worthy had said. Nick thought that if anyone other than Worthy had suggested that Father Joseph headed for Canada, the rest would have dismissed it. But this was Christopher Worthy, the detective known in Detroit and even in Italy as the policeman who was often a step or two ahead of everyone else.

Freya seemed to agree. "It looks like we finally have some breadcrumbs to follow."

"Even though I suggested it, I think the chances are pretty thin that I'm right," Worthy said.

"But Freya is right, my friend," Nick said. "We finally have some breadcrumbs. Those breadcrumbs might not lead us anywhere, but it's better than sitting here."

Clearing his throat again, Henry said, "I think there's a problem to your theory. You said he was an Olympic rower. Like I said, the easiest place to cross the border without running into customs control is the Boundary Waters, but you said he was an Olympic rower. Anyone heading north through the Boundary Waters has to portage dozens of times from one lake to another. I'm talking about carrying what you're traveling in over your head, sometimes for up to a mile or more. You can do that with a canoe, but not a rowboat."

"But wouldn't an accomplished rower be able to handle a canoe?" Nick asked.

Henry shook his head. "No, the skills are completely different. A rower's best bet would be to hitchhike to a lake like this," he suggested, pointing to Rainy Lake, and the Lake of the Woods. "But those are both big bodies of water, maybe too big for a rowboat."

Freya opened her computer and typed in "Lake of the Woods—maps." The image of the lake that appeared on screen looked significantly different from the one in the atlas.

"It's not one big, round lake at all, is it?" Freya asked.

Leaning down to take a closer look, Worthy said, "No, it's more like a hundred small bays, peninsulas, and islands." Pointing at a small dot on the screen, he added, "Look at this town near the border. Warroad, Minnesota. I bet a person could rent a rowboat there or someplace else along the lakeshore."

"Certainly at resorts and campgrounds," Henry said.

Worthy looked up and smiled. "Henry, I'm going to make sure that I write something glowing for your file. For the rest of us, it looks like we have a road trip coming."

It was obvious to Nick that the dark mood in the room had lifted. As Freya had said, there was finally a trail to follow.

After Henry, smiling and looking pleased with himself, left the room, Freya said, "If it's okay with the rest of you, I'm going to stay back and try to contact Natasha. She could still be in danger."

"I feel the same way," Lena said. "I think we owe that to her, if there's any chance her life and the life of her baby are in danger."

FREYA KNEW SHE'D NEED THE AUTHORIZATION from her captain, Sooki Millard, to reach out to Interpol about Natasha, and that raised an ethical dilemma for her. First, she wasn't sure she could justify Father Joseph being considered a missing person. Yes, he was missing, but it seemed obvious now that he'd left of his own volition. Second, there seemed to be no apparent connection between Natasha being in Ukraine and Father Joseph's disappearance from Saginaw. Any appeal for information about Natasha's family could hardly be justified.

Lena and Freya sat in a coffee shop mulling over the problem until Lena said, "How supportive is your boss, in general?"

"I'd say very supportive, but she's also no-nonsense."

"And she'll think your request is just that—nonsense?"

Freya frowned. "If we were talking about asking permission to talk to a police department in Detroit or Chicago, I'd say no. But we're talking about making a request of Interpol. That's not an everyday occurrence in Saginaw. It's a safe bet that no one here has ever even thought of that, much less done it."

Lena nodded, but then smiled. "I understand, but given that we're two bright women, there has to be a way."

"Maybe if we were imbibing a good wine instead of coffee," Freya said, returning the smile.

"Let's take a break. Tell me about the case two years ago, the one where you met Chris and Nick," Lena said.

"Wow, where should I begin," Freya said before pausing. "I suppose I would say I learned more in those weeks than I did in two years at the academy. Of course, I knew the basics of investigations, interviewing techniques, and evaluating evidence from before, but what I didn't know before was how to gauge when it's necessary to take a risk."

"That can't be easy advice to take for a young police officer."

Freya nodded. "To that point, my life goal had been to please everyone above me—teachers, coaches, bosses. But then Chris asks me to go against all that. I don't think I slept a wink that night."

"But it worked, right?"

"At first, I thought my career was in the garbage can. But then, what I did turned out to be important and a help."

"And it led to a transfer to Saginaw."

"Hmm," Freya said, looking out the window. "You know, you're right. If I hadn't taken the risk, I'd probably still be in Houghton fetching coffee for a couple of assholes."

Lena leaned forward. "Remember what I said about our being two intelligent women who could solve our problem? So tell me what taking a risk on this case would be."

"Well, I think my captain sees Father Joseph as more of a runaway than a missing person, but she knows people in Saginaw won't be satisfied until they know for certain why he left. If we still thought there was a link between Father Joseph and Natasha, we'd have a chance. But given what we know—the passport business—I can't say there's a connection. And Captain Millard is too good a boss for me to lie to."

"Linked, but no lying. Linked, but no lying," Lena said. "What if we go back to the link between the two of them before Father Joseph disappeared?"

Freya thought for a moment before saying, "Okay, so we know they met in Thessaloniki when they were in grad school. Let's assume for a moment that Chris is wrong. Let's go with the theory that the two got to know each other, and she felt safe enough to tell him, as a priest, about her troubled marriage. Then came the fateful night when she said that Sergei threatened her, maybe even beat her. She ran to Father Joseph, who, according to both of them, took her in and let her stay the night, though they claim nothing more than that. That's the end."

Freya watched Lena stir another sugar substitute into her coffee before suddenly stopping. "I think there's a way," Lena said.

"Without lying?"

"Yes, without lying. Do you know much about fishing?"

"Fishing?" Freya looked at her, puzzled.

"It's something Chris told me the other day, when I was up at his cabin. He talked about a lake rolling over. Have you ever heard of that?"

"Sure. It's something that happens in the fall. It's when the water at the bottom of a lake becomes warmer than the surface water—"

"Which makes the warmer water rises to the top. Chris described it as everything being upside down," Lena finished the sentence. "So, let's turn our problem upside down. Instead of trying to connect Father Joseph with Natasha, what if we connect Natasha with Father Joseph?"

"You've lost me. There's no difference, is there?"

Lena smiled. "There can be, depending on how you present the problem to your captain. Instead of saying we share Father Joseph's worries about Natasha, what if you told your captain that Natasha is the one person who can best help us understand Father Joseph and maybe shed light on why he disappeared?"

Freya's jaw dropped. "That's brilliant! I don't have to say anything about how worried we are about Natasha. All I have to do is tell my captain what she already knows—that we're worried about Father Joseph's safety. We need Interpol to contact Natasha's family in Ukraine because she knows Father Joseph . . . knows him intimately."

"And while we're not saying that 'intimately' means sexually, you can let your captain think what she wants to think," Lena said.

Freya raised both arms in a gesture of victory, not caring what others in the coffee shop would think. "Hot damn, we are smart!"

✝

THE EIGHTEEN HOURS IT TOOK WORTHY AND NICK TO DRIVE from Saginaw to Warroad, Minnesota, left them plenty of time to talk about the case and other matters.

Eventually, Nick said, "I hope your time at the cabin with Lena was good."

"I won't lie to you, Nick. Things were tense on the way up, which brought back some painful memories."

"I can imagine," Nick said, knowing that both were thinking of Worthy's divorce.

"But Lena isn't Susan," Worthy said. "And there was another surprise. I always thought I understood myself, why I withdraw at a certain point on a case. I discovered that Lena understands that part of me better than I do."

Nick offered a silent prayer of thanksgiving before saying, "If you care to share, I'd be happy to listen."

Over the next fifty miles, Worthy explained how the story of Lena's two sets of grandparents led to her interest in mystics.

"Lena knows I'm no mystic," Worthy said, "but she does believe, because of how I have to turn inward on cases, that I share some traits with resisters."

Nick looked over at Worthy behind the wheel before exploding with laughter.

"What?" Worthy said. "You think she's wrong?"

"No, no, my friend. I'm laughing because in the whole time I've known you, that's what you've been—a resister. You push back against those you work with who take the more traditional approach. Remember your nemesis in your department, Sherrod? Remember Freya's colleagues in Houghton?"

"How can I forget? Yeah, I see that you could be right."

"*Could be?* While they're rushing around after their pet suspects, you deliberately slow down, as if the victims can still communicate."

"Which I believe the victims can," Worthy said.

"Proving Lena's point, my friend. Just proving Lena's point." He slowly and privately made the sign of the cross. Worthy might have lost his faith in God, but Nick had never believed that God had lost faith in his friend. What else could explain why Worthy fell in love with someone who understood his patterns on a case, someone who'd even done research on people much like him?

✝

OCTOBER 21

THE FIRST REPORT BACK FROM THE UKRAINIAN AUTHORITIES through Interpol was disappointing, less a response than a series of questions. But by the second communication, the authorities in Kiev seemed to grasp the importance of locating Natasha Luzinsky. First, the authorities were able to determine from national records that Natasha's maiden name was Orlov. Following that discovery, the authorities contacted the Orlov family, who lived in Brovary, a suburb of Kiev.

Even then, what the Ukrainian authorities passed along was useless. The Orlov family told the authorities that Natasha was still in Thessaloniki pursuing her doctorate. Freya assured Interpol that the information was erroneous, and after another twelve hours, the Ukrainian authorities confirmed that Natasha Luzinsky and her child had returned to Ukraine a little over two months before.

When Lena expressed frustration at what the Orlovs were doing, Freya said, "No, it's good news that Natasha's family is misleading the authorities. If she'd returned to Sergei or, worse, if Sergei had found her, there'd be no reason to lie.

Even better, I keep seeing one name on the Interpol reports, that of a Ukrainian official named Alexandra Kronsky who seems to have taken a personal interest in our case."

"Can we reach out to this woman?" Lena said.

"I already have. I've given Interpol permission to tell Kronsky that she can email me directly. Now let's hope she speaks some English."

Two and a half hours later, an email came through from Alexandra Kronsky. It read: "Forgive poor English. I visit Orlovs tomorrow. Then write."

Freya typed a response as soon as she finished reading the email. "We appreciate your help. While Natasha Orlov Luzinsky might help us with our missing person's case, her life and the life of her child could also be in danger from her estranged husband. It is likely that the Orlov family are hiding Natasha to keep her safe and might not divulge where she is."

OCTOBER 22

WHILE FREYA AND LENA AWAITED A SECOND COMMUNICATION from their contact in Ukraine, Worthy and Nick arrived in Warroad late that night and checked into a local motel. Their first step the next morning was to contact the local police department, located in the center of town. When Worthy presented his credentials and asked for names of places that rented boats and then, as an afterthought, for any reports of thefts of boats in the last five to six weeks, Sergeant Carl Olmstead checked on his computer before yawning and shaking his head.

"No, no thefts reported, but that's a pretty big category. What make of boat?"

"We don't know, but it's likely to be a rowboat. I don't think it would be a boat with a motor," Worthy replied.

Sergeant held up his hands in mock surrender. "Look, it's late October. Resorts and cabin owners stack your rowboats up on shore after Labor Day. We won't know if a boat like that has been stolen until next May when owners open up. And in terms of records of people renting a rowboat, I can't help you with that."

For Worthy, the sergeant fulfilled some of the stereotypes of a small-town cop—the ill-fitting uniform, a box of donuts on the desk—and Worthy imagined him playing checkers with the local drunk in one of the cells below. *Mayberry, Minnesota*, he thought.

When Olmstead closed his computer without saying another word, Worthy and Nick moved toward the door. But before they left, Worthy asked another question. "Every boat, even a rowboat, has to be registered, right?"

Resting his feet on his desk, the sergeant replied, "Aa-yup, with the DNR. Every boat has the letters MN—that's for Minnesota—and seven numbers."

Outside the police department, they stood on the sidewalk and looked out at the lake. "I refuse to believe we came all this way just to be told the trip was wasted," Worthy said, even as he glanced down the town's main street and noted that the place looked deserted. Warroad might be a hopping place in the summer months, but the town now looked as sleepy as Sergeant Olmstead.

In the next block, Worthy and Nick found a small restaurant open, and there they nursed mugs of hot chocolate while they ate coffee cake. "Why did you ask about the boats being registered, Christopher?"

Worthy shrugged. "Probably out of spite. I just wanted to make Andy Griffith answer another question."

"I suppose we should have called before we took the trip."

"No, Nick, I wanted to see the lake, check to see if our theory about Aris Kouris rowing into Canada from a place like this is possible."

Looking out at the lake, which seemed to go on forever, Nick asked, "And do you think it is?"

"I think it's possible. As you know, you and I don't see Aris . . . Father Joseph in the same way. But if we don't know who he is really, I believe in my bones that we know the 'where.' I think he came this way, or to a town along the lake like this one. Look at all those bays and islands out there. A good rower could row from island to island, even if it were windy."

"How long do you think it would it take Father Joseph to get to Canada?"

"That would depend on the weather, especially the direction of the wind, but I'd say no more than two or three days."

"Which means he would need a sleeping bag, food, and other supplies, wouldn't it?"

Worthy smiled. "Nick, you're right, and he sure didn't bring those things with him. We need to check the outdoor supply businesses here to see if they remember anyone buying a sleeping bag, dried food, and maybe a tarp in the last five to six weeks."

Worthy and Nick were in luck when they found several stores that remained open for fall duck hunters and in anticipation of snowmobiling and ice fishing. While the first two suppliers they tried admitted selling quite a few sleeping bags late in the summer to autumn campers, it was at the third store, "Camper Heaven," where the owner thought he remembered Father Joseph from the photo Worthy showed him.

"A nice feller," Mrs. Horner said. "Wasn't from up this way, that's for sure. He bought some food packets and a map of the lake, as I remember. But I get confused, so I might be mixing him up with somebody else."

"Not very solid as evidence goes," Worthy said, as they returned to their car.

After starting the car, Worthy turned toward Nick and said, "I'm still thinking about the boat's registration. The policeman said it had the letters MN and then some numbers."

"Right, but how does that help us?"

"What I'm thinking about now is Aris rowing into Canada. Wouldn't he have left the rowboat somewhere along the shore up that way?"

"Huh." Nick gazed out the windshield at the massive lake. "And the registration letters and numbers would still be on it."

"So, if we drive into Canada, we can ask the authorities if an abandoned rowboat from Minnesota has been found." Worthy started the car and revved the engine. "So much for reaching a dead end, Nick. Let's hope the Canadian authorities are a bit more helpful than Sergeant Olmstead."

"What about our not having passports?" Nick asked.

"There's such a thing as law enforcement cooperation, Nick. Once we establish that we're both working on a missing person's case, we should be good to go."

It didn't take more than forty-five minutes to drive north along the lake and reach the border where they entered the customs office. After the Canadian border guards verified Worthy's story with Freya at the Saginaw police department, they crossed into Canada on the stipulation that they report regularly on their activities and location.

As Worthy and Father Nick drove north on Canada Rt. 503, Worthy looked out at the lake and imagined Father Joseph, to be less obvious, rowing farther than just four or five miles into Canada before coming ashore. At the next gas station, Worthy asked for directions to the nearest authorities.

Malcolm McGregor, the chief ranger in the Cat Mountain Provincial Park that bordered the lake, was a welcome change from Sergeant Olmstead. His Scottish brogue suggested that Inspector McGregor had recently emigrated. The one-room office at the main gate to the park was tidy, with a mural of Lake of the Woods in its various seasons on one wall. When Worthy made his request, Inspector McGregor consulted his computer to find reports of abandoned marine equipment, not just in in his jurisdiction but also twenty miles farther along the shore.

"It's usually oars, fishing nets, or life vests that wash up on the shore, but occasionally we have the odd boat that breaks free from mooring and floats away, depending on the direction of the wind. It's not so common, however, for a boat from the States to make it this far north."

"We're looking for a boat, probably a basic rowboat, that might have turned up sometime five or six weeks ago," Worthy said.

"With Minnesota registration, we shouldn't have too many," the inspector noted. After a few moments, he looked up and said, "No boats found along the shore, but there was a rowboat found about three miles up the lake floating off one of the islands. That was five and a half weeks ago."

"Can you show us on a map?"

McGregor took them over to a large map on one of the other walls. "We're here, and this is the island where the boat was found."

"How far is the island from the shore?" Nick asked.

"About half a mile, no more."

"If a person landed here and didn't tie up," Worthy said, pointing to the nearest place on shore to where the rowboat was found, "could the wind have taken the boat over to the island?"

"Oh, aye, that could happen, given the prevailing westerlies," McGregor acknowledged. Returning to his computer, he added after a moment. "Now, this is odd. The boat didn't have any registration markings on it. It was one of those old green rowboats, but there's something else. There was a layer of dirt about two inches deep inside the hull. If I didn't know better, I'd say . . ."

"What?" Nick asked.

"I'd say it was an old rowboat that someone had in their front yard. You know, one with flowers and plants in it."

Worthy thought for a moment before he said, "So if that boat was in front of a house or cabin along shore, a person could tip it over, empty as much of the dirt as possible, and use it."

"If your man had oars. But it would be risky. If the rowboat's bottom was rotten, the boat wouldn't be seaworthy."

"But it might be a boat that an owner wouldn't care about if it went missing," Nick said.

"Aye, that's true enough. You say the person you're trying to find is a priest, a runaway priest? Are you sure your priest is up here?"

"Honestly, I prefer not to answer that question," Worthy confessed.

"And you?" McGregor asked Nick.

"I'm seventy to seventy-five percent certain. But then I'm the optimist."

"Well, it makes a good story, though back in Aberdeen, we'd say it's all a 'wee bit unco'—a mite unusual."

"It's unusual, but other than his coming into Canada illegally, I don't think it's criminal. If we're right about him being up here, we think he's here to try to help someone he thinks is in trouble," Worthy explained.

"And you don't know who that is or what kind of trouble this person is in?"

"No, not yet," Worthy admitted.

"Be that as it may, I need to send in an official report, given his illegal entry. Now, if the owner of the rowboat comes forward and wants to press charges, that would be handled down in Minnesota. So, if there's nothing else, I'd appreciate seeing a photo of the priest so I can make a copy. And I promise you this—I'll send the photo out to provincial police not just here in Manitoba but also in Ontario and Saskatchewan."

After obliging the inspector with the photo, Worthy and Nick stood outside the station and gazed out at the lake.

"You're seventy to seventy-five percent, huh?" Worthy asked.

"Maybe I stretched it a bit. But you can't deny that we keep finding breadcrumbs, and I take that to mean we're on the right track. Now, where does that leave us?"

"We have no legitimate reason to stay in Canada. Who knows if or when someone will recognize Aris Kouris' photo? But at least it's in their system."

After returning to the car, Worthy said, "Last chance."

"Last chance for what?"

"For finding a reason to stay up here in Canada."

"Well, I am hungry. Maybe we could drive to the next town and see if Canadian food tastes any different," Nick said.

Leaving the provincial park, they had to travel another half hour before they came to the town of Braintree. Worthy slowed as he looked for a burger joint or pizza parlor. They passed a few signs before Worthy jammed on the brakes and pulled over to the side of the street.

"Is it possible?" he asked, staring into the rearview mirror.

"Is what possible?"

"Nick, did you see that sign back there?"

"No, what sign?"

Instead of answering, Worthy turned the car around and drove back to the last intersection. "There," he said, pointing to a sign on a lamppost.

"Saint Theodor Ukrainian Orthodox Church. So . . . wait a minute. Ukrainian? Up here in Canada? Well, I believe in signs, and I don't mean street signs."

Neither of them said a word as Worthy drove down the side street. Four blocks later, on the left side of the road was a massive high-peaked church with a copper onion-shaped dome.

"Well, the church looks large for such a small town," Nick said, "which leads me to think there might be a lot of Ukrainians up this way."

Worthy pulled into the parking lot and stepped from the car. Nick was already on his way to a side door marked "office."

Inside, Nick approached an icon of the church's patron saint and bowed to kiss it. Straightening, he said, "Give me a minute to catch my breath."

"This could all be just coincidence, Nick."

"As you so wisely said to me the other day, 'Oh ye of little faith,'" Nick said. They walked down a hallway lined with photos of priests and hierarchs in the direction of a well-lit and open door. Stepping into the office, Nick introduced Worthy and himself to the woman behind the desk before saying, "I'm wondering if you can answer a question for us."

The woman, whose fair complexion and piercing blue eyes suggested to Nick that she was Slavic, was clearly startled by the two unexpected visitors.

"If I can, Father," she said.

"We're visiting in Canada for a few . . . well, I'm not sure how long, but we're from down in the States. We noticed that Saint Theodor is quite a large church. Are we right in thinking Ukrainians might be common in this part of Canada?"

The woman's first reaction was to frown, as if Nick had said something insulting. Then, she nodded as she reached into a drawer on her desk and produced a flyer about the church. "Seeing as you come up from the States, I'll forgive you. As this pamphlet explains, Ukrainians mostly settled in Manitoba and Saskatchewan, not just in the cities but also in rural areas. In some places, I'm proud to say we're dominant."

Nick and Worthy didn't say anything for a moment.

"Is that your only question?" the woman asked.

"One more," Worthy said. "Do many families in the parish have close relatives back in the home country?"

The secretary thought for a moment. "Not so many among the older families, and there I'm talking about people who emigrated in the nineteenth century. But parishioners who've emigrated since the Soviet Union went kaput, well, yes, they are often close to relatives in Ukraine."

Offering a weak smile, Nick looked at Worthy. "What do you think, my friend?"

Worthy shook his head. "It's a long shot, but what's one more long shot on top of the others?"

Nick looked back to the puzzled secretary. "Thank you, and bless you, my child. You've been a big help."

"Okay, if you say so," she said, seeming unconvinced. "Before you leave, Father, would you like to see the sanctuary? Say a prayer, perhaps?"

Nick laughed. "Yes, I'd like that more than you know."

CHAPTER FIFTEEN

THAT AFTERNOON, WHILE FREYA AND LENA AWAITED another email from Alexandra Kronsky, Worthy called from on the road. On speakerphone, Worthy said, "Freya, do you remember the conversation we had in the UP two years ago? The one about the effect of the word 'if' on a theory."

"How can I forget? You said for every 'if' in a case, the likelihood of a theory being correct lessens twenty-five percent."

"So, I'm going to tell you something, and I want you to count how many 'ifs' you hear. Okay?"

"Is this some sort of puzzle?" Freya asked.

"Could be or maybe not. Anyway, here goes. "*If* we're right about Aris hitchhiking to northern Minnesota, and *if* we're right in thinking he stole a boat and rowed into Canada, and *if* we're right in thinking he managed to avoid border patrols, and here's the big if, *if* Natasha Luzinsky's family has Ukrainian relatives in Canada—"

"What did you just say?" Freya shouted into the phone.

"Just what you heard. There's a pretty big population of Ukrainians in Manitoba and Saskatchewan. So, that's no 'if.' But let me continue. *If* Natasha's relatives in Ukraine have relatives in this part of Canada, and *if*, for her own safety and the baby's, she's in Canada, and *if* she managed to get a message to Aris about her plight, and *if* Aris and Natasha managed to find one another in Canada, and *if* we can track them down, then guess what? It doesn't matter if you all are right about Father Joseph being a caring priest or I'm right about both Aris and Natasha being narcissists. But how many 'ifs' was that, Freya?"

Freya looked up at the ceiling. "I counted eight, maybe nine. At a reduced probability of twenty-five percent for every 'if,' the chances of you being right is . . . about negative one hundred percent. That's like saying your theory is impossible four times over."

"That's what I thought. But Nick is the optimist, as you know. I'll let him explain."

After a pause, Nick said, "Everyone we've talked to here in Minnesota and Canada says it's possible that Father Joseph came this way and did everything Christopher just mentioned. The way I'm thinking, we keep finding breadcrumbs."

"Just enough to keep us going, right, Nick?" Freya said.

"That's what I'm thinking, Freya. The clues keep adding up."

"But then again," Worthy said, "maybe you've heard something from the Ukrainian authorities that disproves everything we just said."

Freya picked up her notes on Natasha. "Obviously, if Natasha Orlov—that's her maiden name—and baby are still in Ukraine, your theory is a pipedream. We just don't have an answer to that question yet. Natasha's relatives aren't being cooperative. The good news is that there's a Ukrainian official who seems committed to finding out what really happened to Natasha. She promised to visit the Orlov family outside Kiev sometime tomorrow."

"So more waiting," Worthy said.

"Maybe there's something we can do from this end that will confirm or sink your theory, Chris," Freya said. "Alexandra Kronsky, the official we're working with in Ukraine, should be able to find out if Natasha's family has relatives in that part of Canada."

"Go with it, then," Worthy said.

"Right," she said. "One more thing. Are you still there, Nick?"

"Yes, I am."

"For what it's worth, I'm a big believer in breadcrumbs."

OCTOBER 23

THE NEXT EVENING IN FREYA'S OFFICE, with Worthy and Nick back from driving through the night, Lena was unsure what to feel. Should she hope that Father Joseph's disappearance was caused by a message from Natasha? What if Alexandra Kronsky proved Worthy right, that Natasha was never in any danger from her husband?

She studied the others in the room, all who'd been through the waiting game before. Freya was bustling in and out of her office, flipping through files of other cases and making notes.

In contrast, Worthy alternated between looking out the office window and doodling on a pad of paper. When he left at one point to use the bathroom,

Lena stole looks at his scribbles, which were a series of spirals. She wondered if the spirals symbolized something to Worthy. Could they mean, maybe, despite the small odds, that Worthy believed they were on a path that was slowly working its way to a center—to a solution to the case?

In contrast, Nick's hand moved rapidly over his knotted prayer rope. He was also popping spearmint candies into his mouth. When he glanced over and offered a weak smile in Lena's direction, she signaled for him to join her outside.

The late October morning was sunny and crisp, and Lena suggested a short walk.

"I'm so glad you appreciate Christopher's pattern on cases," he said.

"Yes, I think I understand. Freya seems to have the same need to withdraw. And what about you, Nick? I assumed monks are trained for the inner life. But you—"

Nick laughed. "No, not me. And remember this, Lena, understanding another person is a two-way street. Yes, I think my being a monk makes it easier for me to understand Christopher when he descends into himself. But please know that Christopher understands me better than my own abbot. If I get him, he gets me."

"I think I know what you mean."

"We all assume we understand ourselves, don't we? But then we meet someone who says something about us that we've never realized. Christopher has never said what's obvious about me, that I'm an extrovert. I'd been told all my life, from my second-grade teacher to my abbots, that I talk too much. Then one day, Christopher told me something that brought me to tears. 'Nick, your abbot is dead wrong. When you're talking, you're also listening.'"

"And he's right, Nick."

"I know he is—now—but I didn't accept it until then. I think that's probably what Christopher felt when you described him as a resister. I forget who said it—some philosopher or writer—but it's this: each of us holds a key to a cage. What's critical is accepting that the key we hold doesn't open our own cage, but someone else's. And that means that someone else holds the key to the cage we're in."

At the end of the block, they crossed the street and began to walk back toward the station.

"What you said might help us understand Father Joseph as well," Lena said.

"Oh?"

"I assume that Father Joseph is like most priests in believing his mission would be to open the cages of others. That would fit with what Freya and you learned about is role in the diner in Saginaw. But I'm also thinking something else could be going on with him. What if, consciously or unconsciously, Father

Joseph is hoping Natasha—or whoever he's searching for—holds the key to unlock his cage?"

FROM THE WINDOW, WORTHY WATCHED AS Lena and Nick walked back to the police station. He could understand their need to talk to one another, even as he accepted Freya's and his need *not* to talk about the case. Someone entering Freya's tiny office might assume the two of them were strangers. Glancing over at Freya, he knew she was perusing other case files in order to distract herself from this investigation. And he? He was asking himself why he judged Aris Kouris so differently from his three companions.

As Lena and Nick reentered the office, Freya looked up from her computer and said, "Good timing. We just got an email from Alexandra. Bear with me. Alexi's English is minimal, but then again, my Russian, or maybe it's Ukrainian, is non-existent. She writes, 'One thing of Soviets to thank. Good records for emigres. Before see family, I find this. Natasha Orlov, her two cousins, emigrated 1977. One New Zealand, one in Canada, Winnipeg. Names: Vladimir and Marina (Orlov) for Canada. Maybe also a child. Visit to Orlovs here in Kiev not helpful. Admit cousins in Canada, but say Natasha and baby not there. First say she with husband, then say no, not with him. Later say they don't know where is Natasha. They look away when I ask if they see Sergei Luzinsky recently. Say he bad man. Criminal. Say I should arrest him. I best suggest—check airplanes Canada.'"

No one said anything until Nick asked, "Another breadcrumb?"

Under a stack of papers on her desk, Freya retrieved the plat map for Manitoba. Pointing to where Worthy and Nick were told the rowboat was found, she said, "If he got a ride from the provincial park to route 503, he could have gotten a ride up to Route 1, and going west, that would take him right into Winnipeg."

"How many miles are you talking about?" Nick asked.

"It can't be more than a hundred fifty miles, maybe less."

Worthy nodded. "So at least we know this: if Aris rowed into Canada from Minnesota, getting to Winnipeg looks doable. None of that is a certainty, but it's better than a maybe."

Freya sat back in her chair. "For me, the last point in the email, the one about checking airline lists into Canada for people with Ukrainian passports, is what we should do next."

FINALLY, FREYA THOUGHT, AS SHE WARMED UP MEATBALLS for supper in her microwave, *we're finally going to be standing on firm ground. If Natasha and her baby flew into Canada, then Father Joseph's disappearance makes sense. If she didn't fly into Canada, then Father Joseph might or might not be in Canada, but he's looking to help someone else. Either way, we'll know something instead of speculating.*

While working with Worthy, Nick, and Lena on this case, Freya recalled from her training what made missing persons cases so difficult. With a homicide, there is a body, a place where the body is discovered, a known cause of death, and usually a community so filled with outrage or fear that the media never lets up.

With a missing person, however, there is none of that—no body, no certain place, no knowledge if the person is alive or dead, and too often a community, after a few days or weeks, that no longer cares. The other difficulty was that, unless that person was a minor, had been kidnapped, or had received threats, there wasn't technically a crime at all. And Father Joseph didn't fit any of those categories.

She had to agree with Worthy that there was much about the priest's disappearance that was troubling. Data from the FBI revealed that clergy rarely went missing, and when a priest or minister did, it was almost always a feeble attempt to flee arrest for embezzlement or pedophilia. Nothing like that had surfaced in Father Joseph's case.

From all they'd discovered, Father Joseph was a healthy young man, a former athlete who stayed in good shape by cycling. There was no hint of suicide, no prior depression or despair that others noticed, nor any significant conflict in his parish. He liked people and was seemingly easy to like. In all, Father Joseph stood out in a crowd, like one of those people in everyday life whom others think could have become a movie or rock star. Yet, this same good-looking and likeable young man had not just run away, but managed to stay hidden for almost two months.

When Worthy uttered the words "I have a bad feeling about this case," Freya's first thought had been to imagine the worst-case scenario, that Father Joseph had put himself in danger. What if Father Joseph, in trying to help someone, had run into someone who thought nothing of killing a nosy priest? At the end of their search, would they find Father Joseph, but as a corpse?

CHAPTER SIXTEEN

────────◆────────

OCTOBER 24

To Nick's surprise, Freya asked if she could go with him to the Sunday service the next morning at St. George in Saginaw. "Canadian customs and the airlines aren't likely to call us back on Sunday," she explained.

They met outside the church at 9:30, the time the service was to start, and entered a sanctuary less than half full. As they sat down toward the left side, Father Gregory chanted the first part of the service facing the altar, with his back to the parishioners.

In a whisper, Nick asked, "Did you attend a service two years ago on our case at the monastery in the Upper Peninsula?"

"No, not unless you count the funeral service," Freya whispered in return.

"No, that doesn't count. Don't be surprised if some of the service confuses you. That was Worthy's reaction after his first visit to an Orthodox church."

"I hope it's not too confusing, Nick. I thought being here might help me understand Father Joseph better."

Nick nodded. "It just might do that." He looked around and saw that some of the parishioners had noticed his monastic robes and clerical collar. *They're wondering why I'm not serving with Father Gregory in the altar,* he thought. He'd intended to do that, but when Freya asked to accompany him, he thought it better to sit with her.

As the service progressed, Nick wasn't surprised that Father Gregory didn't mention Father Joseph. Father Gregory would have been given clear direction from the Metropolitan-Bishop in Detroit to do whatever he could to help the community move past their recent trauma.

Nick knew, however, that moving on wouldn't be as simple or quick a process as the Metropolitan-Bishop hoped. He thought of the parish president, Mr.

Fragouli, who represented those in the parish who had already pushed Father Joseph out of their minds. But he suspected that some parishioners at St. George that morning would be wishing for the Christmas gift of Father Joseph's return.

As he considered this, Nick looked toward the other side of the sanctuary and was surprised to see Connie Ferwerda, the waitress and Father Joseph's accomplice. He'd never imagined that she might be a parishioner at St. George, and, after watching her for a few moments, he could tell that she was probably a visitor, like Freya.

Throughout the service, Nick thought Father Gregory had been a competent and safe choice for the parish. Recalling the most recent photo of Father Joseph, however, Nick could see that St. George's new priest couldn't compete in looks or charisma.

At the end of the Orthodox service, when Father Gregory was about to give out blessed bread to all who were there, the young priest did something that raised him in Nick's estimation. Instead of following the standard practice of most parishes, where the priest stands at the front to hand out the small pieces of bread, Father Gregory took the silver bowl of blessed bread and stepped down into the congregation, meeting parishioners in the center aisle. As he moved slowly to the rear and handed out pieces of bread, Father Gregory paused and chatted with the people about their health, job, or other individual concerns.

To Nick, the gesture wasn't small. The truth about St. George, whether members were doing their best to forget Father Joseph or were painfully missing him, was that everyone in the parish needed healing. A morsel of food along with a personal word from a caring priest was certainly a healing touch.

When Father Gregory came to Freya and Nick, Nick commented on the young priest's loving gesture.

Father Gregory leaned closer to him and whispered, "Yes, I think it's important. Maybe it's not practical in a large parish, but here, it's something the parishioners tell me they appreciate."

"Do they teach that now in seminary?" Nick asked.

Father Gregory shook his head. "No, it's something Father Joseph started here at St. George. They asked me to continue it."

Nick felt a lump in his throat. He nodded and walked out of the church, remembering what he'd said to Freya as the service started, that he hoped she would learn something important about Father Joseph. Something more had happened. He'd learned something about Father Joseph. For a moment, he wished Worthy could have seen the gesture, thinking it might have altered his opinion about the missing priest. *But perhaps,* he thought, *Christopher would interpret the gesture as a stunt, just another attempt to draw attention to himself.*

Outside, in the parking lot, Nick said, "Did you see that Connie Ferwerda was in the service?"

"I did, and I also saw her slip out. I don't think she said a word to anyone."

As Freya was pulling her car keys from her purse, Nick asked, "Are you interested in stopping by the diner to see if she's there?"

Freya glanced up at Nick. "You think she has more to tell us?"

Nick thought for a moment before answering. "Maybe. I'd at least like to know why she came to St. George this morning."

Freya nodded. "Let's do it."

LENA CAME OUT OF THE SHOWER and began to towel-dry her hair. Worthy was sitting at the one table in their motel room, poring over his notes. Coming up behind him, she began to massage his shoulders.

"With us closing in on Father Joseph, I thought you'd feel. . . I don't know, more relaxed. But you're so tight," she said as she rubbed his neck on both sides, where his neck met his shoulders. "Right there."

Worthy sat back and groaned softly. "Whatever you're doing feels good, but I don't think the tightness is going to go away soon. In police work, we say that no two cases are the same, but the truth is that a lot of burglaries, even murders, share aspects in common. Even missing person cases can be similar. This case? There's little about it that reminds me of anything. I mean, who is Aris Kouris, really?"

"Judging by the fact that you insist on calling him Aris Kouris instead of Father Joseph, you must still think the rest of us are blind to his motives."

"Look, I know Freya and you agree with Nick, that he deserves to be trusted, that if he's not a saint, he's at least someone motivated by a desire to help someone in trouble."

"I might be leaning in that direction, but Father Joseph remains a mystery for me. But you seem convinced that he has a Messiah complex," Lena said.

"That might be a bit strong, but yes, I think he feels he needs to save people. That explains what happened back in Thessaloniki as well why he left Saginaw."

Lena continued to massage Worthy's back. "If you're right, it might also explain why he became a priest. But, for you, he's not helping people so much as causing pain."

Worthy groaned, causing Lena to stop the massage.

"No, please keep doing that. I'm just thinking about all the suffering this guy has left in his wake—the fiancés, his family, the people in Saginaw—both in the church and in the community. I think a case can be made that he's even caused pain for Sergei, Natasha's husband, back in Thessaloniki. We have only Natasha's word that her husband was abusive."

"But for you, Father Joseph—or Aris as you call him—didn't cause pain for Natasha. She's as narcissistic as he is."

"You're the psychologist, Lena, but don't narcissists attract other narcissists?"

Lena didn't say anything for a moment. "If you're right, Chris, we're not the only ones who've been taken in by the two of them. There's Irene Nestoris, Natasha's friend in Thessaloniki; the housemother there; Brother Paulus; Connie, his accomplice in Saginaw; Natasha's family in Kiev; and, for all we know, maybe her relatives in Winnipeg. All those people believe that Natasha is really in danger and that Father Joseph is trying to help her. That's a lot of people."

"Look, Lena, I know the three of you think I'm too pessimistic, but there's something more that I haven't shared yet with the others. I think it's possible that Aris—okay, Father Joseph—and Natasha are enjoying all this. Both of them could be together somewhere right now, relishing the fact that people are looking for them. That could explain why another clue surfaces just when we think we've come to a dead end."

Lena stopped massaging Worthy's back.

"Now you understand what I meant before, Lena, about the dark places I have to go to in my mind."

✝

In a booth in Cappy's Diner, Freya sat with Nick and looked around, hoping to see Connie Ferwerda. When another waitress brought them water, Freya asked if Connie was scheduled to work that afternoon.

"She'll clock in at one," the waitress said, as she left them menus.

"Good, only thirty minutes," Nick whispered to Freya.

"If we saw her in the church, Nick, I'm thinking she saw both of us."

"No doubt. Unlike you, Freya, I can't blend into a crowd and disappear. I'm not sure I could even do that as a teenager."

"That's what I find so puzzling about Father Joseph. Women notice men with looks like him, so how is he blending into the woodwork?"

Nick studied the menu for a moment before closing it. "Most people spend a lot of time choosing hairstyles and outfits in order to attract attention. We have to imagine Father Joseph is trying to do the opposite—he wants to be overlooked. But can you imagine a priest trying not to look like one? We're a dead giveaway. That's going to be the hardest part for Father Joseph—to pretend he's not a priest."

For the next half-hour, they ate burgers and fries as they discussed the possibility that Father Joseph had somehow disguised himself. Finally, Freya saw Connie Ferwerda drive up in an old Corolla and walk toward the diner.

Five minutes later, having changed into her uniform, Connie appeared behind the counter, looking at both of them steadily before offering more coffee to other patrons.

Leaning across the table, Nick whispered, "When we talk to her, Freya, I'm going to ask you to listen to what she says with Christopher's point of view."

"You mean the one where he calls Aris Kouris a fraud?"

"I suppose that's one way to describe it."

"I don't remember you two disagreeing on the case two years ago in the Upper Peninsula," Freya said.

A pained look crossed Nick's face. "We've had our differences before, but we've never been this far apart. Frankly, Christopher surprises me, but we have to remember that he could be right and we're the ones who are off base."

Freya realized that she was no longer sure what she thought of Father Joseph. In the first forty-eight hours of the case, she thought it likely he'd had an accident on a bike ride. In the days that followed, after she heard about what happened in Greece, she pictured a womanizer.

Her view changed once Worthy and Nick arrived, after having talked with his brother, Paulus. Father Joseph then seemed to be a misunderstood priest, one who sacrificed his own career in Greece to help an abused woman. Connie Ferwerda's memory of what Father Joseph said when they parted near Marquette made it seem that his disappearance was another example of self-sacrifice for the sake of someone in danger.

But now, Freya found it difficult to decide which assessment of Father Joseph—Worthy's or Nick's—was more likely to be true. Nick's view was supported by Father Joseph's brother Paulus; Connie Ferwerda; the Velonises, the estranged couple in the parish; from Dennis Sevreen, the president of the cycle club; and Irene Nestoris in Thessaloniki.

Worthy's view of the priest was based on the comments of the other brother, Soter; the two fiancés, Candace Jakes and Phyllida Tsimanakis; the parish council president, Mr. Fragouli; and the church hierarchy in Thessaloniki, Detroit, and New York. All of them saw Father Joseph as a charismatic, good-looking, but self-absorbed man who leaves a trail of broken hearts wherever he goes.

And Lena's view? She'd said repeatedly that she didn't have enough information about Father Joseph to say she understood him. Was that Lena being a cautious psychologist, or did she think there was something lacking in Worthy's and Nick's theories?

Freya wondered if finding Father Joseph would, by itself, settle the disagreement. If beauty is in the eye of the beholder, then another person's deepest motivations might be as well. No, the person she was counting on to reveal the real Father Joseph was Natasha Luzinsky. *Who and what she is will reveal who Father Joseph is,* she thought.

Cappy's Diner was a small structure, built to resemble an oversized train dining car from the forties, which made it was difficult for Connie Ferwerda to avoid Nick and Freya. Finally, when the two had finished their meals and were clearly waiting for something, Connie approached them. "If you're here for more than the food, I don't have my first break for another forty-five minutes."

"That's fine, Connie, we'll wait. We have just a few questions," Nick said.

Connie shrugged. "Suit yourself, but this isn't a waiting room. You'll have to order something else."

After Freya and Nick ordered slices of strawberry pie, Connie left to serve other customers.

Freya asked, "What are you hoping she'll tell us, Nick?"

"Actually, I'm going to reverse the conversation. I plan to tell her what we've discovered—or think we've discovered—about Father Joseph's whereabouts in Canada. The least that we'll gain is seeing her reaction, but it's possible that what we've discovered might lead her to tell us *everything* she knows."

Freya sat back in the booth and glanced at Connie behind the counter. "Nick, the word that comes to mind about you is 'sly.' I don't mean you're devious, but your strategy is clever."

"You give me far too much credit, my dear."

"Oh, I don't think so. I think you want us to believe it's just dumb luck when one of your suggestion works."

Nick smiled. "Maybe it's more the mercy of God than dumb luck, then. And I take comfort in knowing that when I do fall on my face, that same mercy remains with me."

"So, if Chris ends up being right about Father Joseph?" Freya asked.

"That will be sad, but I don't say that because I will be wrong. I'll be sad because of what it will mean for Father Joseph, Natasha, and everyone who cares about them. I still picture him serving a parish someday in the future."

"You are such an optimist, Nick."

He nodded. "Perhaps. You certainly aren't the first one to slap that label on me. But then again, I think God must be an optimist."

"I wish I were one," Freya said. "For example, I might sound a lot like Chris, but if Father Joseph imagines he can be a priest again, then he's exactly what Chris says he is—a narcissist. People aren't going to forget what he's done, Nick."

"No, Freya. I'm not saying Father Joseph believes he'll be a priest again. And I'm not saying people will ever forget what he's done. Forgetting is out of the question, but forgiveness is always possible."

By the time they finished dessert and another cup of coffee, it was time for Connie's break. She motioned for them to follow her outside where she lit a cigarette.

"Your car or mine?" she asked.

"Yours is fine," Freya replied.

This time, Connie sat behind the wheel, leaving Nick to sit in the passenger seat and Freya in the back. Connie lowered her window, which Freya realized not only allowed the waitress to blow the smoke out from her cigarette but also meant she didn't have to face the two of them.

"We want to update you on what we've found out about Father Joseph," Nick said.

Connie didn't react other than to blow more smoke out the window.

"After you dropped him off outside Marquette, we believe he hitchhiked to northern Minnesota and then crossed over into Canada. We also think he went there to help a woman, maybe a woman he met in Greece the year before."

Without turning, Connie asked, "Is she the one in trouble?"

"It's possible," Freya said.

Connie didn't say anything more until, in a voice that sounded like a challenge, she said, "Canada's a big country."

"Yes, but the woman we think he went to help is with relatives near Winnipeg."

Connie flicked ash out the window. "Last I heard, Winnipeg is a big city."

Freya paused, hoping Nick could find another way to break the ice.

"We saw you at St. George this morning," he said.

"Yeah, so what?"

"Are you a member or just visiting, Connie?"

After a pause, Connie replied, "I've been there before."

"When Father Joseph was the priest?"

Connie flicked the cigarette out the window. "Yeah, back then."

"You must miss him," Nick said.

"Must I?" She let the sarcasm hang in the air before adding, "What if I do?"

"It just makes you human," Nick said. "The way you describe Father Joseph being a regular fixture at the diner, I suspect a lot of people miss him."

Looking down at the steering wheel, Connie said, "If you're from Saginaw, you're used to being disappointed."

Remembering the assignment Nick had given her, Freya decided to take a risk. "Connie, what if you've been used by Father Joseph?"

Connie swung around and glared at Freya. "Do you hear me complaining?"

"No, we hear you hurting," Freya replied. "But you said you were disappointed."

Just as quickly, Connie swung back around. "The town owes Joe more than he owes us."

"But he does owe you and others an explanation, Connie," Freya said.

"The only thing he owes us is for him to be happy . . . and safe. So, don't expect me or a lot of other people to be hoping you find him. He's not the enemy."

"But we are, is that it?" Freya asked.

"You'll get no argument from me. Why can't you just leave him alone?" Then, in the lull that followed, Connie said, "If that's all, I'm due back in."

She started to open the door of the car, when Nick laid a hand on her arm. "Connie, you seem to forget what he told you. He wasn't running away on a lark. He left to help a person in a life-or-death situation. That means that his own life could be in danger. Right now, Father Joseph might be hoping we'll find him."

Connie looked over to Nick. "And if he doesn't need your help? What then? Will you drag him back here?"

Freya paused. Those were good questions. "You're right, Connie, he's not a runaway teenager, but an adult. If he doesn't need help, if he and the person he's with aren't in danger, then we have no right to force him to come back. He'll have to settle the problem of going into Canada without a passport, but that's a decision for their authorities, not us."

Connie didn't say anything, and Freya guessed she was weighing a decision.

"I'm hoping for something more," Nick said. "Father Joseph is a fellow priest, and I believe he went to left Saginaw to help someone because he *is* a priest."

Freya heard a sniffle and then Connie bent down to open her purse. Holding a folded piece of paper in her hand, she turned around and looked at Freya.

"What you said about leaving Joe alone if he isn't in trouble, is that a promise?"

"Yes, it's a promise."

Connie looked at the piece of paper for a moment before handing it to Nick. "This came three weeks ago. Don't make me regret trusting you."

BACK IN FREYA'S OFFICE, Worthy read the note out loud.

"Dear Connie,

"I'm sure the only reason no one has tracked me down is because of your faithful silence. You can see from the postmark where I sent this note from, but, in case the police or others think the postmark will help them, I want you to know that's not where we are. Yes, I said "we." I found the person who needs my help. I think we're safe, but all that might be changing. We've heard that someone who means us harm is coming for us.

"Thank you for not betraying me to the police. Giving you my bike falls far short of expressing my gratitude. If you're willing, I ask one more favor of you. Please go to St. George some Sunday and say a prayer for both the parish and for me. In my heart, they are still my flock, though they might not consider me their shepherd any longer."

Worthy handed the note to Nick before walking to the window and looking outside as the afternoon sunlight illuminated the autumn leaves on the ground. What Aris Kouris had written in the note raised more questions for him than answers.

Nick looked at the note again before saying, "Connie Ferwerda said the note came from some small town in Manitoba."

"And it was sent on October seventh," Freya added. "The note proves you were right, Chris, in tracing him to Canada. But that's not all the note tells us, is it?"

"It seems that he found the person he went to help," Lena, said, "although it sounds like they could be in danger. Is that Natasha or someone else?" Lena asked.

"We'll know about that tomorrow from the airlines or customs," Nick said. "But for me, there is something equally important in the note. Father Joseph still considers himself to be a priest."

Worthy remained silent until Freya asked, "What do you think, Chris?"

Turning to face the others, he shook his head slowly. "If he really wanted to be left alone, why write the note? And that bit about the police getting ahold of the note and discovering it came from somewhere in Manitoba, doesn't that mean he hoped we'd do just that?"

"Of course it's possible, Chris, but we'd have never seen the note if Freya and I hadn't questioned Connie again," Nick said.

Worthy remembered being outnumbered before on cases; in fact, he was almost used to it. But it bothered him that these three, and especially Nick, were convinced that he was wrong. *Why do we see Aris Kouris—Father Joseph so differently?* he thought. *And why am I beginning to hope that I, not Nick, am in the wrong?*

✟

OCTOBER 25

BY THE TIME LENA, WORTHY, AND NICK ARRIVED at Freya's office the next morning, the Canadian authorities had responded. Smiling, Freya shared that on September first, a Ukrainian woman using the name of Natasha Orlov and a male child, Mitya, had entered the country in Toronto.

"Finally, finally!" Nick shouted as he raised his arms in the air. "This is more than a breadcrumb, my friends." Nick said. "What else do the authorities say? Do they have the address of where she's staying?"

Freya shook her head. "That wasn't required, since she came in on a tourist visa."

Worthy looked at the email message on Freya's computer. "The dates work. Natasha Orlov entered Canada on the first of September, and Aris Kouris left Saginaw on September tenth."

The computer dinged, indicating another email. Freya studied it and exhaled slowly. "After I received that first email, I sent one back, asking if a Russian by the name of Sergei Luzinsky, a male in his thirties, had entered Canada about the same time or a little after that. This email says I struck gold, but I wish I were wrong. Sergei Luzinsky arrived in Toronto on October seventeenth."

"But no record of Natasha and the baby or Sergei going to Winnipeg?" Lena asked.

"No, but perhaps Natasha's relatives from Winnipeg met her in Toronto," Freya suggested.

"That's quite a hike," Worthy said.

Freya hit a few keys and began typing. In fewer than two minutes, she said, "It's almost 1400 miles."

"Not impossible, if her relatives believed she and the baby are in danger," Nick said. "But it means Sergei has been on her trail in Canada for a week, and we're just starting."

No one said anything until Worthy nodded at Freya and said, "You take the lead, Freya."

Freya blushed but recovered quickly. "As soon as we get the address of the Orlov family in Winnipeg, we should head to Canada. I brought my passport to work today for good luck."

"And I have mine—of course," Lena said, removing her Italian passport from her purse.

"The border authorities already know about Nick and me," Worthy said, "so we're set."

Freya felt the new energy in the room. For the first time on the case, they weren't just following breadcrumbs but heading toward a specific destination.

After agreeing on a time to leave Saginaw, Worthy said, "I feel I should say something. If it turns out the three of you are right about Aris Kouris . . . Father Joseph, I want you to know that's an outcome I'll be happy with."

LATER THAT DAY, AS THE POLICE SUV crossed over the Mackinac Bridge into Michigan's Upper Peninsula, Lena glanced at her friends in the vehicle and wondered who among them would find, at the end of their search, what they were hoping for. She could feel from Freya, who was driving, the excitement of coming to the end of the hunt. The young police officer, Lena reasoned, would be satisfied with any result as long as Father Joseph, Natasha, and Natasha's baby were found alive and safe.

Glancing over at Nick, who shared the second row of the SUV with her and was fingering his prayer beads, Lena was reminded of her mother, whose religious faith had made Lena bristle when she was a teenager. "Too many chil-dren end up with cancer or die in war zones for me to believe there's a God who's in control," Lena had said in one of their spats.

Her mother had shaken her head. "I don't say I understand God's ways, Lena, and I don't believe in a God who has everything mapped out. But believ-ing in God isn't the irresponsible, easy path you seem to think it is. Belief is hard, especially when we don't understand."

"Then going to Mass, the prayers, the novenas, the lining up for confession, calling on the saints—why bother with it all?"

"If I sound patronizing, I apologize, but I'm not sure your generation un-derstands, Lena. I was younger than you are now during the war, so I never grew up imagining that life should be fair. Belief in God makes sense to me because life is so often hard and, yes, unfair."

Lena had spent enough time with Nick, on the case in Rome and now in Michigan, to know that he'd agree with her mother. Yet, Nick was anything but fatalistic. Instead, when others fell into despair, Nick seemed to tap into some hidden reserve, as if disappointment held possibilities within it. The search for Father Joseph and Natasha might not end the way that Nick hoped, but even as he would accept such a result, he wouldn't accept that outcome as the last word.

She thought finally of Chris, whom she was watching most closely. Over the last few days, she'd struggled with his insistence that Father Joseph—and maybe also Natasha—were caught up in a drama of their own making. Stubbornness and an inflated male ego had been the ruin of her marriage. If Chris had played the "I'm the only seasoned detective among us" card, she'd have made plane reservation before the day was out.

But then, at the same moment that morning when they all realized that the end of their search was near, Chris had surprised them by acknowledging that he could be wrong. Everything in her, in that moment, told her his admission had been genuine. If Chris turned out to be right about Father Joseph, she knew he wouldn't gloat or celebrate. The specter of another male ego in her life faded, and she felt her heart open even more to him.

And me—what am I hoping for? She let the question go unanswered for a few moments. In a way, she already received what she'd hoped for from the case—that she could contribute and not be a burden. She knew that the others in the SUV were genuinely grateful for her insights into Father Joseph, Natasha, and even Sergei.

Looking out the window at the dense forests, she realized that she had come this time to the US with another item on her agenda, something she hadn't shared with anyone, even Chris. The last time she'd spent this much time in the US was back in the late 90s, when she was a grad student and married to

Stefano. The pain of their marriage and divorce had led to a promise that she would never live in the US again.

She remembered the culture shock she felt when she first arrived at Notre Dame in 1996. She'd taken Rome's international flavor for granted, its attraction to tourists from around the world, until she found herself in the bland landscape of the American Midwest. The only thing that Rome and South Bend, Indiana, had in common was the Catholic faith, but the ubiquity of priests at the University of Notre Dame meant little to her.

To make friends at the university, she'd hidden her feelings from everyone but other international students. Once every six to eight weeks, however, she'd steal away by train to Chicago for a weekend of art museums, live theater, decent Italian restaurants, and, on warmer visits, the shore of Lake Michigan. Chicago wasn't Rome, but the busy city reminded her of home.

In her final year of her doctoral studies and against all her plans, she'd fallen in love with Stefano, an Italian-American from St. Louis, Missouri, and a fellow grad student in her department. By the time they graduated, they were engaged, Stefano having promised that they'd divide their future life together between the US and Rome.

Marrying a month after graduation, they returned from their honeymoon in San Francisco to what seemed to be wonderful news. Stefano had been offered a position at his college alma mater in St. Louis to teach medieval studies, the college's offer including an administrative position for Lena in the school's travel-abroad program.

As Stefano threw himself into his role as a lecturer, Lena realized that their good fortune came with a price. Although the college had a program for students to spend a semester in Rome, Stefano wouldn't qualify to teach in that program for five years. In her own role in the college's travel-abroad program, Lena worked fifty weeks a year organizing semester-long study-abroad student trips to Italy, Spain, and France.

Slowly, Lena was forced to acknowledge the pain she felt. There was, first of all, the pain every morning of watching Stefano getting ready for his lectures and every evening grading papers and exams. It smarted to see him enjoying what she was just as qualified, if not more qualified, for. But as a known quantity at the college, Stefano had won a position Lena wouldn't have even been considered for.

She felt another level of pain in her daily job, one that had her organizing and arranging travel experiences for students to her beloved Italy as well as to Spain and France. Travel companies would send her emails and brochures that were meant to tantalize college students but triggered for her a longing that she gradually realized wouldn't be satisfied.

The worst part of being newly married, however, was the Sunday afternoons and evenings she spent at the homes of Stefano's parents and siblings. Both

Stefano's parents and two brothers lived on the same street in the Italian neighborhood of St. Louis known as "The Hill." Despite how Stefano had described the neighborhood, "The Hill" was like no part of Italy Lena had ever seen. When Stefano's mother hinted that Lena and her son should consider buying on "The Hill," Lena felt panic rise within her. That night in bed, she made the mistake of telling Stefano that "The Hill" seemed to be a cheap Disneyland version of Italy.

She didn't realize how much her comment irritated Stefano until the following Sunday, when Stefano's momma again brought up the subject of Stefano and Lena buying in the neighborhood. Stefano, with a sneer on his face, shared with his whole family Lena's comment about "The Hill" and Disneyland.

That Lena's mother-in-law resented her from that moment on didn't surprise her, but Stefano's betrayal took her off-guard, proving that there would be no boundaries in their marriage. When she confronted Stefano on his indiscretion, Stefano flew into a rage and declared that buying a bungalow on "The Hill" made sense. Lena didn't do well controlling her own temper as she reminded him of his promise to split their married life between Rome and the US. When he screamed back, "Grow up, Lena. That was a fantasy; this is real life," Lena knew the marriage was over. The divorce was resolved speedily, giving Lena the impression that Stefano was as relieved as she to be free of each other.

In the subsequent years, Lena focused on her career, believing marriage would always mean a compromise she was unwilling to make. An additional pledge she'd made to herself at the time—and had kept—was to stay clear of American men.

Then Chris came into her life, and now she found herself traveling through a country she'd promised herself to avoid and in love with another American man. Chris' and her future wouldn't be resolved by her saying she loved him more than she'd loved Stefano. She had to know if she could ever love the US.

CHAPTER SEVENTEEN

———————◆———————

OCTOBER 27

ALTHOUGH FREYA HAD TRACKED DOWN THE ADDRESS of Natasha's relatives outside Winnipeg, she suggested that they begin in the suburban police station in Stonewall. Not knowing what they would discover as they drew closer to Father Joseph, Natasha, and especially Sergei, Freya didn't want to have to explain to the authorities how the four of them had stumbled onto a crime scene.

That was the one topic none of them had raised on their two-day drive into Canada—the possibility that they might be too late, Sergei having already taken his revenge. What Freya hoped for seemed less and less likely, that they'd find mother, child, and protector living in peace, somehow no longer hounded by Sergei. *The problem with that is that life isn't a Christmas card,* she thought.

As they presented their identification in the Stonewall police station, the desk sergeant looked up from Worthy's picture.

"I've read about you," Sergeant Singh said.

"Don't believe everything you read," Worthy replied.

The sergeant smiled. "The article was kind, Lieutenant, more of a tribute as I remember. And if what I read was accurate, that would make you," he said, looking in Nick's direction, "his partner."

Nick blushed. "Just a helper."

"And I see you've brought others with you. Are you also helpers, a detective from Saginaw, Michigan, and a professor from Italy?" he asked the women as he studied their passports and IDs.

Before they could answer, Worthy said, "We're here as a unit."

A puzzled look crossed the sergeant's face.

"I can explain," Freya said, as she began to summarize what they hoped to find in Canada.

When she finished, the sergeant frowned. "Unless I missed something, you're searching for a priest who's committed a felony by crossing the border without documentation. In addition to that, you're primarily concerned about a Russian husband who, from our standpoint, entered Canada legally and hasn't committed any crime, to our knowledge."

Nick fingered the pectoral cross on his chest, knowing the sergeant was technically correct. "Our chief concern, sergeant, is the mother and child," he said in explanation. "If we find them safe, we'll also find Father Joseph, the priest, and be able to convince him to turn himself in."

"Do you know for a fact that this priest is even in the country?"

"I can assure you that his trail leads here," Worthy said.

Nick could accept that the known facts of the case might point to Father Joseph being the lawbreaker and Sergei being the concerned husband in search of his family. If the sergeant hadn't known about Worthy's reputation, Nick was sure they'd be turned away.

After a moment, the sergeant handed the IDs back before saying, "Lieutenant and Sergeant, you have no legal status in our country. No one is required to answer your questions. In fact, you can make no demands at all. Even if you see a crime being committed, you are to do nothing but report it. If you cross the line, you'll be subject to arrest."

"We understand. We're simply tourists," Worthy said.

"But tourists on a mission," the sergeant said as he handed a card to Worthy. "Report on anything you find. No matter what time of day or night, call this number if you need assistance. If I don't answer, leave a message. Agreed?"

"Yes," Freya replied.

Back in the car, Freya turned to the others. "Shall we head for the Orlovs'?"

"Not until we decide how we're going to proceed," Worthy said. "I don't think the four of us suddenly showing up at the door is going to work. And of the four of us, I'm probably the last person to make a good first impression."

"Why, Chris?" Lena said. "You and Freya have the badges."

"Which is exactly what could make the Orlovs clam up. Freya and I both know how people react when law enforcement shows up unannounced."

"Which leaves you and Nick, Lena," Freya said.

"Hold on a second," Lena said. "Who am I, an Italian from Rome, to ask about Natasha and Father Joseph, two people I've never met?"

"And I have my own doubts," Nick added. "Assuming they're Orthodox, won't my presence have an effect about as bad as police knocking ringing the doorbell? For many people, seeing an unknown priest at the door is like having a black cat cross their path. Their first thought is that someone has died."

"What if the person who rings the doorbell is their own priest?" Lena asked.

Freya turned around in the driver's seat. "Go on, Lena."

"We're all strangers to the family, but what if you talk to their priest, Nick, and explain why we need to talk with the Orlovs? Maybe he'd agree to accompany you."

Worthy nodded. "I like the idea. The Orlovs aren't going to shut the door on own priest."

"And there's another advantage," Nick said. "The Orlovs aren't going to lie about Natasha and Father Joseph in front of their priest," Nick said.

STONEWALL, MANITOBA, WAS BLESSED WITH TWO Ukrainian Orthodox churches, and at the second one Nick contacted that morning, St. Seraphim of Sarov, a secretary said she couldn't answer any question about parishioners over the phone. If Father Fortis were willing to come by the church, however, their presiding priest, Father Nilus, would be happy to meet with him. Just the way the secretary thanked Nick for the call gave him the impression that St. Seraphim was the right church.

Leaving Worthy and Lena at the motel, Freya dropped Nick off at the church that afternoon. As he exited the car, Nick turned to Freya and said, "God willing, one more breadcrumb."

Instead of going immediately to the parish office, Nick entered the sanctuary to offer a prayer. As he offered a worried prayer before the icon of Christ for the safety of Father Joseph, Natasha, and her child, he felt an ever-so-slight warm breath on the left side of his face. Thinking someone had entered the sanctuary from a side door, he looked in that direction but saw no one. As his attention slowly returned to the icon of Christ, his eye stopped on the icon of the Theotokos, the icon of the Virgin Mary holding the Christ child.

It was just a vague feeling, but it seemed in that moment that the Virgin Mary was looking at him. He half expected the Theotokos to say something to him, but as he continued to feel her gaze upon him, he realized she was speaking through her silence.

Of course, he thought, *a mother's love. Warmth, love, but most of all protection.* He felt the warmth enter him as he realized that his concern for the welfare of Father Joseph, Natasha, and baby Mitya was in the Virgin Mary's safe hands.

He rose from his knees, feeling at peace for the first time since the case began. *We are being led; we are being led,* he thought, as he made the sign of the cross and left the sanctuary to find the parish office.

Father Nilus was a big man, equal to Nick in both girth and beard length, and so Nick thought their embrace as fellow priests must look, to the parish secretary, as if they were grizzly bears in a zoo. Father Nilus greeted him with the traditional "Father, bless," to which Nick responded in kind.

"I took the opportunity to pray before the icons," Nick said. "I was blessed to feel the presence of the Theotokos very strongly."

Father Nilus made the sign of the cross and motioned for Nick to sit in one of the two chairs before sitting himself. "Did you feel a warm breeze?"

"Yes, that's exactly how it felt," Nick said.

"Others have had the same experience with that icon. Maybe someday, I will too." Father Nilus smiled before adding, "Please explain your mission, Father."

Nick summarized how the search for Father Joseph had led to a concern for Natasha Orlov and her child. While he described how this had led Worthy, Freya, Lena, and him to Stonewall, Father Nilus looked down at his hands.

When Nick finished, Father Nilus sighed. "What a sad tale. A priest who leaves his flock, that is serious. If this woman is truly in danger, please tell me how I can help."

"Natasha Orlov has relatives who live in Stonewall. I am hoping that maybe they are in your parish. Is so, would you be willing to accompany me when I question them?"

"We have a number of Orlovs here at St. Seraphim. Do you know the first names of the relatives?"

"It's Vladimir and Marina."

"Ah, then I do know them. Sad to say, they have a child with cerebral palsy, and that prevents them attending Divine Liturgy on a regular basis. I bring the Eucharist to them when I can, so they're used to seeing me."

"Have you been to their home recently, Father?"

"Now that you mention it, no. They cancelled my last two visits. They've had the flu and didn't want to expose me to that. Do you think . . .?"

"I don't know," Nick said. "They might be protecting Natasha, or they could be telling the truth."

Father Nilus didn't say anything for a moment. Pulling on his beard, he said, "The Orlovs are farmers and live outside of town. Like all farmers, they have outbuildings on their property. Perhaps . . ."

"Perhaps they could be hiding the couple?"

"That's what I'm wondering. Unfortunately, I have a funeral this afternoon. Actually, more than a funeral. It's a sad one, a young mother killed in a car crash. I'll be with the family until late tonight." After a moment, Father Nilus added, "I can be free tomorrow morning."

Being this close to Father Joseph and Natasha made it difficult for Nick to wait even a half day.

"Of course, of course," he said. "I should tell you that three others are with me, two who are police officers in the States. But it will just be me accompanying you."

Father Nilus looked up. "Two police officers? The matter is that serious?"

"We just don't know. We did find out that Natasha Orlov's estranged husband flew to Canada from Ukraine, not Russia, about six weeks after Natasha and the child arrived. We don't know where he is right now, but it's certain that he's been involved in criminal activity before."

Making the sign of the cross, Father Nilus said, "I can see why you're concerned. I could call the Orlovs right now if you want and simply put the question to them—are Natasha, her baby, and a priest staying with them?"

Thinking that such a message might prompt Father Joseph and Natasha to panic and flee, Nick said, "No, no, we'll wait until tomorrow. Is eight in the morning too early?"

"Let me pick you up at seven, Father. The Orlovs are farmers, so they'll be up. And, in light of what you've told me, I don't think I'm going to sleep all that well anyway."

CHAPTER EIGHTEEN

———— ◆ ————

OCTOBER 28

A FTER A RESTLESS NIGHT, NICK ROSE EARLY the next morning to offer his prayers before making coffee in his motel room. As he prayed, he remembered what Worthy had said the night before over supper.

"Tomorrow could be the end of our search, one way or another."

None of the others had to ask what "one way or another" meant. They might find Natasha and her child with Father Joseph huddled in the back of a barn, but safe. Or, they might find something much worse.

Wrapping his hands around the coffee mug, Nick looked down at the photo of Sergei Luzinsky from Interpol and whispered, "Kyrie eleison, Lord, have mercy."

✝

WORTHY AND LENA WERE ALSO STUDYING THE PHOTO of Sergei early that morning as they drank coffee in their motel room.

"That picture gives me the shivers," Lena said. "I think it's the eyes."

Worthy nodded. "A lot of people look ashamed in their mug shots. I've even seen some where the person is laughing, but that's usually because they're high on something. Now, this look?" he asked, pointing to the photo. "That's the look of someone who knows the drill because he's been through it before."

"It's like he's dead inside," Lena added as she closed her eyes and shook her head. "What does Interpol say about him?"

Worthy turned the photo over. "No official record until he was discharged from the military. Then, two years ago, he was arrested for war profiteering.

He's also suspected of having links with Russian organized crime. So, Sergei isn't exactly a patriot. But Natasha must have agreed to marry him."

"You still think it's possible he's a misunderstood and decent husband?"

"Is it possible? Yes, but, as you say, when you look at those eyes, he looks like trouble. It's not impossible that all three of them—Aris, Natasha, and Sergei—are messed up in their different ways. But I grant you that if we're lucky, Sergei won't cross paths with any of us—Natasha, her child, Aris, and us. If we're lucky."

Promptly at seven, Father Nilus picked Nick up. As Nick stepped into the four-wheel-drive Jeep, he expressed his gratitude.

"I'm just grateful for the chance to help, Father. The Orlovs are part of my flock, and if they're in trouble . . . . Well, I'm sure you understand."

"I do."

They settled into a comfortable silence until Father Nilus asked, "Are you concerned that the priest you're looking for has broken his vows with this woman?"

Looking out the window as industrial buildings gave way to farmland, Nick shared the incident in Thessaloniki that caused Father Joseph's abrupt return to the States. At the end, Nick said, "A lot of people, including the Metropolitan-Bishop in Detroit, believe Father Joseph has betrayed his calling, but if you're asking me personally, my answer is no, I don't believe that."

"Can I ask why?"

Glancing over at Father Nilus, Nick thought this fellow priest would give him a fair hearing. "I've interviewed several of his parishioners in Michigan. I can't deny that a few of them, after they heard about the incident in Greece, have written him off. My partner, Lieutenant Christopher Worthy, feels the same. But I can't believe that because of the way Father Joseph lived out his vocation. Not only some of his parishioners, but some of the town's people still believe in him, and I think that's because he cared deeply about them."

Nick paused as something else became clear to him. "I think leaving his parish was the hardest decision Father Joseph ever made."

The Orlov farmhouse and buildings looked no different to Nick from farms near his monastery in Ohio. The stubble in the fields, however, a bright almost neon yellow, was new to him.

"It's rapeseed," Father Nilus explained as he drove down the lane leading to the main house. "It suits our climate."

Other than a pickup truck parked beside a John Deere tractor, Nick noticed that there were no other vehicles by the house.

"Could they be gone?" he asked.

"Maybe, given the season."

They walked slowly up to the porch, giving whoever was inside—if some-one was inside—a chance to see them approach. Father Nilus rang the bell and, when there was no response, rang a second time, this time bringing the sound of dogs barking from the back of the house.

"Vladi, it's Father Nilus. I need to talk with you."

They waited another moment before a middle-aged man in bib overalls, his face creased with wrinkles, opened the door halfway. "Father Nilus, what is it?" the man said.

"Nothing to worry about, Vladi, but can we come in?"

Mr. Orlov studied Nick for a moment before opening the door wide enough for the two priests to enter. As Nick entered the first room, a parlor, he saw a rifle leaning against the wall by the door.

"Is Marina here?" Father Nilus asked.

Mr. Orlov shook his head. "She's taken Nicholai to the city for physical ther-apy, Father." He motioned for the two priests to take seats even as he remained standing, shifting his weight from one foot to the other.

"Is everybody over the flu, Vladi?" Father Nilus asked.

For a second, Mr. Orlov gave a puzzled look, and Nick understood that the man had forgotten the excuse he'd given to keep his priest away from the house. Looking down, he said, "We're over the worst of it, Father."

"Good, good. This is Father Nicholas Fortis from the United States. I brought him out here because he has a few questions to ask you, Vladi."

Giving Nick a quick glance, the farmer said, "Me?"

"You're not in any trouble, Vladi, so why don't you sit down too," Father Nilus said.

Vladimir Orlov seemed to weigh the request before obliging. *He's already on the defensive, so how can I put him at ease?* Nick thought as Mr. Orlov's eyes focused on the room's braided rug.

"I'm a monk from Ohio, Mr. Orlov, and one of my fellow monks in the monastery is worried about his brother. The brother's name is Father Joseph, a priest from Michigan, and he's gone missing."

Nick thought he detected Mr. Orlov's shoulders relax as he looked up. "That's a real shame; yes, it truly is."

If he knows Father Joseph, he doesn't know him by that name. He thinks I'm here on a fool's errand, Nick thought. *Time to force the issue.*

"A little over a year ago, Father Joseph was studying at a university in Greece, Mr. Orlov. That's where he befriended a woman whose life, we've been told, was in danger. An abusive husband, you see."

Mr. Orlov's gaze returned to the rug as he clasped his hands in front of them.

The room was silent until Father Nilus said, "Vladi, I know you are a good man. And I know you wouldn't lie to me, would you?"

Without saying anything, Mr. Orlov shook his head.

"Father Fortis knows that the woman he's talking about is a relative of yours. And he knows that she arrived in Canada about six weeks ago. So, Vladi, is she here with her child, or has she been here?"

The farmer sat frozen in his chair, before whispering, "Don't ask me that, Father. Please."

Father Nilus looked at Nick and shook his head. After a moment, Nick said, "I think I know why you have a rifle by the front door, Mr. Orlov."

Wringing his hands, Mr. Orlov cleared his throat but said nothing.

"You're worried Natasha's ex-husband, Sergei, could show up." Nick said before pausing, his heart beating faster as another thought struck him. "Or has he already been here, Mr. Orlov?"

The farmer looked up, his jaw set. "It wouldn't do him any good if he did come. No, please, can't you leave this alone?"

Nick shook his head. "I can't leave until I know if there's a priest with Natasha and the baby."

Looking genuinely confused, Mr. Orlov said, "A priest? No, no, there's no priest with her."

The farmer's face turned even redder, and Nick could see that Mr. Orlov realized what he'd given away.

"The man with her is a priest, Mr. Orlov. His name is Father Joseph Kouris. He's a Greek Orthodox priest from the States."

Shaking his head, Mr. Orlov said, "I can't . . . I can't believe it."

"It's the truth, Vladi," Father Nilus said.

Mr. Orlov rose and walked to the window. With his back to the two priests, he said, "He was mute and deaf, didn't say a word. Natasha told us to expect him, someone she knew in Greece. An American. Sure enough, a couple days after she and the baby got here—that was a little over four weeks ago—he showed up at the door. But a priest?"

"You said he didn't say a word. Does that mean he's no longer here?" Father Nilus asked.

"They're all gone, and no, I don't know where they went. I took them to the train station, and she told me to leave them, said she wouldn't tell me where they were headed. Said it would put us in more danger."

"Why'd they leave?" Nick asked.

Mr. Orlov glanced toward the rifle. "Natasha got a call from Kiev, from her brother. Sergei had shown up, searching for Natasha and the baby but not finding out anything. Then, the day before, Sergei came to the brother's house with a couple of others of his type. They beat her brother up pretty bad, said they'd break his legs unless he told them where Natasha and the baby were. The brother told them they'd left the country, but he didn't know where. But he said Sergei was wild and took a hockey stick to his kneecap. Eventually, he confessed that he gave them our name and where we live."

"When was this?" Nick asked.

"Five days ago. They left the next day."

Father Nilus rose and walked over to stand by the farmer. "Are Marina and your boy really in town for physical therapy?"

"It's the truth, but not the whole of it, Father. The missus and the boy are staying with a cousin of hers until . . . until I know it's safe."

"And you've been here alone waiting, is that right, Vladi?" Father Nilus asked.

Walking to a roll-top desk, Mr. Orlov raised the lid and took out a pair of binoculars. "About three days ago, there was someone over that way in the woods. I felt it in my bones. Whoever it was, well, he was keeping an eye on the place. My dogs barked pretty bad one night, so maybe he was looking in the barns. If he'd broken into the house, I'd have shot him, no questions asked. But then yesterday, there was nothing, like he's gone. But I'm still watching."

"So Natasha and Father Joseph have about a week's head start on us," Freya said that afternoon after Nick told them what he'd learned from Mr. Orlov. They were huddled in Worthy's and Lena's motel room, the only one with a sofa, chairs, and a kitchenette.

"And Sergei could be one or two days ahead of us," Worthy added. "We have to hope he's as clueless about the whereabouts of Natasha, Aris, and the baby as we are."

Lena got up from the sofa and entered the kitchenette. While filling a kettle for tea, she said, "That business about Father Joseph pretending to be mute—why was that?"

"If the Orlovs and Natasha spoke Ukrainian or Russian, maybe he just seemed mute," Worthy replied.

"I'm wondering if there's another reason," Nick said. "If Father Joseph talked with the Orlovs, there'd be the chance that he'd slip and give something away. We priests have certain phrases that come as naturally to us as breathing, such as 'God willing' or 'Lord, have mercy.'"

"And a priest isn't as likely to use the colorful language of a lot of men, which might also make him stand out," Worthy agreed.

After they had cups of tea, Freya asked, "If Natasha, the baby, and Father Joseph didn't stay in the house, does that mean they stayed in one of the outbuildings?"

"Huh. I wonder," Worthy said.

"What?" Lena asked.

"I think we need to see where they stayed out there."

"You think they might have left a clue, Christopher?"

"Nick, you said they had to leave in a hurry. I'm not even sure they knew where they were going when Mr. Orlov dropped them at the train depot. But I'm hoping they left some sort of clue."

✝

MR. ORLOV LOOKED SURPRISED TO SEE NICK AT HIS DOOR AGAIN, especially accompanied by three others. And he didn't look that willing to help when Nick explained that they wouldn't know if Natasha and her baby were safe until they found them.

"You said you were convinced Sergei was watching the farm, maybe even looking in some of your outbuildings," Worthy said. Stretching what they knew for sure, he added, "We're pretty sure he hasn't left Canada. That means if he found something they left behind, he could be closing in on them."

Mr. Orlov considered this for a moment, before walking them out to one of the larger barns. Inside, the farmer walked them past bundled hay stacked against one wall and farming tools on another. At the far end of the barn, Mr. Orlov opened a door to an enclosure.

Just inside the doorway, Mr. Orlov turned on a light. "It's a bunkhouse, pretty basic as you can see, but it's heated and has its own bathroom. Natasha said they were comfortable."

Before Mr. Orlov could enter the room, Worthy reached out and caught his arm. "I'd appreciate it if you'd let Sergeant Maaki and me look things over first."

Mr. Orlov stepped back. "Be my guest."

Leaning in the doorway, but not entering, Nick gave a quick glance around the room. There were two single beds, obviously slept in, with a crib in between. He tried to imagine the three living in safety for over a month before they heard about Sergei coming for them.

From inside the room, Worthy asked, "Is the door ever locked?"

"No, I've never seen the need."

Worthy and Freya divided the room as they began their search. The most obvious item they found was a photo album that lay on one of the beds. Opening it, Worthy saw pages of black and white snapshots.

"Natasha and my wife loved looking at photos of the first Orlovs who emigrated here after the war," Mr. Orlov explained.

Freya found the second item, the top part of an empty package of diapers. "No surprise," she said.

They found nothing more for the next five minutes before Worthy, on his knees, gently probed a small mound of straw. Using a ballpoint pen, he lifted the circular object and brought it to the door from where Nick, Lena, and Mr. Orlov were watching. "Recognize it, Nick?"

Without touching it, Nick replied, "It's a very small prayer rope."

"A what?" Freya asked.

"It's something like a rosary, but it's a cord with knots. And you can see a tiny cross at one end. Do you recognize it, Mr. Orlov?"

"I think I saw it on the baby."

Sniffing the object, Worthy returned to where he'd found it and knelt down again. "There's evidence of quite a bit of urine here. It's on the straw, the floor, and the prayer rope."

"From a diaper?" Mr. Orlov asked, now as curious as the rest of them.

"Too much for that," Worthy replied.

Shaking his head, Nick said in a low voice, "I think Sergei broke into the room and found the baby's prayer rope. The urine is his."

Worthy looked up. "I agree, Nick. It's his signature."

"I'm sorry to say it's more than that," Lena said. "It's a classic expression of rage."

☦

Later that afternoon, they went to Winnipeg's train station to show photos of Father Joseph and Natasha to the train agent.

"Sure, I remember him. He paid for the tickets in US dollars. Didn't even seem to mind that he was overpaying with the exchange rate."

Freya felt a twinge in her stomach. "Do you remember their destination?"

"Funny you should ask that. He paid for tickets all the way to Vancouver, but then he asked if he could get off before that—if he changed his mind, you see. I told him he could, but I couldn't guarantee he'd get a refund."

"What did he say to that?" Worthy asked.

"Not a word. It was like the money wasn't important to him."

"If this man did decide to get off the train at one of the other stops, would he have to show his ticket to anyone?" Freya asked.

"No. He could just step off the train and be on his way."

After feeling hopeful just a moment ago, Freya fought off a wave of frustration. If Natasha, the baby, and Father Joseph left the train at one of the stops, they could now be anywhere.

She felt Nick pat her arm as he asked the ticket agent, "Can we have a list of the stops on the train to Vancouver?"

"Of course. Just stops or junction points?"

"A junction means what?" Lena asked.

"They're stops where travelers can change trains, ma'am."

"If the man we're looking for got off at one of the junctions, would his tickets to Vancouver still have value?" Nick asked.

Handing out timetables for the Vancouver-bound train, along with contact information, the ticket agent said, "Yes, but he'd have to show them to the agent at the junction for re-ticketing."

More breadcrumbs, Freya thought. *But it's better than no trail at all.*

As they were about to leave, Freya showed the ticket agent the photo of Sergei and specified the dates between October 24 and 27. The ticket agent shook his head. "No, ma'am. I've never seen him, but I only work days. You need to ask Cam. He works second shift."

"Is there a third shift?" she asked.

"No, the ticket office closes at midnight."

"Do you have contact information for Cam?"

The ticket agent tapped on his computer before writing down the phone number and address of Cameron Rostovich.

Sitting down in the station's lobby, Nick asked the others what they should do next.

Freya shrugged. "I wish I knew. We need to contact all the junction stations, and then someone needs to show Sergei's photo to Mr. Rostovich."

"Okay, let's do this," Worthy said. "Give Rostovich's address to me, and Lena and I will show him Sergei's photo. Meanwhile, you two stay here and start contacting junction stations."

After calling the first junction stations and discovering nothing valuable, Freya said, "Of course, if Father Joseph and Natasha left the train at one of the other stops, we're going to be left in the dark."

"Listen, Freya," Nick said, "look how much closer we are today than even two days ago. Don't ask me to explain, but something happened to me the other day that has me believing that we're meant to find them."

"I hope you're right, Nick."

CAM ROSTOVICH, A STOCKY BALDING MAN in his fifties who limped slightly, ushered Worthy and Lena into his small apartment and offered them coffee. Both accepted, and soon they were seated in a room whose walls were covered with hockey memorabilia.

"Did you play the sport yourself?" Worthy asked.

"I made it to the minor leagues before this knee," Rostovich said, patting his right knee, "had enough. You two like the sport?"

"Sorry, I'm Italian," Lena said. "I've heard they've started playing hockey up in the north of my country, but I've never seen it played."

"Honey, you've missed one of the truly great pleasures of life. And you, Lieutenant?"

"I didn't much care for the sport on TV until a friend took me to a Redwings game. I couldn't believe the speed of the sport. It was crazy."

Rostovich closed his eyes and swayed back and forth as if he were moving down the ice, before turning to point to a pair of beat-up child's skates hanging on the wall. "That's my first pair, and my two older brothers used them before me. I'd have those blades sharpened before every game." He paused before adding, "Never had any kids myself, so I couldn't pass them on. But you didn't come here to talk hockey with me, more's the pity."

Worthy produced the photo of Sergei and placed it on the coffee table. The ticket agent picked the photo up, studied it, then placed it back down.

"Sure, I remember him. His English was bad, but my grandparents were from the same country, so we could understand each other. Said he'd played hockey on one of Russia's national teams, and I thought, yeah, people say a lot of things, but he was a bruiser. Anyway, I wouldn't want to be forechecked by him."

"Do you remember where he was headed?" Worthy asked.

Rostovich nodded. "It's funny what he asked me. I saw him twice. That first time, he pulled out a map of Canada and asked me where most Ukrainians settled. He didn't like it when I laughed and pointed from Ontario to Alberta. You see, my first thought was that he was a tourist, a Russian with Ukrainian connections who wanted to see our part of the country. But the way he looked at me, I thought, 'This guy ain't no tourist.'"

Lena leaned forward. "If not a tourist, then what do you think he is?"

"Well, when he showed me a photo of a woman and a child and said he was looking for them, I thought maybe he was a cop or . . ."

"Or what?" Lena pressed.

"To tell you the truth, I didn't want to think of what he might be if he wasn't police. Like I said, the guy was a bruiser." After a moment, he added, "Now that I think about it, he reminded me of one of those bounty hunters in westerns."

Worthy nodded. "You're not far off. He's the woman's husband or ex-husband, and we're trying to find her before he does. Did he end up buying a train ticket?"

"Not the first time, that was three days ago, but he came back the next day. He acted like we hadn't met and asked to buy a ticket for Denby."

"Denby?"

"It's not much of a town, just a few buildings on the north shore of Lake Winnipegosis." Rostovich pulled himself up and went to a bookshelf. He returned with a road atlas and opened it to the map of the province.

"Here it is," he said.

"Why there?" Worthy said, as much to himself as to Lena and the ticket agent.

"Is it possible to take a train up there?" Lena asked.

Rostovich pointed to a town close by. "One train every two days stops there, but no farther."

"Have you ever been up there yourself," Worthy asked him.

"Nah, I'm not much of a fisherman. That's the main attraction, if not on Lake Winnipegosis, then you can hire a float plane to fly you into some of the smaller lakes. Not that any of the lakes up that way are small."

Worthy looked down on the lake-studded map. "So, one day, this man is looking at a map covering most of Canada, and then the next day, he comes back to your window and says, 'I want a ticket to Denby.' Like he was certain of the place. Is that right?"

"Yep, just like you said. Whatever he was looking for, he knew where he wanted to start."

✝

WHEN THEY WERE ALL CROWDED INTO A BOOTH in a fish and chips shop for supper, Freya looked out the window and said to Worthy, "So, in just one day, Sergei somehow figured out that Father Joseph and Natasha are up near Denby?"

"Or Natasha, the baby, and Aris went to Denby on their way to somewhere else, maybe by float plane or car," Worthy explained.

Nick wiped his hands on his napkin and took a swig of beer. "Why Denby?"

Lena sat back in the booth. "The ticket agent made it sound like it's a destination for fishermen, but that hardly helps us. Unless . . ."

"Unless what, Lena?" Freya asked.

"I was remembering when the two of us, Chris, were at your cabin on the lake. Fishermen need boats, but they also need cabins, right? Maybe Natasha and Father Joseph headed that way to hide in one of those cabins."

"That might explain why they took a train in that direction, but how did Sergei know they headed that way?" Nick asked.

"Whatever he learned about Denby, it was something he figured out in a day," Worthy said.

Freya pulled out her notepad and turned a few pages. "The only thing we know about those days is what Mr. Orlov said—that he thought Sergei was watching the farm."

"But don't we know that he also broke into the barn?" Lena asked.

"That's right, so that means that unless he took something from the barn, what we saw there was the same as what he saw," Freya said.

Everyone looked at Worthy who seemed to be lost as he stared at his plate. When Freya started to say something, Nick raised his hand to stop her. The three waited until Worthy seemed to shake himself out of a dream.

"He found that photo album," he said in little more than a whisper. "Something in those old photos must have pointed him toward Denby."

CHAPTER NINETEEN

———————◆———————

OCTOBER 29

THE NEXT MORNING, LENA FELT A MIX OF EXCITEMENT and fatigue as the four of them hurried through a breakfast of coffee, toast, and fruit before returning to the Orlov farm. Freya had torn off a bit of her toast and held it up, saying, "Speaking for myself, I'd like to find something bigger than another breadcrumb today."

"You speak for all of us," Nick said. "At some point, the trail ends. But is that at Denby or somewhere else?"

"What we know is that Sergei headed there after he broke into the barn. The photo album or something else in the barn must somehow explain the Denby connection," Worthy said.

At the Orlov farm, it was their good fortune to find that Marina Orlov and their son Nicholai had returned home. To Lena, the tall woman in jeans and a flannel shirt looked like what a North American pioneering farm wife should look like. Her hair was cut short, her hands calloused. *No polish on those nails,* Lena noted. With a smile, the farm woman invited them into the kitchen for pastries and coffee. She sat between Freya and Lena, with Worthy and Nick standing behind, and pointed out the photos in the album that Natasha and the man with her, whom they knew as Clark, had seemed most interested in.

The grainy photos reminded Lena of pictures in her own grandmother's albums. It wasn't until Lena was at university that she realized her grandmother never offered to show her photos from the war years, the same years when both she and Lena's grandfather had supported Mussolini. She wondered how many Ukrainian immigrants in Canada had similar albums with empty pages covering life under Soviet rule.

"Natasha was especially drawn to the photos from the thirties, like these," she said, lingering on several of the earliest photos. "These are of the first Orlovs who arrived in Manitoba as homesteaders. She couldn't get over how hard they had it back then—shacks, donkeys, and babies, that's about all they had—immigrants landing in the middle of the Great Depression. I remember that she especially liked the photos of the babushkas, the women who wore their best scarves for the pictures. It didn't take me long to realize that she was homesick."

"Do you know if any of the family settled up near a place called Denby?" Worthy asked.

Mrs. Orlov called to her husband and repeated the question.

Standing in the doorway, Mr. Orlov rubbed his chin and said, "Denby, let me think. We Orlovs have always been farmers, and what's up there is mainly forests. But wait a minute. Marina, show them the photos of my great-uncle Andrei, the monk. I think he lived at a monastery up that way in the forties and fifties. He'd been imprisoned by the Soviets for being a priest and was happy to get out when he did."

Marian Orlov turned several pages of family photos until she came to a page showing three monks standing on the shore of a big lake.

"Could that be Lake Winnipegosis?" Nick asked.

Mr. Orlov approached the table and squinted down at the photo. "Well, I'll be. How'd you know that?"

Mrs. Orlov turned the page and paused. "Vladi, there are some photos missing. I think they must have fallen out in the barn."

"I doubt it, Mrs. Orlov," Worthy said. "We checked every inch of that room."

"Can you remember who was in those photos?" Freya asked.

"I seem to remember there was a small wooden chapel, much like those back in the old days in Ukraine," Mr. Orlov answered. "I think it had an onion-shaped dome."

"And I remember several more photos of huts behind the chapel," Marina Orlov added.

"Is there still a monastery up there?" Nick asked.

"Sorry, I have no idea," Mr. Orlov said.

"That's okay. We can check on the Internet," Worthy said.

After they finished the pastries and coffee, Worthy said, "I think you've given us what we need to go on. Thanks for all your help."

Marina Orlov spoke for both herself and her husband at the front door. "We're so grateful you're looking for the poor thing and her baby. The thought of her husband tracking her all the way from Ukraine, well, it scares me to death."

As they started toward the SUV, Lena turned back to the Orlovs and asked, "I wanted to ask you what you thought of the man who was with Natasha, the one called Clark. We know he didn't say anything, but what was he like?"

Mrs. Orlov looked at her husband. "He was a lovely man. He held that baby like Mitya was his own. Didn't matter if the baby fussed or not, he just loved holding that child."

As WORTHY AND LENA PACKED, LENA SAID, "There's no guarantee Father Joseph and Natasha are up in Denby, is there?"

"No, but it's where Sergei thinks they are."

"What can you do if we find him there instead of Father Joseph and Natasha?"

Worthy shook his head. "Freya's and my hands are tied, officially, that is. And I don't see Sergei as the type we could scare off." Pausing, he said, "The odd thing is that I find Sergei a lot easier to understand than Aris. It's clear what Sergei's goal is, but I can't say the same for him."

Lena stopped packing for a moment and sat on the bed. "So you still think Father Joseph could be getting something out of this running and hiding?"

Worthy shrugged. "Maybe so; maybe not. The Orlovs clearly believe Natasha is in trouble. They take the phone message supposedly from Natasha's brother as genuine. On the other hand, it does seem like a fifties' romantic movie in a lot of ways."

Lena sighed heavily. "I don't know about a movie, but Nick said something like that the other day. He said it all seemed like a story he'd read a thousand times before, but he couldn't think of what it was."

In the bathroom to pack up his toiletries, Worthy said, "Maybe it will come to him once we get to Denby. Nick and I have been on cases before where little made sense until the end."

Lena felt a tug on her heart with Worthy's last words "the end." *When we arrive at the end, I'll be on my way home,* she thought. Not wanting to think about that, she said, "The ending I'd like would be for Father Joseph, Natasha, and the baby to live happily ever after. And you don't have to tell me that that also makes me a romantic."

"My hope," Worthy said, "is that we find them before Sergei does. If we do, Natasha should go to the police and make her case that Sergei is a threat to her and the baby. Maybe she could even apply for asylum, although I think it's more likely she could get a protection order against Sergei. The police could then arrest Sergei and put him on a plane back to Russia."

"And Father Joseph? What happens to him?"

Worthy left the bathroom and sat down next to Lena. "Assuming Natasha and the baby are safe, he'll be deported, since he's in Canada illegally. She and the baby might be able to remain in Canada, even apply for citizenship, but Aris will be sent back to the States. They're bound to be separated."

"Then what?" Lena asked.

"That's the question—then what? Has Aris even thought about the future? I know Nick is hanging on to the belief that Father Joseph still considers himself a priest, but I can't see the church buying that."

"If Natasha and Father Joseph got married, would they be able to live in the same country?"

"I don't believe Canada would let him back in, so it would have to be in the States. That would be the end of him being a priest."

Neither said anything until Lena asked, "Do you remember how the beds were set up in the barns?"

"Separate with the crib in between. Yeah, I noticed that. They still could have been having sex, but you'd think they'd have pulled the beds together. It's possible nothing has been going on between them."

Lena put her head on Worthy's shoulder. "That would fit with what Father Joseph said happened back in Thessaloniki. He let Natasha stay the night because she was in danger."

"One thing became clear to me after looking at the old photos. I was thinking about how those immigrants burned their bridges to come to a new country. They left everything behind. That made me wonder what Aris thought when he looked at the photos. I wonder if he saw that he'd done the same thing—from his failed engagements in college to what happened in Greece to running away from Saginaw, he's burnt every bridge behind him."

ON THE INTERNET, NICK FOUND THE WEBPAGE for St. Mary of Egypt's Skete. The small community of monks remained active, their mailing address being in Denby. The small chapel in the Orlovs' photo album was still being used, but according to the website, the huts where the monks once lived had been replaced by newer log cabins. The formal photo of the community showed eight monks standing behind the seated figure of the abbot, who appeared to be elderly.

In the photo of the chapel, he could see a large body of water, the lake, he presumed, behind it. *Beautiful in the summer,* he thought, *but how much summer do they get that far north?* He shivered, trying to imagine trudging through deep drifts of snow to early morning prayers in an icy chapel. *No, not for me,* he admitted, thankful that he was a Greek monk, not Ukrainian.

If the monastery was Father Joseph's and Natasha's destination, Nick wondered which of them had made that choice. *Did one of them consider St. Mary of Egypt's Skete their last stand or simply their latest stopping point?* he asked himself. Maybe Father Joseph thought that the monks could shield them, but the monks pictured on St. Mary of Egypt's webpage would hardly be able to deter Sergei for long.

He arose from the desk in his motel room to face the icon of the Virgin Mary he'd brought with him. Making the sign of the cross, he prayed for Natasha, her baby, and Father Joseph before remembering to pray for Sergei as well.

As he ended his prayer, he found himself hoping that Sergei didn't know that Father Joseph was with Natasha. That might be possible if Natasha and Father Joseph left the Orlov farm before Sergei arrived to spy on the place. That hope dissolved when he remembered that Sergei had broken into the barn where the three had stayed. Sergei had seen that both single beds had been slept in. Nick realized that Sergei's urinating on the prayer cord, like a dog marking his territory, meant that he must have put two and two together. Perhaps the jilted husband had even guessed that his old nemesis from Thessaloniki, Father Joseph, was with Natasha.

OCTOBER 30

FREYA LOOKED AT THE LIGHTED DIAL ON HER WATCH as she lay in bed in her motel room. She'd been nervous since they'd agreed over dinner the night before to drive to Denby in the morning. She would have preferred to pack up and drive north immediately, even if that meant driving through the night.

The worry that kept her tossing and turning was the issue of the ticking clock. If St. Mary of Egypt's Skete was Father Joseph's and Natasha's destination, they would likely have arrived four or five days before. Based on Cam Rostovich's memory of when Sergei bought a train ticket, Sergei could have arrived in Denby just days later. That meant Sergei, Father Joseph, and Natasha could have been in the same rural, isolated area for several days.

Worthy, however, had convinced the group that it would be better to leave in the morning, reasoning that driving two hundred and forty miles through the night would leave them exhausted. He repeated something all police recruits learned at the police academy, that lack of sleep was a major cause of poor decisions and botched cases.

Of course, she knew that Worthy was right, but she couldn't ignore another truth. If Father Joseph and Natasha had been able so far to avoid someone as desperate and angry as Sergei, how long could that situation continue? Didn't every hour matter? She was sure that none of them would forgive themselves if they found out that if they'd arrived a day, even a couple of hours, too late.

She tried to focus on what Nick had said: *Don't ask me to explain, but something happened to me the other day that makes me believe we're meant to find them.*

How she wished she could believe him. But that was the challenge Nick posed for her. What Nick asked of her was far harder than what Worthy asked of her two years before—to take a risk. Nick asked her to believe, to not give up hope.

✝

For Nick, it seemed that with every mile on the road to Denby the tension in the car increased as the temperature outside decreased. Worthy was mainly silent, which wasn't surprising. Freya, too, was quiet as she focused on driving.

Sitting together in the second row of seats, Lena and Nick carried on an intermittent conversation about the rugged scenery that they were passing. The farther they went north, the fewer cars and trucks they noticed. For many miles, their SUV was the only vehicle in sight, giving Nick the feeling that the world was flat and they were coming to its edge. Running parallel to the road were the train tracks on which Sergei and maybe Natasha and Father Joseph had traveled on their journeys north.

Halfway to Denby, Lena interrupted Nick's reverie by saying, "I remember seeing this American film maybe fifteen years ago. I remember it because it had this weird ending—a serial killer is heading for a police trap when he's involved in an accident. The car bursts into flames, and the killer dies instantly. But because the police don't know the identity of the killer, they think he just outsmarted them and got away."

"I saw that film," Freya said from the front seat. "I think Jack Nicholson was in it. What made you think of that?"

"I was imagining arriving in Denby and finding out that Sergei was in that kind of accident and had died. I admit that if that happened, I'd feel only relief for Natasha and the baby."

Nick looked down at his hands, then up to see Lena looking at him.

"But you wouldn't feel that would you, Nick?"

"You give me too much credit, my dear. If something like that happened, I pray I wouldn't rejoice, but I might."

The exchange hung over Nick like a cloud, from which unsettling questions began to rain down. *Have I even prayed for Sergei? Yes, the once. But have I thought of him as someone who deserved the chance to change? No. Have I thought of our search ending with Sergei's death, even at my hands? More times than I can recall.*

Looking out the side window and into the growing darkness, Nick saw his reflection—the beard, the monastic robes, and the silver cross around his neck—and thought what a poor monk he was.

✝

IF WORTHY HAD HOPES OF FINDING A POLICE STATION or a Chamber of Commerce in Denby, he was disappointed. Denby was a small cluster of buildings: two bars, a bait shop, a real estate business specializing in lakeside cabins, and a gas station that also sold groceries.

Asking Nick and Lena to make inquiries in one of the bars, Worthy and Freya walked to the gas station.

The proprietor, an older man in need of a shave, looked suspiciously at Worthy's and Freya's IDs. "Law enforcement? What, you got some crime to report?"

"No, sir, but we're here looking for a couple with a baby. We also looking a man who might have asked about the couple," Worthy explained.

"Are they Crees, by any chance?"

"Crees?" Worthy asked.

"The Chemawawin Crees, over on the Rez," the man explained.

"No, two Ukrainians and an American," Freya said. "Do the Cree have their own tribal police?"

"Yes, indeed. Take the road a mile back toward Easterville and you'll come to the station."

"What about the monastery—St. Mary of Egypt? How can we get there?" Worthy asked.

The proprietor frowned. "I seem to know a lot more when people buy supplies."

Worthy smiled. "That's good, because we need supplies, and you look like the closest thing to a shopping mall."

"We probably got what you need. And if we don't . . ."

"Then we probably don't need it," Freya said, completing the comment.

Taking hand-held shopping baskets, Worthy and Freya loaded up with supplies for supper. Returning to the counter, Worthy said, "Now, about my questions. Where can we find a place to stay around here? And how do we get to the monastery?"

"Well, you're in luck. One of the monks is due in tomorrow around noon. They come in twice a week, and tomorrow's one of their days."

"Just tell us what road to take, and we'll find the place on our own."

The proprietor laughed. "Not unless you're hauling a boat, mister. St. Mary of Egypt is on an island about a mile out in the lake."

✝

LENA NOTICED THE HEADS OF THE MEN TURN as she and Nick entered the oddly-named "Tropical Keys Bar and Grill." Although it was only noon, the patrons looked like they'd been perched on barstools for hours. Several whispered among themselves as they looked with blurry eyes more at Nick than at her.

"You sure you're allowed to be in here?" the bartender said as he glanced up at Nick.

A few of the men laughed as one of them motioned for Nick to come to the bar. "Let me buy you and the pretty lady a drink, Brother-what's-your-name."

If Nick was uncomfortable with the attention, Lena didn't notice. He approached the bar to lay down photos of Natasha, Father Joseph, and Sergei in front of the bartender. "Have you seen any of these people?"

The bartender glanced briefly at the photos and then back at the two of them. "You're not from the monastery, are you?"

"Not this one," Nick said.

"What have these two done?" the bartender asked as he studied the photos of Natasha and Father Joseph.

Lena stepped up and said, "These two have done nothing, other than maybe try to get away from this man. Has he been in here?"

Wiping the bar with a not-all-that-clean towel, the bartender replied, "A lot of guys come in here. Guys up for the fishing, some like yourselves from the States."

Lena saw no need to correct the bartender about her nationality. Instead, she said, "He speaks with a pretty heavy accent—Russian or Ukrainian. Does that ring a bell?"

The bartender stopped wiping the counter but didn't look up. "We get a lot of Ukes from Winnipeg up this way. For the fishing, like I said, except the season is closed."

"I'll tell you why I think you recognize him," Nick said. "You moved these two pictures away from this one and asked what the two had done. You didn't ask what this guy had done."

The patrons stopped their chatter and listened for what would follow. The bartender turned away to place the towel by a sink.

A couple of customers laughed when the bartender said, "So what if he was in here? I don't think he's coming back."

"What do you mean?" Nick asked.

"One of my regulars said something about his accent. Just like that, he had a gutting knife up by the guy's face. The long-blade Rapala, not the short one."

"What happened?" Lena asked. "Did you call the police?"

"What police? You mean the cops from the Rez? No, we handle our own problems here. I told the guy that guns and knives aren't allowed in my bar, so if he wanted to stay and drink, he'd have to hand over the knife. I had to tell him twice; his English wasn't all that good."

"What did he do?" Lena asked.

"He made the mistake of believing me. Hell, most of the guys in here have knives on them. When he handed over the knife, four of my regulars escorted the guy outside and beat the shit out of him. Although, when they came back in, it looked like he'd done some serious damage too."

"When was this?" Nick asked.

"I'd say two nights ago, maybe three."

"And he hasn't been back?" Lena asked.

"His English wasn't very good, missy, but he didn't strike me as the stupid kind."

Nick picked up the photos. "So, all this happened after he asked about a couple and a baby?"

"That's right. I'm thinking he caught a ride from one of the truckers and got the hell away from here."

"I hope you're right, but I have my doubts," Nick said.

WITH WORTHY AND FREYA DRAWING A BLANK AT THE OTHER BAR, one more appropriately named "The Fireside Bar," they all rendezvoused at the bait shop. As soon as Freya entered, the overpowering smell of live bait brought back childhood memories of fishing with her grandfather.

A flickering overhead fluorescent light made the colorful lures lining the walls seem to dance. Working alone in the shop behind a counter was a man Freya assumed was indigenous, from the Cree community.

Looking up at the group, the man smiled when he saw Nick. "I like your ponytail."

Nick laughed and replied, "I like yours."

It struck Freya that she couldn't remember the last time any of them had laughed. Homicide cases and cases of missing persons, like this one, were grim by nature, which meant that anything that broke the tension was welcome.

The owner laughed and said, "People call me 'Bait-Man Billy' and my prices are the best in town. Ice fishing season is due to start in a month or so, so I guess I can't sell you licenses, tackle, or lures."

Nick placed the photos of Natasha, Father Joseph, and Sergei on the counter. "We're looking for these people, Billy."

Billy put on a pair of glasses and studied the photos before putting his finger on Sergei's. "That's 'Two Knives.' Not that I called him that to his face, seeing how it was all bloody the second time."

At the same moment that Nick replied with "two knives?" Worthy asked, "The second time?"

Bait-Man Billy held up both hands in mock surrender. "Whoa, one at a time. It was like this. He came in and bought a fish-gutting knife, a Rapala. He wasn't very talkative, but that's okay. It ain't more than an hour later and he waltzes in a second time, blood from his ear to his chin and all down his shirt. And what does he do? He buys the same knife all over again."

"What did you think when he did that?" Worthy asked.

"That he wasn't in a mood for me to ask why. To be honest, I thought he might be going back to finish a fight. But, as far as I know, nothing happened that day or anytime afterwards. So that's the tale of Two Knives."

Worthy nodded. "So, if a guy like that wanted to stay around Denby for a while, where could he do that?"

"Usually, when I'm asked that, I ask if the person has money. But I already saw that this guy had plenty of cash. His wallet was bulging when he bought the knives."

Freya caught Worthy's glance. *Yes, this is new information,* she thought. *Sergei came to Canada with plenty of money.*

Bait-Man Billy continued. "So a guy with money like Two Knives could rent a cabin from Millie, the real-estate lady, just down the street. Same goes for you if you're looking for a place to bed down."

"How about the monks out at St. Mary of Egypt?" Nick asked.

"You still talking about lodgings?"

Nick nodded.

"Sure, a few folks head out there for retreats. I don't see Two Knives as that type."

Lena stepped forward and pointed toward the photos of Natasha and Father Joseph. "But you haven't seen these two, along with a baby?"

The bait shop owner shook his head. "They didn't come in here. Are you sure they came to Denby?"

They all looked at each other, realizing that there was plenty of evidence of Sergei coming to this town, but, so far, no evidence that Father Joseph, Natasha, and the baby had ever set foot in Denby.

CHAPTER TWENTY

———◆———

Sharing the supper supplies, they sat in the SUV with the heat on high and looked out from the shore of the lake toward the island and the lights of the monastery.

"It's possible, I suppose, that Sergei made a mistake in coming up this way," Nick said between mouthfuls.

"Which would mean we made the same mistake," Freya said.

"Maybe that's good news," Lena said. "If that's what happened, Sergei might have already gone back to Russia."

"He's come a long way to give up," Worthy replied.

"And we've come a long way, too. And I don't think we're going to give up if Natasha and Father Joseph aren't here," Nick added, deciding not to mention the obvious—if Natasha, the baby, and Father Joseph weren't here, where were they?

Worthy opened a bag of chips and offered it to the others. "As far as I can tell," he said, "we have three more stops here in Denby before we give up hope. The first is the train station. Maybe someone remembers seeing Father Joseph, Natasha, and the baby get off the train there. The second is the real estate office to see if they rented a cabin when they arrived. And the third is the monastery."

Freya looked at her watch. "It's now nearly seven o'clock. The boat out to St. Mary's comes in tomorrow, so what can we do tonight?"

Knowing that they'd need lodging for the night, they went to the real estate office, a ranch-style house nestled by the lake. Outside, a neon "Open" sign flashed.

"Looks like someone's still here," Freya said. Inside, they met Millie McConnell, the single real estate agent for Denby and the north shore of Lake Winnipegosis. Worthy and Freya started by showing their IDs and then the photos of the three adults, which Nick could see clearly disappointed Ms. McConnell. Worthy figured the woman had little business this late in the fall.

Ms. McConnell raised a pair of glasses, which were dangling from around her neck, and squinted at the three photos. To Nick's surprise, her first reaction was to put the photo of Father Joseph to the side, even as she picked up the other two.

"I can't say I ever saw this woman," she said, turning around the photo of Natasha, "but this man here," she added, now turning around Sergei's photo, "showed me a picture a lot like it. At least, I think it was the same woman."

"But this man," Freya asked, pointing to the photo of Sergei, "didn't show you the photo of this other man?"

"No, I've never seen him or this photo before. And I think I'd remember. He's a looker. I hope he's not a bad guy."

"No, but the man you met might be," Nick replied.

"Oh, dear. Well, he was a scary one."

"He didn't rent a cabin from you for a night or two?" Freya asked.

Millie shook her head. "Now you have me concerned. He didn't rent a cabin, but the tribal police left me a message a couple of days back, saying that there'd been a report that one of our cabins looked like it was broken into. I'm sorry to say that's not uncommon, so I didn't put the two things together."

"Do you mind if we look into it?" Worthy asked.

"You want to search the cabin?"

"Yes, ma'am," Worthy replied.

"Frankly, that would be a relief."

By the time they left, Ms. McConnell had given them the key to the suspicious cabin as well as the key to the cabin next door. "Stay as long as you need and use all the firewood you need. It's on me," she said.

ON THEIR WAY BACK INTO DENBY, Worthy said, "It's hard to know how much time we'll have tomorrow before the monk arrives in town. Even though it's late, let's check out the train station." They found the station deserted, a light shining down on a notice board. Tacked to the board, they found a sign with "Need a Ride to Denby (3 miles) or Easterville (14 miles)?—Day or Night." written on it and a phone number with the name Conrad below.

"Might as well call the number," Worthy said, wondering if this was another breadcrumb or a dead-end.

A man's voice answered immediately. "What can I do for you?"

"Hello, Mr. Conrad. This is—"

"Not Mr. Conrad. Just Conrad," the man on the other end of the line clarified.

"Okay. My name is Lieutenant Christopher Worthy. I'm a police officer from the States, and I'm enquiring about some folks who might have gotten off the train in Denby about a week ago, maybe less. If they did, I'm wondering if you gave them a ride."

"You say 'about a week ago?'"

"Yes, but maybe less than that. A man, woman, and a baby."

"Are they on the run?"

"In a way, but they haven't done anything wrong. We're trying to find them to make sure they're safe."

There was a pause long enough on the line for Worthy to say, "Hello? Are you still there?"

"Yep, I'm here. Where are you right now?"

"My colleagues and I are at the train station."

"This late? You must be really worried about them."

"We are, Conrad," Worthy said.

"I'll be there in ten minutes," Conrad said, before ringing off.

Worthy turned to the others. "You probably heard. He doesn't trust us, which I take as a good sign."

"It seems unlikely that he'd drive out here this late at night unless he knew something," Freya added.

With the time approaching eleven in the evening, they all felt the cold and retreated to the SUV.

Almost exactly at the ten-minute mark, a Chevy Suburban pulled up in the train stop's parking lot. A man who could have been Bait-Man Billy's older brother rolled down his driver's side window and called out, "Hop in."

Inside the vehicle, Worthy and Freya handed over their IDs. Conrad studied them and said, "I just needed to check. My cousin Billy said you were in the bait shop, but I had to make sure."

"We appreciate your caution," Freya said, as she handed the photos to Conrad.

"Yep, I gave rides to them all, but not on the same day."

Worthy counted to five silently before pointing to the photos of Natasha and Father Joseph and saying, "You're sure about these two? They had a baby."

"Of course, I'm sure. They asked me how to get to the monastery. I told them it would be a couple of days before the monk boat came into town, but the guy insisted that I drop them down at the wharf. He seemed to know something, but I never heard another thing about them. I think I was the only one in town who saw them."

"How did they seem?" Lena asked.

"Tired. Yep, they were tired, and the baby was fussy."

"You said the man insisted you take them down to the wharf. Was he the one making the decisions?" Worthy asked.

"Well, he's the one who said it, but the two of them had been whispering before that. She didn't give me the impression that she thought otherwise."

"What day and time did you drop them there?" Nick asked.

"That was four days ago, I think. But I remember the time. It was about one-thirty in the afternoon."

"So, there were still a few more hours of light," Nick said.

"Oh, yes. Three hours at least. Now, do you want to hear about the other fella?"

"Yes, we do," Freya said.

"He's the reason I had to see you in person. You see, he got off the train two days ago, and he called me for a ride. The same time of day, because that's when the train comes in. Well, I have to be careful about who I pick up. I've been robbed before, you see. Anyway, I pull up here in the parking lot, and this guy is sitting on his suitcase and he's glaring at me. I'm thinking, 'What did I do to piss this guy off?' I ask if he's the guy who called me, and he just nodded. He got in my car, and I have to tell you, I wasn't feeling all that good about him. He'd been drinking on the train, that's for sure, and drinking was one of my demons in the past. The smell of it, it brings some bad days back. Anyway, before I could ask him where he wanted me to drop him, he pushes a picture of this lady into my face."

"This man had an accent, right?" Worthy asked.

"A heavy one. He said something like, 'You see her—maybe with baby?'"

Worthy could feel the tension in the vehicle as they waited for Conrad to finish the story.

"All I could think about was that little baby with her parents, and I thought, 'Lord, forgive me, but I'm going to lie.' And I did. I said I'd never seen them, and if they'd come in on the train, I'd have been the one to pick them up."

Conrad turned to look at Nick in the second seat, "Father, this probably won't surprise you, but I did a lot of lying in my drinking days. I ended up being pretty good at it."

"So you think the man believed you?" Nick asked.

"Don't really know, but then he scared me about out of my wits. He asked me to take him to St. Mary of Egypt Skete. So that's when I doubled down and lied again. I told him the monastery was six miles out in the lake on an island and what we call 'the monk boat' wouldn't be coming into town for supplies for another week. You see, I was hoping he'd believe me and catch the train back to Winnipeg yesterday."

"Where'd you drop him?" Freya asked.

"In Denby. He asked me to take him to the best bar in town. So, I fibbed a third time. I took him to the 'Tropical Keys' because I know the crowd there is pretty rough. But when I dropped him there, he went next door to my cousin's at the bait shop. I found out later what happened."

"Two knives, you mean," Lena asked.

"Billy told you, I see. I'm not sorry he got a licking, but I made sure I didn't run into him over the next couple of days. He'd have known by then that I lied about the monastery and the monk boat. And I thought he might be the type of guy who'd try to beat the truth out of me, so I laid low."

"So, he never called you back," Nick said.

"If he had, I'd have hung up on him. I just hoped he hitchhiked out of town, but looking at your faces, I guess you think he's still here."

ALTHOUGH TIRED FROM THE TWO DAYS OF TRAVELING, they were also ener-gized by what they'd discovered. Father Joseph, Natasha, and the baby had indeed come to Denby. Then, just two days later, Sergei had arrived. And all of them had been interested in the island monastery. Too keyed up for sleep, Worthy and Freya searched the cabin that had been broken into as carefully as they'd inspected the Orlovs' barn. The simple log cabin was one of several set along the shore of the lake and sheltered by tall pines. Two bedrooms and a bathroom were set behind a larger front room that also contained a kitch-enette. Worthy and Freya could see immediately that one of the beds had been slept in and towels in the bathroom had been used.

"I wish we could ask for forensics to go over the place for prints, but we don't have any actual evidence of a crime," Worthy said.

"Not yet, anyway," Freya added, as she pulled out two empty bottles of whis-ky from underneath one of the beds. "Like Conrad said, Sergei likes his booze. It's hard to know if his being under the influence will make him more accident-prone or more dangerous."

"Could be both," Worthy observed.

After finding some empty Twinkie packages on the floor in the kitchenette, Freya said, "There's something I want to ask you, Chris. It's about Natasha."

"Why she hasn't gone to the Canadian police, right?"

"That's it. I can understand why she didn't go the authorities back in Ukraine. Sergei is the kind of guy who probably owns police and politicians. But when she came to Winnipeg, why didn't she apply for asylum or at least have a restraining order when she heard Sergei was on his way?"

"It's part of the mystery," Worthy said. "She must have a reason, something that convinced Father Joseph as well. I'm also wondering why the story ends here. They had tickets valid all the way to Vancouver. That gave them a lot of options. But coming here—I mean, out at the monastery on an island—there's nowhere else to go."

Freya sat down at the small table in the kitchenette. "Maybe it makes sense. Natasha left Greece with the baby, but not with Sergei. She realized she wasn't safe in Ukraine and flew to Canada to get away from him. She arrived in Winnipeg, hoping she'd be safe with the Orlovs, but then she had to run away again. At some point, maybe she just couldn't face a life of running and accepted that facing Sergei was inevitable."

"And Aris . . . Father Joseph, a priest and a brother of a monk, decides St. Mary of Egypt is that place," Worthy said. "That makes a kind of sense."

"Does it?"

"Have you ever heard of the concept of sanctuary, Freya?"

OCTOBER 31

EARLY THE NEXT MORNING, WORTHY, FREYA, AND LENA LEFT Nick to his prayers and drove west along the lakeshore to the tribal police station on the Cree Reservation. Soon, the road signs were printed in both Cree and English, and Freya followed the one pointing to tribal headquarters.

Like the cabin from the previous night but larger, the tribal headquarters was a log construction. Inside, a young Cree woman in uniform sat behind a desk.

Looking up, she asked, "What can I do for you?"

After they introduced themselves, and the officer introduced herself as Captain Lilly Song, Freya explained how the real estate agent, Millie McConnell, had given them permission to inspect the cabin that had been broken into.

"I've seen worse," Captain Song said. "Did you find anything interesting?"

"Just a couple of empty whisky bottles," Freya replied. "We were wondering if you had a suspect in mind for that."

"Not really. It looked to me like someone broke in to sleep off a drunk. It's more common for a break-in to be a robbery, but it didn't look like that."

Freya set down the photo of Sergei. "The bartender at 'Tropical Keys' said this guy got into a fight a couple of days ago. We were wondering if you've had any dealings with him."

Captain Song studied the photo. "No, but fights in a bar, well, that comes with the territory. You thinking he did the break-in?"

"Can't be sure, but it seems likely," Freya said.

"What do I need to know about him, in case our paths cross?"

"He's Russian, been in the country not all that long, and we're pretty sure he's stalking these two plus a baby," Worthy said as he put down the photos of Natasha and Father Joseph.

"Huh," Captain Song said, looking at the two photos one at a time. "Why didn't they report him?"

"We're not sure, except this guy," Worthy said, pointing to Sergei's photo, "is her husband, or maybe by now her ex-husband. These other two have been in the country a few weeks longer than this guy."

"And the baby is his?"

Lena answered this question. "It's complicated, but the woman came to Canada because she thought her ex-husband might harm her and the baby."

Captain Song took a moment before picking up the photo of Father Joseph and asking, "And this man? Is this her boyfriend?"

Lena waited for Worthy to answer the question, but it was Freya who said, "That's complicated as well. He's a priest, and we think he came up from the States to protect her and the baby."

"Shit, really? A priest? He looks pretty buff for a priest. So, you think the priest, this woman, and her baby could all be up in Denby, and this guy is looking for them?"

"We know these two got off the train here and got a ride to the wharf with Conrad," Worthy explained.

"The wharf? Why there?"

"We're thinking they wanted to go out to the monastery—St. Mary of Egypt Skete," Worthy said.

"And when would this have been?"

"We think the 26th or 27th of this month," Freya said.

"Well, that's interesting," Captain Song said, returning to her desk and finding a folder. Opening it, she said, "An owner on that same day reported his rowboat went missing. A couple of days later, one of the monks brought it back, saying he'd found it floating off the island."

They looked at each other for a moment before Worthy asked, "How far is it from the wharf to where the boat was taken?"

"I'd say about two hundred yards. You think this guy could have rowed them out to the island? If the wind was up, the water would have been pretty choppy."

"That wouldn't have mattered to him," Freya said.

CONVINCED THAT THEY'D FIND FATHER JOSEPH, Natasha, and the baby out at St. Mary of Egypt, they knew that there was only one remaining question—where was Sergei?

They drove back to the wharf in time to meet the "monk boat" as it arrived. A young monk, his beard still coming in and his cheeks red from the cold, was alone in the boat. As he stepped onto the dock, Freya presented her badge before showing him Sergei's photo.

By the way the young monk looked at each of them before settling on Nick, Freya could see that the young monk was surprised by the confrontation.

"Did you give this man a ride out to St. Mary's?" Freya asked.

The monk glanced at the photo before saying, "No."

"Have you seen him at the monastery?"

The monk still seemed uncomfortable as he shook his head again. "Has he done something?" he asked.

Freya was about to show the monk the photos of Natasha and Father Joseph when she changed her mind.

"We're not sure he's done anything, but we'd like to talk to him," she said. "We'd also like to visit St. Mary's, if we can ride back with you."

The monk considered this for a moment before saying, "I'm in town about an hour for supplies. Meet me here, and don't be late."

They watched the monk walk toward the gas station-convenience store before Freya explained. "I remembered what you said, Chris, about Father Joseph and Natasha choosing the monastery for sanctuary. If he rowed them out to the island so they could ask for the monastery's protection, I wasn't sure this monk would tell us."

"He did seem a bit nervous. Do you think he recognized Sergei from the photo and didn't want to tell us?" Lena asked.

"I can't see why he'd lie about that," Nick said. "But I agree that something is troubling him."

"Okay, we have an hour before he comes back. I suggest we go back to the bait shop," Worthy said.

"What for?" Freya asked.

"We have to figure out how someone without a boat, like Sergei, could have gotten out to the island. And I bet Bait-Man Billy can tell us."

BAIT-MAN BILLY SMILED WHEN HE SAW THEM come into his shop. "You still fishing for information?"

"Yes, we are. So, Billy," Worthy said, "if I wanted to hire someone to take me out on the lake, where could I do that?"

"I can do that, or you can go down to the Rez. A lot of the men down there work as fishing guides during the season. But the season is over. Won't be open until ice fishing starts."

If Sergei had worked out a ride to the island through Billy, Worthy knew the bait shop owner would have said something on their earlier visit.

"Okay. If someone wanted to go out to the monastery, I imagine that would be easy," Worthy said.

"Sure, the season being over doesn't mean men on the Rez aren't looking to make some cash. I can ask if you want to come back in a day or two."

"Thanks, but we don't have that much time. There's something else. Could someone also buy supplies—food, water, maybe a blanket or two—on the reservation?"

"Of course. There's a store there. Not as nice as mine, though."

They all thanked Billy and started toward the door. A thought, however, made Worthy turn to ask, "How hard would it be for someone visiting the area to buy a gun?"

Bait-Man Billy pursed his lips. "Getting a gun license up here isn't like it is in the States. It takes time."

"What if a person didn't have time but lots of money?" Worthy asked.

"Ah. So hypothetically, we're talking about Two Knives?"

"I could be."

"He'd need a lot of money, but I saw Two Knives had that. His best bet would be on the Rez again."

"Maybe even from the same guy with the boat?" Freya asked.

"Hmm, are we still speaking hypothetically? Then, yes, that'd be possible."

✝

SHIVERING AS THE COLD WIND HIT THE BOAT, Lena looked toward the island and St. Mary of Egypt Skete. This wouldn't be her first visit to a monastery, as she'd stayed at monasteries in Europe when she was conducting research.

From her first visit to a monastery in her university days, she felt an attraction that was hard to explain. Going to Mass with her mother always led to a flood of questions as she observed those around her. *Do I believe what these people believe? Do all these people, including the priest, believe everything they're mouthing? Do any of these people think about the atrocities that have been committed by the Church throughout history? Do any of them question Jesus being divine, born of a virgin, and now existing somewhere with God?*

What surprised her when she began visiting monasteries was how differently the monks lived out the same faith. She never had the sense that they were struggling to hang on to belief in a skeptical world. Instead, many of them lived in a kind of playful contentment despite their lives being far from easy. And more than one monk had admitted that there was a great deal about the Divine that he didn't understand. Instead of being defensive about this, however, they seemed happy with the mystery.

In the boat, Lena's gaze fell upon Nick, and she thought, *Haven't I just described Nick? She remembered what he'd say once, that he was "happy to be in customer service instead of sales."* That must be the reason, she figured, so many people—even those without faith—fled to monasteries for solace. The monks weren't selling anything. Living simply and simply living, the monks were there to serve. *And maybe that's why Father Joseph and Natasha decided to end their running here,* she thought, looking toward St. Mary of Egypt.

✠

AS MUCH AS WORTHY ENJOYED BEING ON WATER AGAIN, he used the boat ride to the monastery to ask the monk about the island. When looking out from Denby at the island, he's noticed that it was shaped like a tilting table with high cliffs on the side facing the town. And above the cliffs were clouds that promised snow. Although the young monk was hardly talkative, he did share that the island was five miles long by three miles wide. St. Mary of Egypt owned the entire island, even though the monastery proper covered only twenty-five acres. The rest was forest, he said, except for a clearing above the cliffs.

Worthy realized that a person with military training like Sergei would use the dense cover to his advantage. Worthy pictured him somewhere on the island with a cache of supplies and maybe a gun, hiding as he watched the monastery without being seen.

If time were not a factor, Worthy thought Freya and he might be able to tempt Sergei from hiding. But they didn't have unlimited time. The monks might have agreed to shelter Father Joseph, Natasha, and the baby, but the monks would hardly allow them to remain on the island for long. All Sergei had to do was wait for the monks' hospitality to end.

Worthy did see one glimmer of hope. Nothing about the demeanor of the monk piloting the boat led him to believe that Sergei had already made his move against Father Joseph and Natasha. *He's still waiting for something,* Worthy thought, as he studied the high cliffs and the dense forest of the island.

CHAPTER TWENTY-ONE

———————•———————

T HE WORDS THIS PLACE LOOKS LIKE *the end of the world,* floated through Nick's mind as the motor died and the boat glided toward the monastery's dock. *St. Mary of Egypt Monastery will at least be the end of Natasha's and Father Joseph's flight,* he thought, shivering with the fear of how close Sergei might be.

It seemed strange to Nick that a monastic community this far north would take the name of an ancient saint from the desert of Egypt. The only link Nick could see connecting the two contrasting settings, the late autumn chill of the Canadian forest and the heat of the desert, was the intense solitude that underlay the legend of the saint. "A woman of "ill-repute," a euphemism in the ancient world for a prostitute, Mary of Egypt experienced a sudden conversion when she tried to enter a church and felt a divine force repelling her. Leaving her old life for the desert, she lived alone for the rest of her life. After her death, this Mary was venerated as a model of repentance and humility, providing an example and challenge for the monks on this Canadian island.

As they left the boat and walked up a path to the monastery's chapel, Nick stopped to let the sound of monks chanting wash over him like a soothing antidote to his worries. It had been more than three weeks since he'd been surrounded by his brother monks in Ohio. His own daily prayers had been as vital to him as eating or sleeping, but now, as he closed his eyes and listened to the chant emanating from the chapel, he realized how much he missed praying in a community. That made him wonder if Father Joseph felt the same spiritual loneliness while he'd been on the run. Was that why he chose a monastery as the place to end their running? Perhaps, even after weeks of running and hiding, Father Joseph remembered the prayer from the Orthodox liturgy, when the petitioner asks to die in a state of grace. Nick knew Father Joseph would have said that same prayer in every service he offered. And didn't many monks, nuns, and priests, Nick wondered, add a silent addition to that prayer, that God would let them die not just in a state of grace, but also in a *place* of grace?

Nick thought that Father Joseph must have realized that Sergei would eventually track them down. If Father Joseph, Natasha, or both, had chosen this monastery to be the end of their running, Nick knew there'd be no more breadcrumbs.

☦

BEFORE LEAVING DENBY, THEY ALL AGREED WITH NICK that they'd be honest with the abbot about why they were there. "If we lie to him, we're not likely to get his cooperation when we need it."

Now, after waiting twenty minutes for the service in the chapel to end, they entered the warm chapel together. Candles provided the only light in a room with icons covering the walls from floor to ceiling. The others hung back while Nick took a candle off a table and added it to others below the icons.

As Nick turned and whispered to the others to give him a few minutes to pray, Worthy had a memory return from his first case with Nick. As they had closed in on the killer, Worthy was totally focused on making the arrest. That was when Nick surprised him by saying, "If it's possible, I'd like to hear his confession."

Worthy remembered his response. "Sure, Nick, once he's in custody."

"I'm hoping to hear his confession before he's arrested," Nick replied.

Worthy had been dumbfounded. "No way, Nick. That's a crazy idea."

"Don't you see, my friend? If he lets me hear his confession, then he'll surrender. That's different from being captured."

"Nick, it won't affect his sentencing one bit."

Worthy knew he'd never forget Nick's response. "I'm thinking of his soul."

Growing up as a minister's son, Worthy had been surrounded by religious language both in church and at home. With his Dad, words like "God," "soul," and "repentance" were uttered in a certain tone, as if his father had to change gears inwardly before uttering those words. In Worthy's ten years of working with Nick, he'd often heard those same words, but with a naturalness, almost a childlike innocence.

There was another difference. Worthy knew if his father had ever been asked to pray for a killer on the loose, he'd have prayed that the police would apprehend the culprit before he killed again. Nick's prayer, he knew, would be different. Nick would pray that the killer would have a chance to be set free spiritually, even though his arrest and incarceration were certain.

As a homicide detective, Worthy accepted that he'd always view killers as his father did—brazen or scarred persons with little to lose and who needed to be stopped. But that didn't keep him from wishing he was more like Nick, who he knew was praying not just for Father Joseph, Natasha, and the baby, but also for Sergei.

His thoughts were interrupted by Lena squeezing his hand. He bent down to hear her whisper, "Do you ever wish it wasn't too late to believe in all this like Nick does?"

He'd never expected to hear those words from Lena, and they rocked him. Had she commented on the darkness of the chapel as "medieval" or even "disturbing," he'd have understood. Had she observed that the chant, the icons, and the incense were powerful means to manipulate a person's emotions, he'd have understood that as well.

But Lena's words stunned him. He felt an urge to leave the chapel, go out into the light of day, and breathe fresh air. He reminded himself that he'd visited and even stayed in monasteries on previous cases with Nick. In those places, he'd felt nothing but the old emptiness, and he wondered if what he felt now was a sense of betrayal by Lena or something more.

All he knew for certain was that he'd heard longing in Lena's voice. Until that moment, he'd assumed, from what Lena had shared about her mother's piety and then her later study of mystics, that she'd simply outgrown belief in God. Now he realized that at some level Lena lived with regrets. Perhaps, he reasoned, Lena's faith was like one of the candles at the front of the chapel, which, as he was thinking about Lena's unexpected comment, had burned to the bottom and then gone out with hardly a spark, leaving behind it only a ribbon of smoke. *Or maybe I've just described what happened to me ten years ago,* he thought.

NICK HAD FINISHED HIS PRAYERS AND had gone through a side door, telling the others that he would look for the abbot. After waiting fifteen minutes, Freya began to feel claustrophobic. The faces in the icons seemed to stare at her. Her urge to wait outside was relieved by Nick returning with another monk, who was bald and little more than half Nick's height. Introducing himself as Abbot Jakovi, he invited them to sit while they talked. Freya appreciated the abbot walking to a wall switch and turning up the lights. The faces on the walls seemed to recede and give her more air to breathe.

"Father Fortis has told me about your mission," the abbot began, in a voice Freya found unexpectedly strong given his shortness and advanced age. "On rare occasions, we have given sanctuary and protection, but it is always with an assurance that we will neither confirm nor deny anyone's presence. Of course, we draw the line if someone has broken the law, but Father Fortis assures me that this isn't the case here."

Freya weighed the abbot's words. Despite his promise of anonymity, had his words "the case here" hinted that the monastery *was* sheltering Father Joseph and Natasha?

"Reverend Father, we appreciate your stance, but we think there is someone on the island who intends to harm the people whom we think you're sheltering," Freya said.

The abbot nodded. "Yes, I can understand your concern, but as Father Nicholas knows, the principle of sanctuary has clear guidelines. We invite anyone who has a complaint against someone who might be sheltering here to come forward and make his case. You see, we can't mediate and seek a solution that is agreeable to everyone until a person does that."

Freya had a hard time believing that Father Joseph and Natasha came to the monastery with the hope of reaching an agreement with Sergei. And she could see from the expression on Lena's face that she agreed.

"We think the man we're concerned about could have a weapon, maybe two," Lena said. "Can you see how that changes the situation?"

"'The situation?'" the abbot repeated. "That possibility was true in ancient times as well as now. We would ask such a person to put down his weapons before any negotiations can begin."

"And if such a person came with a desire for revenge instead of reconciliation, then what?" Freya pressed.

"Then our duty is to stand between the two parties until the weapons are set aside."

Freya felt her face redden. The abbot was holding on to a rule that endangered not only Father Joseph, Natasha, and the baby, but also the monks of his community.

In the tense silence that followed, no one spoke before Worthy said, "Let's say that somebody came here for sanctuary. Would you let that person know if others came who wanted to help him?"

Abbot Jakovi looked at Worthy with a slight smile. "I would have to think about that. I won't say no, but . . . I won't say yes."

AN HOUR LATER AND AFTER HAVING been assigned rooms, they walked to the library to plan the rest of the day and the evening.

"Assuming Sergei is watching, I wonder what he makes of us being here," Freya said.

"I've been wondering the same thing," Worthy added. "Four people arrive a couple of days after he comes to the island. Does he get suspicious?"

"The good thing is that we know what he looks like, but he's never seen us before," Freya said.

"If we want to keep him guessing, we need to behave like the people who come to this monastery on retreat," Nick said. "We can't be too obvious in looking for him."

"Does that mean we should be going to the services, Nick?" Lena asked.

"Not all of them, but each of us should be seen going to one of the daily services," he explained.

"Can we search the island at all?" Freya asked.

Nick nodded. "I think we can, if we're not too obvious. People who come on retreat to my monastery in Ohio love to walk the grounds. For many people, being in nature is their form of prayer."

"In case you haven't looked in the desk in your room, there's one of these," Worthy said waving a map of the monastery's grounds. "Sergei won't have a map, so that's one point in our favor. But obviously we can't all be searching the island at the same time."

Just as they began to make a schedule of who would go to a prayer service or on a walk, Lena asked, "Do we believe Father Joseph and Natasha will contact us if the abbot tells them that we're here?"

"I don't hold out much hope for that. If I was in their shoes and the abbot told me that four people had showed up claiming to want to protect me, my first thought would be that they could be working with Sergei."

"Does that mean you've changed your mind about Father Joseph and Natasha?" Lena asked.

"It's fairer to say I've changed my mind about Sergei. We have no proof that he's on the island, but if he is, he's not here to reunite with his family. But Aris—okay, Father Joseph—still bothers me. If he sees himself as the hero, the knight in shining armor, there's no telling what he'll do."

Worthy placed the map of the island on the table and, with a pen, underlined the paths branching out from the monastery buildings.

"We have to assume that Sergei, with his military training and his cache of supplies, could be hiding anywhere on the island, but probably somewhere near the monastery," he said. "If he's smart, he's probably changing his location frequently."

"I'm wondering if the map can help us with something else," Lena said. Pointing to the cluster of monastery buildings, she said, "Can't we use the map to figure out where Father Joseph and Natasha are most likely hiding?"

Studying the map, Nick pointed out the chapel, the refectory or dining hall, the library, and the guesthouse. That left an equal number of buildings unmarked and reserved for the monks.

"Father Joseph and Natasha could be in any of those buildings," Freya said. "And I don't see them venturing out."

"Maybe not, but the baby needs diapers and baby food, and Father Joseph and Natasha need food as well," Lena said. "Somebody has to be bringing all that to them."

Worthy leaned back and groaned. "I'm so stupid. Why didn't I think of that when we were on the boat this morning? I just assumed the monk had been buying normal supplies for the monastery. He must have had supplies, like diapers, under the tarps the whole time. All I would have needed to do was watch the monk when he unloaded everything."

"None of us thought of that, Chris," Freya said.

"That's right," Nick added. "Yes, we missed that chance, but what you said, Lena, can still be helpful. Given the way most monasteries are laid out, one of these unmarked buildings must be the infirmary. Others will be for storage. And I remember a flyer in my room describing monks making candles. They must make those candles in one or two of the other buildings. If I were to guess, I'd say Father Joseph, Natasha, and the baby are staying in either the infirmary or one of the storage buildings. If we watch those buildings at mealtime, wouldn't we see a monk carrying food to one of the buildings?"

Freya pointed to a dotted line on the map. "This is the fence that encloses the buildings we're talking about. As far as I can tell, it's solid wood and about eight feet high. So we can't see where the monk goes . . ."unless . . ."

"Unless what?" Lena asked.

"Unless one of us climbs to the rise on this side of the monastery," Freya said. "From there, one of us can see where a monk is taking them food."

No one spoke until Nick said, "Christopher and Freya, let's assume we do find which building they're hiding in. What do we do next?"

Worthy glanced at Freya and waited. Clearing her throat, she said, "Given what the abbot said, I think we wait. If Sergei makes his move, we'll have solid grounds to break through the fence to rescue them. That is, unless we're too late."

THEY DECIDED THAT NICK, IN HIS ROBES, would be the least suspicious to take the path to the overlook during the evening meal.

With a smile, Freya said, "Maybe you can kneel and pretend to pray."

"Oh, I won't need to pretend," Nick replied.

That left the others decide who would attend the prayer service before the evening meal. Before anyone else could volunteer, Worthy said, "I'll go."

With their plan set, they all went back to their rooms. Worthy tried to take a short nap but couldn't sleep. How he longed for the case to be over. When he would look back on these weeks in the future, he thought that he'd regret spending every moment of his time with Lena searching for a couple who, in the final analysis, had made a series of poor choices.

Because wasn't that what had happened? Natasha might have had good reason for believing she and her baby were in danger in Ukraine, but why, when she was at the Orlov farm, hadn't she gone to the Canadian authorities for protection? Worthy wondered if the answer to that question would be found in another poor decision, this one by Aris Kouris, a man and a priest who needed to play the role of rescuer.

An hour and a half later, Worthy entered the chapel to find it again dark, the room lit by only the candles set before the icons. After taking a seat in the back row and letting his eyes adjust, he realized slowly that he wasn't alone. In the front row, a monk with a cowl was kneeling and, more than once, making the sign of the cross. The monk's prayer sounded like a faint hum in the room, and Worthy wondered what it would be like to feel that someone was listening to his thoughts, instead of this emptiness.

When his life imploded a decade before, after his wife asked for a divorce and his older daughter ran away, he prayed but felt no one there. He hadn't expected a voice or a sign in the sky, but he'd hoped for and needed something. As those first days of shock turned into weeks and then the weeks turned into months, his sense of abandonment deepened. He would wake from dreams in which he was still married and surrounded by his family to face the bleak walls of his apartment. At work, he watched himself as if he were a different person as his proficiency declined to the point of his nearly being dismissed. At night, alone in his apartment, he'd stare at the walls or at the bottle of whisky, as he tried to figure out what he'd done to lose everything.

Finally, he accepted that the loss of his marriage would be the one mystery he would never solve. From that day on, by throwing himself into his work, he slowly felt his job skills return. Once again, he was the cop who had a knack with cold cases. As he solved case after case, colleagues who'd failed at those same cases distanced themselves from him. He became known as a "headline cop." But he didn't care. He wasn't pouring himself into his cases because he wanted the accolades. He stayed busy because work filled the emptiness better than the whisky.

Two years later, he met Nick and, unexpectedly, they formed a close friendship. Nick contributed more than he knew to their cases, and he became the one partner who hadn't ended up resenting Worthy. Nick had also been instrumental in helping him recover a relationship, strained though it often was, with his daughter Allyson.

Then, last year on a case that took Nick and him to Rome and Jerusalem, he met Lena, and love came back into his life. He was no longer, to use Nick's phrase, "living in the graveyard of failed marriages."

As Worthy sat with himself in the darkness of the chapel, he thought back on the past decade, of what he'd lost—wife, home, and the love of his older daughter—and what he'd recovered—a challenging job, friendship, and love.

Aren't I one of the lucky ones? Wouldn't millions of people be happy to have even a piece of what I have? he asked himself. He looked at the somber faces of the saints in the icons of the chapel. As if he were addressing them, he whispered, "Why can't what I have be enough?"

AT THE TOP OF THE OVERLOOK, Nick was relieved to find a small shrine containing an icon of St. Mary of Egypt. As snow began to fall, he knelt in prayer while keeping an eye on the buildings below.

Nevertheless, with an eerie feeling that Sergei was watching him, Nick devoted his prayers to the man whom they all feared. Following Sergei to Denby and hearing about the brawl the man had gotten into in town, Nick was convinced that Sergei wouldn't be satisfied with anything but blood.

When he heard the monastery bell chime for supper, Nick watched for anyone leaving the dining hall with a tray. He wondered if Sergei had stumbled onto the same clue, only perhaps a day or even two before. If he had, did Sergei already know where Natasha and Father Joseph were hiding? And if Sergei did know, what was he waiting for?

Sergei would be out for revenge, but Nick wondered where he would begin his revenge. Then it hit him that Sergei's revenge would begin with Father Joseph. The question was, did Father Joseph realize that as well?

FREYA'S TURN TO ATTEND A PRAYER service was for the final prayers of the evening. She wasn't sure if Sergei would recognize her in the fading light as one of the people who'd arrived on the boat that morning, but she knew she had to act as if he would.

At night, the chapel was even darker than on her earlier visit. But she was prepared for the darkness this time, and she focused her thoughts on the monastery's arcane rules that prevented them contacting Father Joseph and Natasha. Didn't the abbot understand that his policy would mean nothing to someone like Sergei and that the naïve rule worked in the man's favor?

Freya knew that she would never forgive herself if they'd arrived in time to protect Father Joseph, Natasha, and the baby but, by bowing to an ancient custom, had given Sergei the opportunity to fulfill his mission.

Hardly paying attention to the chanting of the monks in the service, she thought, *No, we can't let that happen.* Worthy, she knew, would agree with her and was probably formulating a plan at that very moment. He might have already shared his plan with Lena who, she believed, would also opt for action instead of waiting.

The chanting of the monks, instead of distracting her, helped her concentrate. She tried to hold on to what she considered the optimum outcome, that they would thwart Sergei by escorting Father Joseph, Natasha, and the baby back to the mainland and to the Canadian authorities. Once there, Natasha could do what she should have done before—ask for asylum for herself and her child. At the same time, Father Joseph could explain his illegal entry into Canada and hope for clemency.

The only obstacle preventing that optimistic outcome was the wooden fence cordoning off the "Monastics Only" area of St. Mary of Egypt. *If a building behind that fence was on fire, wouldn't we have the right to smash through the barricade to save lives?* she asked herself. If that was true for a fire, why wasn't it true for a potential killer?

Slowly, she realized that the service had ended and the monks had filed out. She approached the front, where candles left by the monks beneath the icon screen gave the room a bit of light. She looked at the parade of icons, her gaze resting on the image of the Virgin Mary and the Christ child. A vague thought began to surface when she heard the door leading to the off-limits area squeak.

She turned to see a figure slowly emerge from the shadows. Her first thought was that it was the abbot, come to tell her to leave the chapel. But as the figure approached and came farther into the light, she realized she was wrong.

Before her stood Natasha Orlov cradling her baby.

CHAPTER TWENTY-TWO

———◆———

LENA WAS READING A BROCHURE ABOUT THE LEGEND of St. Mary of Egypt when Freya called on her cellphone and told her to come to the chapel immediately. When she asked, "What if Sergei sees me?" Freya answered, "It's too late to worry about that."

By the time Lena arrived, Worthy and Nick were already there, standing next to Freya, who was holding the baby. Natasha was crying softly as she slumped in a chair. What first struck Lena about Natasha was her thinness and the dark circles around her eyes. Her cheekbones, so prominent in her photo, were now even more so. In all, she looked like she hadn't eaten or slept much in days. Her second thought was, *Where is Father Joseph?*

Kneeling at the feet of Natasha, Lena heard her repeat, "I'm so tired." Glancing up at Worthy, Lena saw that his face was pale, and she knew he understood that this wasn't someone faking terror.

Lena rose to her feet and sat down in the chair next to Natasha, and, for a few moments, did nothing but pat her arm as the woman sobbed. Finally, when Natasha's tears subsided a bit, Lena said in a soft voice, "You can stop running now, Natasha. You and your baby are safe."

If Lena expected Natasha to show relief, she was mistaken. Natasha shook her head and moaned before saying, "No. Sergei, he is here. He watches."

"It's okay; it's okay, Natasha. If he's on the island, we can protect you until the authorities send him back to Russia," Lena said.

Again, Natasha shook her head. "No, I cannot go to authorities."

Nick sat down on the other side of Natasha. In an equally soft voice, he said, "My dear, this isn't Ukraine or Russia. You can trust the authorities here. Canada is different."

As if she were too exhausted to argue, Natasha just shook her head and began crying again. After a few moments, she said, "They will take my baby."

Lena put her arm around Natasha. She could feel the woman's bones as she shivered. "When was the last time you ate something, Natasha?"

"I not hungry."

"But you must eat. We'll get you something to eat. Now, please listen to me. The Canadian authorities won't take your baby."

Natasha slumped further in the chair. "You do not understand. Sergei, he will not give me divorce. That is why I find Joseph on internet, send letter. I tell him everything, about rape, about Mitya being born, about Mitya and me, how we in danger from Sergei, how we here with family in Canada, in Winnipeg."

"You don't have to stay with Sergei," Freya said.

"No, it is not me. It is my baby. With no divorce, Sergei, he tell authorities Mitya is his child. Authorities, they take my baby. Joseph, he agrees."

Lena looked up at Worthy, and she could see that he understood. Father Joseph and Natasha had failed to go to the Canadian authorities not because of poor judgment, but because they understood what was likely to happen if they did. With Natasha and Sergei both claiming the right to Mitya, the Canadian authorities would have no choice but to take the baby into care until the opposing claims could be investigated. Even a DNA test for paternity could take days, and when such a test proved Mitya wasn't Sergei's biological child, Sergei could still claim in the courts that he was the child's parent. Hadn't he and Natasha lived together in Greece before and after the child was born?

Grasping all this as she listened to Natasha moan again, Lena saw that the abbot's offer of negotiating an agreement between Natasha and Sergei would only lead to a tragic end. When the abbot discovered that Natasha and Sergei were still married and Natasha was living with another man, a wayward priest at that, the abbot would likely side with Sergei.

As she was wondering how any of them could convince the abbot of Sergei's true intent, Worthy stood in front of Natasha to ask the question Lena knew was on all their minds.

"Where is Joseph?"

✝

WORTHY MOVED AS QUIETLY AS HE COULD along the path Natasha had pointed to on the map, using the flashlight only when the forest's density made it impossible for him to see the way forward. In his other hand, he held the only weapon he could find in the monastery kitchen—a knife for cutting vegetables.

I might as well be unarmed, he thought, shivering in the cold. His only hope was to find Father Joseph before Sergei did.

Natasha had cried so loudly when he asked his question—"Where is Joseph?"—that the baby had begun to wail. It took Natasha a few moments to stop crying long enough to explain that Father Joseph had left to confront Sergei.

"We not know Sergei here until Abbot Jakovi tell us about you coming," Natasha had said, looking from Lena to Freya who was still holding the baby. "The abbot say you tell us we in danger. Because Sergei is here, on island."

Natasha gathered her strength. "Joseph say he find Sergei, talk to him. I hold Joseph. I say 'Sergei is crazy.' But he say Sergei, he be satisfied with him. Joseph, he say he make things right."

Worthy stopped on the path to catch his breath and blow on his cold hands. He felt a twinge of guilt, knowing that the message they'd given the abbot was what prompted Father Joseph to leave the safety of the monastery. Worthy inhaled deeply as he thought, *Forget about Sergei for now. Put yourself in Father Joseph's shoes.*

It seemed a peculiar thought, to put himself in Father Joseph's place, and he wondered why it now seemed right to think of him as Father Joseph, not Aris Kouris. He thought back on when he was first convinced that the priest was self-absorbed, an unstable narcissist. Had it been when he heard the story of what happened in Greece?

In the cold air, his mind cleared, and he realized what had been the starting point of his view of Father Joseph as a narcissist, a view so at odds with Nick's view as well as Lena's. It was the pain he heard in the voices of the two fiancés, the women to whom Father Joseph had been engaged. Though their stories were different, both described being cheated by Aris.

Being cheated, being cheated. Worthy leaned against a tree as the realization hit him. Being cheated was how he'd felt when his ex-wife, Susan, had walked away from their marriage. She'd never given him a reason, and for months, then years, he'd felt abandoned by everyone, including God, alone in a dark cave trying to find the way out.

When Phyllida Tismanakis had described the Christmas card that Father Joseph had sent to her seven months after he broke off their engagement, when he'd written that he hoped she had a Merry Christmas and then ended the note with a request that she pray for him, it had been as if Worthy had received that card. He could now see that from that moment forward, he'd imagined the case ending with them finding someone who reminded him of his ex-wife.

If he thought that he'd gotten over the pain of his divorce, this case proved that the wound did not simply remain, but was capable of clouding his vision. Looking ahead into the deep woods, he realized that he really didn't know Father Joseph at all. If he did find him alive, he knew he'd be meeting a perfect stranger.

But now he had to focus on a different matter. If Father Joseph were trying to draw Sergei away from the monastery, how would he do that? The answer came quickly, as if it were obvious. Father Joseph would do what he could to draw Sergei away from Natasha and the baby. He would make noise. He would call out Sergei's name. And then he'd lure Sergei as far away from the monastery as he could. *I'd be moving fast and heading . . . heading where?* he asked himself.

He turned on the flashlight, the image of the cliffs seemed to jump off the map he was holding. The cliffs were a good fifteen to twenty minutes ahead of him, even as he remembered Father Joseph's last words to Natasha—"I make things right." Those words meant that Father Joseph intended to stop Sergei one way or another. There would be no more running, no more looking over their shoulders. Instead, there would be an ending. Worthy knew that Father Joseph might try to reason with Sergei, but he was also prepared to fight.

Aiming his flashlight ahead of him on the path, Worthy hoped to see footprints in the snow. But the wind was blowing away the flakes of snow as soon as they hit the ground. Worthy considered his options and ran toward the end of the island. He knew that if it came to a fight, the clearing above the cliffs would be Father Joseph's best and maybe only chance.

FREYA, LENA, AND NICK REMAINED IN THE MONASTERY'S CHAPEL, forming a protective ring around Natasha and the baby in case Sergei's real target was the two of them.

"Where have you been hiding in the monastery?" Freya asked.

"Infirmary," Natasha replied.

"Alone?"

Natasha nodded.

Turning to Lena and Nick, Freya said, "It's not safe to take her back there, even if we stay with her. If Sergei didn't see Father Joseph head away from the monastery, he probably saw Natasha and the baby come to the chapel."

"Doesn't that mean it's not safe for any of us to stay here?" Lena asked.

"You're right. But if we leave now, we'll be easy to spot, no matter where we go," Freya said. "It looks like we're trapped."

"I have an idea," Nick said, "but I need to find the abbot. Will you be okay for a few minutes?"

Freya looked around the chapel. "I'll wedge chairs up against the two doors. Be sure to knock when you come back."

After Nick left, Freya blockaded the doors before returning to stand with Lena and Natasha. Natasha was soothing the baby by nursing him, and the action seemed to be soothing Natasha as well. In a few seconds, Mitya fell asleep.

Natasha didn't remove her child from her breast as she looked from the women guarding her to the icons at the front and on the walls.

"It so long since I feel safe," she said. "I want feel safe."

Freya looked at the icons, certain that Sergei wouldn't let the saints stand in his way if he broke in.

The tension that built with every minute was broken by the unexpected sound of the monastery's bells. Confused, Freya wondered if the tolling of the bells was somehow part of Nick's plan. Nothing made sense until she heard a knock on the door. Running to it, she opened it to find Nick leading a cluster of monks into the chapel. Silently, the monks formed a half circle in front of the icon screen. The last monk to come through the door was Abbot Jakovi, who approached Natasha and her sleeping child. He stood over them and made the sign of the cross.

As one of the monks lit candles beneath the icon of the Virgin Mary, the abbot said in a low voice to the three women, "For nearly two thousand years, people have prayed to the Theotokos, the Mother of God, whenever they or someone they love is in peril. You are in our care," he said, placing his hand on Natasha's head, "and so we pray for your safety. And we surround you until we know you are safe."

With tears in her eyes, Natasha looked up at the abbot. "Please, pray for Joseph."

✝

OUT OF BREATH AND SHIVERING WHEN HE ARRIVED AT THE CLEARING, and seeing and hearing nothing, Worthy thought that he'd made two terrible mistakes. One mistake was that he'd guessed wrong about where Father Joseph had been headed, but a worse mistake was believing that Sergei had swallowed Father Joseph's bait. Instead of following Father Joseph, Sergei might at that very moment be forcing his way into the chapel where Natasha and her baby were being guarded by Nick, Lena, and Freya.

What can any of them do if Sergei is armed? he asked, even as he knew that none of them would ever desert Natasha. He walked closer to the cliff edge and shone his flashlight in a wide arc over the snow-flecked grass. Seeing nothing, he turned, intending to run back to the monastery when he saw what looked like blood off to his left.

Following the blood trail for ten yards, Worthy came to a shallow gully near the cliff edge, made by rain washing down to the lake below. There, lying face down was a body.

Not knowing if he was looking at Sergei or Father Joseph, he approached cautiously. A pool of blood below the shoulder blades was evidence that the person had been wounded in the torso. Given that he hadn't heard a shot, Worthy assumed he was looking at a man with a stab wound.

He bent down and reached to feel the man's neck. He felt a faint pulse and slowly turned the body over. Even though the man had shaved his head and grown a scruffy beard, Worthy realized he was looking at Father Joseph. The man's eyelids fluttered as he slowly regained consciousness. Worthy had seen enough people die to know from the location of another stab wound in the chest that Father Joseph had only minutes to live.

Seeing that Father Joseph was trying to say something, Worthy lifted the priest's head and rested it in his lap. Looking down at a man who looked years older and pounds thinner than he did in his photo, Worthy remembered his doubts about the priest. Even at that moment, Worthy wondered if confronting Sergei was Father Joseph's only real option or the option of someone who thought of himself as a "knight in shining armor."

Bending down, Worthy said, "Where is Sergei? Is he headed back to the monastery?"

Father Joseph's breathing was so shallow that Worthy didn't at first hear his response. Moving closer to his face, Worthy heard Father Joseph whisper, "It's so cold."

Fearing that Father Joseph would lose consciousness again and die before he said where Sergei was, Worthy bent down farther and asked again about Sergei. In barely a whisper, Father Joseph muttered, "He stabbed me and tripped . . . over the cliff. I think he's dead."

Shining his flashlight on the snow leading to the cliff, Worthy could see where the cliff wall had given way.

"He's dead because of me. That's why . . . why you must hear my confession," Father Joseph said.

Time seemed to stop for Worthy. His mouth was completely dry as tried to take in that Sergei was dead and, at the same time, make sense of the priest's request.

"Sergei's dead? Are you sure?"

"God forgive me. Please, you must hear my confession."

Worthy said, "I can't. You . . . don't understand. No, Father, no."

Father Joseph's eyes brightened momentarily as he offered a slight smile. "I wanted to die as a priest in front of the icons."

Instead, you'll die looking at me, a man without God, Worthy thought.

In a weaker voice, Father Joseph said, "I beg you. Hear my confession."

"No, Father, no. God . . . God is not . . . not with me. I can't."

Father Joseph's eyes fluttered, and Worthy, thinking the priest was drifting into a coma, was surprised to hear the priest say in a stronger voice, "In the Liturgy, I offer incense not only to the altar and icons, but to the people—all the people. Even atheists. Do you know why?"

Worthy estimated that Father Joseph was coming soon to his last breath. *The least I can do is let him talk,* Worthy thought. Shaking from the wind and the cold, he said, "No, Father, I don't know why."

"Every person is an icon, an image of God," Father Joseph managed to say. "I am, Sergei is, you are. I see . . . I see God in you." Pausing to take a couple of labored breaths, he added, "What is your name?"

"No, Father, no. I'm the last person—"

"Your name. Please, your name."

"It's Worthy, Christopher Worthy."

Father Joseph smiled weakly. "Really, is that true?"

"Yes, Father. That's my name."

"Your name . . . it means you are a worthy Christ-bearer. Christopher Worthy, yes, you are meant to hear my confession."

Worthy said nothing for a moment. Finally, seeing the light begin to fade in Father Joseph's eyes, he said, "Tell me what you need to confess."

Father Joseph didn't answer, and Worthy wondered if he'd lost consciousness for the last time. But after a moment, Father Joseph said in a stronger voice, "When I was young, I did a horrible thing. I abandoned a baby, and the baby died. I've never been able to forgive myself, even if I've asked Christ to forgive me so many times."

"Yes, Father, I know about that," Worthy whispered.

"Oh, do you? That's good, good. When I was finishing college, I was all set to marry a wonderful woman." He paused, struggling to breathe. "But then one day—in early May—I woke up remembering that that day was the anniversary of the baby's death. Everything changed in a second, though it felt like something I'd known for a long time but hadn't admitted to myself. I knew I couldn't get married and have other children. I just couldn't. I decided then and there that the best thing I could do would be to become a priest, a celibate one. Penance, you see." The last words were little more than a whisper.

Worthy bent down again. "Is that why you sheltered Natasha and her baby? Penance?"

"At first . . . yes. But then I understood. Not penance, but a chance."

"A chance for what?"

"Don't you see? A chance to protect a baby. God gave me another chance to do one good thing in my life."

Father Joseph's chest gurgled, no doubt with blood, Worthy thought, as the priest feebly sucked in air. "Christopher Worthy, please, I beg you, absolve me in Christ's name."

As tears streamed down Worthy's face, he heard the words come out of his mouth. "Christ forgives you, Father Joseph. Christ forgives you."

CHAPTER TWENTY-THREE

———————◆———————

NOVEMBER 2

TWO NIGHTS LATER, LENA LAY NEXT TO WORTHY in their motel room in Saginaw. Resting her arm across his chest, she said, "I thought it was time for me to make the reservation for my flight home. So I did."

He turned to look at her. "When?"

"When did I make the reservation, or when am I leaving?"

"When are you leaving?" he asked.

"I fly out in four days. I wanted to wait until after the funeral."

Worthy squeezed Lena's hand. "Are you sorry you came? I mean, with the case swallowing up all our time together."

She didn't answer for a moment. "It's hard for me to know what I feel. I'm sorry how everything turned out, and I suppose because of that, part of me wishes I'd been somewhere else—anywhere. But in a year or so, I think I'll look back—no, I think we'll look back—and remember these weeks as . . . I don't know how to put it, maybe we'll remember these weeks as when we each learned a lot about one another. I just hope I wasn't in the way."

"You in the way? I was the one in the way. I was the one who misread Father Joseph."

Lena moved closer and rested her head on his shoulder. "Maybe not completely. All of us are complicated. It's hard for any of us to know everything that drives us."

Knowing she wouldn't see him again for three or four months, she moved in as close to him as she could, feeling his body warmth on her face.

"Do you ever get used to seeing people die?" she whispered.

She heard him inhale deeply and then slowly exhale. "No." After a minute, he added, "I don't think any two people die in exactly the same way."

Lena thought about that for a moment before saying, "If you don't want to tell me, that's okay. But I heard you tell Nick that Father Joseph said some things before he died."

"No, it's something I want you to know. I just didn't know the right moment."

"Hmm. Was he talking about killing Sergei or about saving Natasha and the baby?"

"Neither." He paused again before saying, "He asked me to hear his confession."

Lena raised her head. "He did?"

"Yes. I don't expect anyone to ever ask me that again. As I said, no two people die the same way."

Lena studied the face of the man she loved. "You did that for him, didn't you, Chris. You heard his confession."

He looked at her and nodded. "I don't know why, but I thought I should tell Nick."

"Of course. What did he say?"

"Well, if anyone had the right to tell me I was out of line with what I did, it would be Nick. But Nick is just Nick, which is why we love him, right? He just looked at me, and then I could see tears in his eyes. That's when I told him the rest."

"The rest?"

Worthy raised an arm and rested it across his eyes. "You know my problems with God. How I felt God abandoned me back in the divorce and when Allyson ran away."

"Yes, I know."

"Someone, maybe it was my sister, asked me soon after everything fell apart if I'd become an atheist. I remember saying, 'No, you don't get it. I lost God. It's like God has forgotten me.' That's what it's been for me for the past ten years. I mean, it's hard to work with Nick and not feel that something is pretty close to him. But that something just wasn't with me."

Lena kissed him. "And now?"

"I don't know about 'now,' but two nights ago, when Father Joseph asked me to absolve him, I told him I couldn't. I tried to explain why, but he kept begging. I could see him struggling to breathe, and I knew this was the end for him. I looked at Aris Kouris, Father Joseph, the man we'd been searching for all these weeks, but he looked at me as if he'd been searching for me. So . . . yes, I absolved him."

She saw the tears forming in the corners of his eyes. "Lena, what I'm trying to say is that when I did that, I felt—for the first time in ten years—that God was there . . . that God and I were in the same space."

CHAPTER TWENTY-FOUR

————◆————

NOVEMBER 5

THE LITTLE CHURCH OF ST. GEORGE IN SAGINAW was filled to overflowing for Father Joseph's funeral. Abbot Jakovi from St. Mary of Egypt attended as did the Archdiocesan Chancellor from Detroit.

Father Joseph's parents and his two brothers, Paulus and Soter, sat in the front pew on the right. Behind them, sitting together, were Natasha with Mitya in her arms; the Orlovs from Winnipeg; Connie Ferwerda from the diner; and Mrs. Reston, the parish secretary.

Behind them sat Freya, Worthy, and Lena, who would be flying back to Rome the following day.

Standing in front by the icon screen with Father Gregory, the young priest of St. George, Nick scanned the others attending. He recognized Dennis Sevreen, the bike shop owner; Cappy, the owner of the diner; and the Velonis family. He wondered if this was the first time the Velonis family had returned to St. George, as Father Joseph had once hoped.

Nick looked down at the body in the casket, a person he hardly recognized. In death, Father Joseph seemed to be at peace, his hands cradling a cross.

From what Father Joseph managed to tell Worthy before he died and the subsequent police investigation, they learned what had likely occurred at the clearing by the cliffs. The blood that was found at the scene was solely Father Joseph's. The body at the bottom of the cliff was Sergei's. Near his body was found a fish-gutting knife with Father Joseph's blood on it. The bloodstains in the snow on the clearing above were evidence of a struggle, a fight that ended with Father Joseph mortally wounded and Sergei dead from the fall.

What Nick knew no one would ever know was what, if anything, was said between Father Joseph and Sergei before they died. Had Father Joseph tried to reason with Sergei? Had Sergei accused Father Joseph, as he had in Greece, of sleeping with Natasha? When Father Joseph denied that, as Nick felt sure he had, was that when Sergei initiated the fatal fight?

Father Gregory had invited only two to speak at the funeral: Connie Ferwerda and Nick.

Connie walked slowly to the casket and, for a second, patted the open lid of it. Turning, she began in an uncertain voice. "I'd never met anyone like Joe, and I don't think I ever will again. We learned a lot more about him after he left, but for those of us who loved Joe. . . Father Joe, what we were told about his past didn't matter. Joe would say some pretty odd things in the diner sometimes, things I'm not sure we understood. One time he said, 'The good thing about God is that He can't stop Himself from loving us sinners.' I think what we now understood from what Joe said was the word 'us.' Joe was always just one of us. I think Cappy's Diner was as much his church as this place is."

Connie paused for a moment and looked down at Father Joseph. "When I heard the news, I thought, 'This isn't right.' If Joe's God exists, this just isn't right. But over the past few days, I keep seeing Joe's smile, and I hear him laughing. I'm crying, like I am now, but he's laughing."

Connie shook herself before adding, "I respected Joe so much that I even came to this church. Twice, I think. I'm not saying I remember much of it—it was hard for me to follow—but I do remember a prayer he gave. He prayed that at the end of our lives we'd have a good death, a death without pain or suffering. So, that's what I'm believing today, that even though he was killed, Joe had a good death. I say this because, from what I've been told, he died protecting two people. I think he did the same thing here in Saginaw. He was always protecting us. We won't forget you, Joe . . . Father Joe. I won't forget you."

After Connie sat down, Nick approached the casket. He made the sign of the cross and said a prayer for Father Joseph's soul. Turning, he looked down at baby Mitya and Natasha and could see that Natasha was far from being at peace. Because Sergei was dead, the Canadian authorities were considering sending her and the baby back to Ukraine. But Natasha still feared for her safety and the safety of her child because Sergei's relatives were still a threat.

O Lord, help me say what is your truth to everyone here, for only your truth can heal us, he prayed silently.

Nick cleared his throat and began. "I am a priest who asks your patience as I talk about another priest. To say that Father Joseph's journey as a priest was often rocky is to simply tell the truth. Not everyone understood why he did what he did, and I am sure Father Joseph was often perplexed by some of his own actions. You see, a priest is still a person, and all of us are flawed.

"Over the weeks of our search for Father Joseph, I became convinced that he loved this community, both St. George and Saginaw. He listened to you with an open heart, whether he met you here at St. George, at Cappy's Diner, or the bike club."

Nick took a deep breath and paused. "I know some of you might say that I'm being too kind to the memory of Father Joseph. You might be thinking, 'But Father Joseph abandoned us.' If you're harboring that thought in your hearts, I ask you to remember that a priest is a shepherd.

"Those of us raised in the Church have heard the story of the Good Shepherd. In this parable or story, Jesus teaches us that God isn't Who we often think He is. God is not some heavenly accountant who sits passively and writes down all the good and, especially, all the bad that we do. Jesus taught that God is instead an unusual shepherd, the kind who will leave the ninety-nine sheep in the flock to search for the one sheep who is lost and in trouble. This is what I believe Father Joseph did as a shepherd. He left Saginaw not because he no longer loved you, his friends here, but because he, and only he, could help two others of his flock, this mother and baby here," Nick said, pointing to Natasha and baby Mitya, "who were in danger."

Perhaps it was seeing the tears in Natasha's eyes that made him pause, but in that moment, Nick understood the hope that fueled Father Joseph's journey from beginning to end.

No one stirred as he let the truth of the last weeks wash over him. Finally, he said, "In our limited human understanding, this funeral is hardly the ending that Father Joseph was hoping for. Father Joseph's wish was to return to Saginaw with these two sheep whom he rescued, Natasha and Mitya. He hoped this could be their new home; here, they would find safety and acceptance.

"Can't we all picture Father Joseph bringing this mother and child to Cappy's Diner, to the bike club, and here to St. George, where he would have begged this community's forgiveness and understanding? Because Father Joseph understood being a priest meant being a good shepherd, I believe his message would have been simple—'Now my flock is complete.'

"Let all of us who love Father Joseph finish the story the way he wanted. To Natasha and baby Mitya, to the regulars to Cappy's Diner, to the members of the Bike Club, to all who are part of St. George, and to all who have been estranged from St. George, let us face one another and say, 'Now Father Joseph's flock is complete.'"

EPILOGUE

———◆———

NOVEMBER 6

THE MORNING AFTER FATHER JOSEPH'S FUNERAL, Freya, Lena, Worthy, and Nick sat with Connie Ferwerda at a table in Cappy's diner. There was just enough time before Worthy had to drive Lena to the Detroit airport for them to spend a few moments together.

The mood was subdued, not just at their table but in the diner itself. Black crepe paper covered the seat at the counter where Father Joseph sat when he listened to whatever people needed to tell him. Connie had draped the seat earlier that morning, but she'd also done something else. Right after the funeral, she'd volunteered to work with Father Gregory, Mrs. Reston, Freya, and Cappy on Natasha's request for asylum in the US. If they were successful, Natasha would live and Mitya would grow up in Saginaw surrounded by those who loved Father Joseph.

Lena accepted a second cup of coffee before saying, "Before we go our separate ways, I want to share something that I realized last night. All except you, Connie, know that I was never convinced of either of your theories, Nick and Chris. But last night, I realized that you both had a piece of the truth about Father Joseph but not the whole truth."

Worthy shook his head. "You're being too kind, Lena. I need to apologize to everyone for how badly I misjudged Father Joseph."

"What I'm saying, Chris, is that in one sense you misread him, but in another sense you didn't."

"Go on, Lena," Nick said.

"Before Father Joseph died, he told you, Chris, how guilty he felt about the baby he'd fathered in high school, then abandoned. He must have felt he was carrying the dead baby within him for those nearly twenty years. What I'm saying is that guilt like that can look a lot like narcissism."

When no one said anything, Lena concluded that they weren't following her. "Maybe I can explain it this way. "Have you ever seen a butterfly in someone's collection, thy way it's pinned to a piece of cardboard or wood?"

"I have," Connie said, in little more than a whisper. "The butterfly is stuck there forever."

"Exactly, Connie. Guilt is like that pin. Guilt is what kept Father Joseph stuck with the pain of that memory. Chris, you said Father Joseph was a narcissist, but what you saw more clearly than the rest of us was that he was stuck on himself. No, not 'stuck on himself' in the way that people usually mean that. Father Joseph was stuck, but he was stuck on the memory of the abandoned child who died."

"I think I understand what you're saying, Lena," Nick said. "Father Joseph's guilt explains why his two engagements didn't—no, couldn't last," he said. "He didn't feel he deserved the possibility of having a family and children."

No one said anything until Worthy spoke. "He told me that helping Natasha and Mitya was his 'second chance,' his chance to atone for the past. If he could save Mitya, then he would know that he could be forgiven. But I thought he was a narcissist, someone who saw himself as a knight bent on rescuing Natasha and Mitya."

Lena squeezed Worthy's hand. "You weren't completely wrong, Chris, and Nick wasn't completely right," she said. "Father Joseph's need to rescue others wasn't just about why he became a priest. Helping others must have eased the guilt, the pain of the memory. That's why he let Natasha stay in his apartment that night in Greece."

"And why he sat over there at the counter and listened to everyone else's pain," Connie added, again in little more than a whisper.

Lena looked up to see tears not just in Connie's eyes, but Nick's as well. "What is it, Nick?"

"It's what Christopher did for Father Joseph on the cliff. Christopher, my friend, when you . . . when Christ absolved Father Joseph on the cliff, I believe he was finally released from all that. Father Joseph died free."

THE END

Franklin College in Franklin, Indiana, has been David's home for the past forty-three years. David has been particularly attracted to the topics of faith development, Catholic-Orthodox relations, and Christian-Muslim dialogue. In 2007, he conducted interviews across the country in monasteries and convents about monastic responses to 9/11. The book based on that experience, Peace Be with You: Monastic Wisdom for a Terror-Filled World, was chosen as one of the Best Books of 2011 by Library Journal.

In the past sixteen years, religious terrorism has become an area of specialty. Much of his time in the last ten years has been spent giving talks as well as radio and television interviews on ISIS, Al-Qaeda, and other terrorist organizations.

Now retired, David enjoys writing both non-fiction related to interfaith relations and the award-winning Christopher Worthy/Father Fortis Mystery series.

His wife, Kathy, is a retired English professor, an award-winning artist, and his best editor. Their two sons took parental advice to follow their passions. The older, Leif, is a Fine Arts professor and photographer, and the younger, Marten, is a filmmaker.

www.ingramcontent.com/pod-product-compliance
Lightning Source LLC
Chambersburg PA
CBHW011517100726
47899CB00010BD/3403